'Dick's plastic realities tell us more than we'll ever want to know about the inside of our heads and the view looking out. In his tortured topographies of worlds never made, we see mindscapes that we ourselves, in our madder moments, have glimpsed and thought real. Dick travelled out there on our behalf. It is our duty to read the reports he sent home.' *James Lovegrove*

'Dick quietly produced serious fiction in a popular form and there can be no greater praise.'
Michael Moorcock

'One of the most original practitioners writing any kind of fiction, Philip K. Dick made most of the European avant-garde seem navel-gazers in a cul-de-sac.' *Sunday Times*

'The most consistently brilliant SF writer in the world' *John Brunner*

'Dick's abundant storytelling gifts and the need to express his inner struggles combined to produce some of the most groundbreaking novels and ideas to emerge from SF'
Waterstone's Guide to Science Fiction, Fantasy and Horror

'In all his work he was astonishingly intimate, self exposed, and very dangerous. He was the funniest sf writer of his time, and perhaps the most terrifying. His dreads were our own, spoken as we could not have spoken them' *The Encyclopedia of Science Fiction*

Also by Philip K. Dick

NOVELS

Solar Lottery (1955)

The World Jones Made (1956)

The Man Who Japed (1956)

The Cosmic Puppets (1957)

Eye in the Sky (1957)

Dr. Futurity (1959)

Time Out of Joint (1959)

Vulcan's Hammer (1960)

The Man in the High Castle (1962)

The Game-Players of Titan (1963)

The Penultimate Truth (1964)

The Simulacra (1964)

Martian Time Slip (1964)

Clans of the Alphane Moon (1964)

Dr. Bloodmoney, or How We Got Along After the Bomb (1965)

The Three Stigmata of Palmer Eldritch (1965)

The Ganymede Takeover (with Ray F. Nelson) (1967)

Now Wait for Last Year (1966)

The Crack in Space (1966)

The Zap Gun (1967)

Counter-Clock World (1967)

Do Androids Dream of Electric Sheep? (1968)

Ubik (1969)

Galactic Pot-Healer (1969)

Our Friends From Frolix 8 (1970)

A Maze of Death (1970)

We Can Build You (1972)

Flow My Tears, The Policeman Said (1974)

Confessions of a Crap Artist (1975)

Deus Irae (with Roger Zelazny) (1976)

The Divine Invasion (1981)

Valis (1981)

The Transmigration of Timothy Archer (1982)

Lies, Inc (1984)

The Man Whose Teeth Were All Exactly Alike (1984)

Puttering About in a Small Land (1985)

In Milton Lumky Territory (1985)

Radio Free Albemuth (1985)

Humpty Dumpty in Oakland (1986)

Mary and the Giant (1987)

The Broken Bubble (1988)

SHORT STORY COLLECTIONS:

The Variable Man (1957)

A Handful of Darkness (1966)

The Turning Wheel (1977)

The Best of Philip K. Dick (1977)

The Golden Man (1980)

The Collected Stories of Philip K. Dick:

1. Beyond Lies the Wub (1987

2. Second Variety (1987)

3. The Father Thing (1987)

4. The Days of Perky Pat (1987)

5. We Can Remember It For You Wholesale (1987)

A SCANNER DARKLY

Philip K. Dick

The right of Philip K. Dick to be identified as the author
of this work has been asserted by him in accordance with
the Copyright, Designs and Patents Act 1988.

First published in Great Britain in 1999 by
Millennium
An imprint of Victor Gollancz
Orion House, 5 Upper St Martin's Lane,
London WC2H 9EA

This edition reprinted in Great Britain by
Gollancz
An imprint of the Orion Publishing Group

13

A CIP catalogue record for this
book is available from the British Library

ISBN 13 978 1 85798 847 5

Excerpt from 'The Other Side of the Brain:
An Appositional Mind' by Joseph E. Bogen, M. D.,
which appeared in *Bulletin of Los Angeles Neurological
Societies*, Vol. 34, No. 3, July 1969. Used by permission.
Excerpt from 'The Split Brain in Man'
by Michael S. Gazzaniga which appeared in *Scientific
American*, August 1967, Vol. 217. Used by permission.
Untitled poem reprinted from Heinrich Heine:
Lyric Poems and Ballads, translated by Ernst Feise,
Copyright © 1961 by the University of Pittsburgh Press.
Used by permission of the University of Pittsburgh Press.
Other German quotes from Goethe's *Faust*, Part one,
and from Beethoven's opera *Fidelio*.

Printed in Great Britain by
Clays Ltd, St Ives plc

The Orion Publishing Group's policy is to use papers that
are natural, renewable and recyclable products and
made from wood grown in sustainable forests. The logging
and manufacturing processes are expected to conform to
the environmental regulations of the country of origin.

www.orionbooks.co.uk

CHAPTER ONE

Once a guy stood all day shaking bugs from his hair. The doctor told him there were no bugs in his hair. After he had taken a shower for eight hours, standing under hot water hour after hour suffering the pain of the bugs, he got out and dried himself, and he still had bugs in his hair; in fact, he had bugs all over him. A month later he had bugs in his lungs.

Having nothing else to do or think about, he began to work out theoretically the life cycle of the bugs, and, with the aid of the *Britannica*, try to determine specifically which bugs they were. They now filled his house. He read about many different kinds and finally noticed bugs outdoors, so he concluded they were aphids. After that decision came to his mind it never changed, no matter what other people told him . . . like "Aphids don't bite people."

They said that to him because the endless biting of the bugs kept him in torment. At the 7-11 grocery store, part of a chain spread out over most of California, he bought spray cans of Raid and Black Flag and Yard Guard. First he sprayed the house, then himself. The Yard Guard seemed to work the best.

As to the theoretical side, he perceived three stages in the cycle of the bugs. First, they were carried to him to contaminate him by what he called Carrier-people, which were people who didn't understand their role in distributing the bugs. During that stage the bugs had no jaws or mandibles (he learned that word during his weeks of scholarly research, an unusually bookish occupation for a guy who worked at the Handy Brake and Tire place relining people's brake drums). The Carrier-people therefore felt nothing. He used to sit in the far corner of his living room watching different Carrier-people enter—most of them people he'd known for a while, but some new to him—covered with the aphids in this particular nonbiting stage. He'd sort of smile to himself, because he knew that the person was being used by the bugs and wasn't hip to it.

"What are you grinning about, Jerry?" they'd say.

He'd just smile.

In the next stage the bugs grew wings or something, but they really weren't precisely wings; anyhow, they were appendages of a functional sort permitting them to swarm, which was how they migrated and spread—especially to him. At that point the air was full of them; it made his living room, his whole house, cloudy. During this stage he tried not to inhale them.

Most of all he felt sorry for his dog, because he could see the bugs landing on and settling all over him, and probably getting into the dog's lungs, as they were in his own. Probably—at least so his empathic ability told him—the dog was suffering as much as he was. Should he give the dog away for the dog's own comfort? No, he decided: the dog was now, inadvertently, infected, and would carry the bugs with him everywhere.

Sometimes he stood in the shower with the dog, trying to wash the dog clean too. He had no more success with him than he did with himself. It hurt to feel the dog suffer; he never stopped trying to help him. In some respects this was the worst part, the sufferings of the animal, who could not complain.

"What the fuck are you doing there all day in the shower with the goddamn dog?" his buddy Charles Freck asked one time, coming in during this.

Jerry said, "I got to get the aphids off him." He brought Max, the dog, out of the shower and began drying him. Charles Freck watched, mystified, as Jerry rubbed baby oil and talc into the dog's fur. All over the house, cans of insect spray, bottles of talc and baby oil and skin conditioners were piled and tossed, most of them empty; he used many cans a day now.

"I don't see any aphids," Charles said. "What's an aphid?"

"It eventually kills you," Jerry said. "That's what an aphid is. They're in my hair and my skin and my lungs, and the goddamn pain is unbearable—I'm going to have to go to the hospital."

"How come I can't see them?"

Jerry put down the dog, which was wrapped in a towel, and knelt over the shag rug. "I'll show you one," he said. The rug was covered with aphids; they hopped up everywhere, up and down, some higher than others. He searched for an especially large one, because of the difficulty people had seeing them. "Bring me a bottle or jar," he said, "from under the sink. We'll cap it or put a lid on it and then I can take it with me when I go to the doctor and he can analyze it."

Charles Freck brought him an empty mayonnaise jar. Jerry went on searching, and at last came across an aphid leaping up at least four feet in the air. The aphid was over an inch long. He caught it, carried it to the jar, carefully dropped it in, and screwed on the lid. Then he held it up triumphantly. "See?" he said.

"Yeahhhhh," Charles Freck said, his eyes wide as he scrutinized the contents of the jar. "What a big one! Wow!"

"Help me find more for the doctor to see," Jerry said, again squatting down on the rug, the jar beside him.

"Sure," Charles Freck said, and did so.

Within half an hour they had three jars full of the bugs. Charles, although new at it, found some of the largest.

It was midday, in June of 1994. In California, in a tract area of cheap but durable plastic houses, long ago vacated by the straights. Jerry had at an earlier date sprayed metal paint over all the windows, though, to keep out the light; the illumination for the room came from a pole lamp into which he had screwed nothing but spot lamps, which shone day and night, so as to abolish time for him and his friends. He liked that; he liked to get rid of time. By doing that he could concentrate on important things without interruption. Like this: two men kneeling down on the shag rug, finding bug after bug and putting them into jar after jar.

"What do we get for these," Charles Freck said, later on in the day. "I mean, does the doctor pay a bounty or something? A prize? Any bread?"

"I get to help perfect a cure for them this way," Jerry said. The pain, constant as it was, had become unbearable; he had never gotten used to it, and he knew he never would. The urge, the longing, to take another shower was overwhelming him. "Hey, man," he gasped, straightening up, "you go on putting them in the jars while I take a leak and like that." He started toward the bathroom.

"Okay," Charles said, his long legs wobbling as he swung toward a jar, both hands cupped. An ex-veteran, he still had good muscular control, though; he made it to the jar. But then he said suddenly, "Jerry, hey—these bugs sort of scare me. I don't like it here by myself." He stood up.

"Chickenshit bastard," Jerry said, panting with pain as he halted momentarily at the bathroom.

"Couldn't you—"

"I got to take a leak!" He slammed the door and spun the knobs of the shower. Water poured down.

"I'm afraid out here." Charles Freck's voice came dimly, even though he was evidently yelling loud.

"Then go fuck yourself!" Jerry yelled back, and stepped into the shower. What fucking good are friends? he asked himself bitterly. No good, no good! No fucking good!

"Do these fuckers sting?" Charles yelled, right at the door.

"Yeah, they sting," Jerry said as he rubbed shampoo into his hair.

"That's what I thought." A pause. "Can I wash my hands and get them off and wait for you?"

Chickenshit, Jerry thought with bitter fury. He said nothing; he merely kept on washing. The bastard wasn't worth answering . . . He paid no attention to Charles Freck, only to himself. To his own vital, demanding, terrible, urgent needs. Everything else would have to wait. There was no time, no time; these things could not be postponed. Everything else was secondary. Except the dog; he wondered about Max, the dog.

Charles Freck phoned up somebody who he hoped was holding. "Can you lay about ten deaths on me?"

"Christ, I'm entirely out—I'm looking to score myself. Let me know when you find some, I could use some."

"What's wrong with the supply?"

"Some busts, I guess."

Charles Freck hung up and then ran a fantasy number in his head as he slumped dismally back from the pay phone booth—you never used your home phone for a buy call—to his parked Chevy. In his fantasy number he was driving past the Thrifty Drugstore and they had a huge window display: bottles of slow death, cans of slow death, jars and bathtubs and vats and bowls of slow death, millions of caps and tabs and hits of slow death, slow death mixed with speed and junk and barbiturates and psychedelics, everything—and a giant sign: YOUR CREDIT IS GOOD HERE. Not to mention: LOW LOW PRICES, LOWEST IN TOWN.

But in actuality the Thrifty usually had a display of nothing: combs, bottles of mineral oil, spray cans of deodorant, always crap like that. But I bet the pharmacy in the back has slow death under lock and key in an unstepped-on, pure, unadulterated, uncut form, he thought as he drove from the parking lot onto Harbor Boulevard, into the afternoon traffic. About a fifty-pound bag.

He wondered when and how they unloaded the fifty-pound bag of Substance D at the Thrifty Pharmacy every morning, from wherever it came from—God knew, maybe from Switzerland or maybe from another planet where some wise race lived. They'd deliver probably real early, and with armed guards—the Man standing there with Laser rifles looking mean, the way the Man always did. Anybody rip off my slow death, he thought through the Man's head, I'll snuff them.

Probably Substance D is an ingredient in every legal medication that's worth anything, he thought. A little pinch here and there according to the secret exclusive formula at the issuing house in Germany or Switzerland that invented it. But in actuality he knew better; the authorities snuffed or sent up everybody selling or transporting or using, so in that case the Thrifty Drugstore—all the millions of Thrifty Drugstores—would get shot or bombed out of business or anyhow fined. More likely just fined. The Thrifty had pull. Anyhow, how do you shoot a chain of big drugstores? Or put them away?

They just got ordinary stuff, he thought as he cruised along. He felt lousy because he had only three hundred tabs of slow death left in his stash. Buried in his back yard under his camellia, the hybrid one with the cool big blossoms that didn't burn brown in the spring. I only got a week's supply, he thought. What then when I'm out? Shit.

Suppose everybody in California and parts of Oregon runs out the same day, he thought. Wow.

This was the all-time winning horror-fantasy that he ran in his head, that every doper ran. The whole western part of the United States simultaneously running out and everybody crashing on the same day, probably about 6 A.M. Sunday morning, while the straights were getting dressed up to go fucking pray.

Scene: The First Episcopal Church of Pasadena, at 8:30 A.M. on Crash Sunday.

"Holy parishioners, let us call on God now at this time to request His intervention in the agonies of those who are thrashing about on their beds withdrawing."

"Yeah, yeah." The congregation agreeing with the priest.

"But before He intervenes with a fresh supply of—"

A black-and-white evidently had noticed something in Charles Freck's driving he hadn't noticed; it had taken off from its parking spot and was moving along behind him in traffic, so far without lights or siren, but . . .

Maybe I'm weaving or something, he thought. Fucking goddamn fuzzmobile saw me fucking up. I wonder what.

COP: "All right, what's your name?"

"My *name?*" (CAN'T THINK OF NAME.)

"You don't know your own name?" Cop signals to other cop in prowl car. "This guy is really spaced."

"Don't shoot me here." Charles Freck in his horror-fantasy number induced by the sight of the black-and-white pacing him. "At least take me to the station house and shoot me there, out of sight."

To survive in this fascist police state, he thought, you gotta always be able to come up with a name, your name. At all times. That's the first sign they look for that you're wired, not being able to figure out who the hell you are.

What I'll do, he decided, is I'll pull off soon as I see a parking slot, pull off voluntarily before he flashes his light, or does anything, and then when he glides up beside me I'll say I got a loose wheel or something mechanical.

They always think that's great, he thought. When you give up like that and can't go on. Like throwing yourself on the ground the way an animal does, exposing your soft unprotected defenseless underbelly. I'll do that, he thought.

He did so, peeling off to the right and bumping the front wheels of his car against the curb. The cop car went on by.

Pulled off for nothing, he thought. Now it'll be hard to back out again, traffic's so heavy. He shut off his engine. Maybe I'll just sit here parked for a while, he decided, and alpha meditate or go into various different altered states of consciousness. Possibly by watching the chicks going along on foot. I wonder if they manufacture a bioscope for horny. Rather than alpha. Horny waves, first very short, then longer, larger, larger, finally right off the scale.

This is getting me nowhere, he realized. I should be out trying to locate someone holding. I've got to get my supply or pretty soon I'll be freaking, and then I won't be able to do anything. Even sit at the curb like I am. I not only won't know who I am, I won't even know where I am, or what's happening.

What is happening? he asked himself. What day is this? If I knew what day I'd know everything else; it'd seep back bit by bit.

Wednesday, in downtown L.A., the Westwood section. Ahead, one of those giant shopping malls surrounded by a wall that you bounced off like a rubber ball—unless you had a credit card on you and passed in through the electronic hoop. Owning no credit card for any of the malls, he could depend only on verbal report as to what the shops were like inside. A whole bunch, evidently, selling good products to the straights, especially to the straight wives. He watched the uniformed armed guards at the mall gate checking out each person. Seeing that the man or woman matched his or her credit card and that it hadn't been ripped off, sold, bought, used fraudulently. Lots of people moved on in through the gate, but he figured many were no doubt window-shopping. Not all that many people can have the bread or the urge to buy this time of day, he reflected. It's early, just past two. At night; that was when. The shops all lit up. He could —all the brothers and sisters could—see the lights from without, like showers of sparks, like a fun park for grown-up kids.

Stores this side of the mall, requiring no credit card, with no armed guards, didn't amount to much. Utility stores: a shoe and a TV shop, a bakery, small-appliance repair, a laundromat. He watched a girl who wore a short plastic jacket and stretch pants wander along from store to store; she had nice hair, but he couldn't see her face, see if she was foxy. Not a bad figure, he thought. The girl stopped for a time at a window where leather goods were displayed. She was checking out a purse with tassels; he could see her peering, worrying, scheming on the purse. Bet she goes on in and requests to see it, he thought.

The girl bopped on into the store, as he had figured.

Another girl, amid the sidewalk traffic, came along, this one in a frilly blouse, high heels, with silver hair and too much make-up. Trying to look older than she is, he thought. Probably not out of high school. After her came nothing worth mentioning, so he removed the string that held the glove compartment shut and got out a pack of cigarettes. He lit up and turned on the car radio, to a rock station. Once he had owned a tape-cartridge stereo, but finally, while loaded one day, he had neglected to bring it indoors with him when he locked up the car; naturally, when he returned the whole stereo tape system had been stolen. That's what carelessness gets you, he had thought, and so now he had only the crummy radio. Someday they'd take that too. But he knew where he could get another for almost nothing, used. Anyhow, the car stood to be wrecked any day; its oil rings were shot and compression had dropped way down. Evidently, he had burned a valve on the freeway coming home one night with a whole bunch of good stuff; sometimes when he had really scored heavy he got paranoid—not about the cops so much as about some other heads ripping him off. Some head desperate from withdrawing and dingey as a motherfucker.

A girl walked along now that made him take notice. Black hair, pretty, cruising slow; she wore an open midriff blouse and denim white pants washed a lot. Hey, I know her, he thought. That's Bob Arctor's girl. That's Donna.

He pushed open the car door and stepped out. The girl eyed him and continued on. He followed.

Thinks I'm fixing to grab-ass, he thought as he snaked among the people. How easily she gained speed; he could barely see her now as she glanced back. A firm, calm face . . . He saw large eyes that appraised him. Calculated his speed and would he catch up. Not at this rate, he thought. She can really move.

At the corner people had halted for the sign to say WALK instead of DON'T WALK; cars were making wild left turns. But the girl continued on, fast but with dignity, threading her path among the nut-o cars. The drivers glared at her with indignation. She didn't appear to notice.

"Donna!" When the sign flashed WALK he hurried across after her and caught up with her. She declined to run but merely walked rapidly. "Aren't you Bob's old lady?" he said. He managed to get in front of her to examine her face.

"No," she said. "No." She came toward him, directly at him; he retreated backward, because she held a short knife pointed at his stomach. "Get lost," she said, continuing to move forward without slowing or hesitating.

"Sure you are," he said. "I met you at his place." He could hardly see the knife, only a tiny section of blade metal, but he knew it was there. She would stab him and walk on. He continued to retreat backward, protesting. The girl held the knife so well concealed that probably no one else, the others walking along, could notice. But he did; it was going right at him as she approached without hesitation. He stepped aside, then, and the girl traveled on, in silence.

"Jeez!" he said to the back of her. I know it's Donna, he thought. She just doesn't flash on who I am, that she knows me. Scared, I guess; scared I'm going to hustle her. You got to be careful, he thought, when you come to a strange chick on the street; they're all prepared now. Too much has happened to them.

Funky little knife, he thought. Chicks shouldn't carry those; any guy could turn her wrist and the blade back on her any time he wanted. I could have. If I really wanted to git her. He stood there, feeling angry. I know that was Donna, he thought.

As he started to go back toward his parked car, he realized that the girl had halted, out of the movement of passers-by, and now stood silently gazing at him.

He walked cautiously toward her. "One night," he said, "me and Bob and another chick had some old Simon and Garfunkel tapes, and you were sitting there—" She had been filling capsules with high-grade death, one by one, painstakingly. For over an hour. El Primo. Numero Uno: Death. After she had finished she had laid a cap on each of them and they had dropped them, all of them together. Except her. I just sell them, she had said. If I start dropping them I eat up all my profits.

The girl said, "I thought you were going to knock me down and bang me."

"No," he said. "I just wondered if you . . ." He hesitated. "Like, wanted a ride. On the sidewalk?" he said, startled. "In broad daylight?"

"Maybe in a doorway. Or pull me into a car."

"I *know* you," he protested. "And Arctor would snuff me if I did that."

"Well, I didn't recognize you." She came toward him three steps. "I'm sorta nearsighted."

"You ought to wear contacts." She had, he thought, lovely large dark warm eyes. Which meant she wasn't on junk.

"I did have. But one fell out into a punch bowl. Acid punch, at a party. It sank to the bottom, and I guess someone dipped it up and drank it. I hope it tasted good; it cost me thirty-five dollars, originally."

"You want a ride where you're going?"

"You'll bang me in the car."

"No," he said, "I can't get it on right now, these last couple of weeks. It must be something they're adulterating all the stuff with. Some chemical."

"That's a neat-o line, but I've heard it before. Everybody bangs me." She amended that. "Tries to, anyhow. That's what it's like to be a chick. I'm suing one guy in court right now, for molestation and assault. We're asking punitive damages in excess of forty thousand."

"How far'd he get?"

Donna said, "Got his hand around my boob."

"That isn't worth forty thousand."

Together, they walked back toward his car.

"You got anything to sell?" he asked. "I'm really hurting. I'm virtually out, in fact, hell, I am out, come to think of it. Even a few, if you could spare a few."

"I can get you some."

"Tabs," he said. "I don't shoot up."

"Yes." She nodded intently, head down. "But, see, they're real scarce right now—the supply's temporarily dried up. You probably discovered that already. I can't get you very many, but—"

"When?" he broke in. They had reached his car; he halted, opened the door, got in. On the far side Donna got in. They sat side by side.

"Day after tomorrow," Donna said. "If I can git ahold of this guy. I think I can."

Shit, he thought. Day after tomorrow. "No sooner? Not like, say, tonight?"

"Tomorrow at the earliest."

"How much?"

"Sixty dollars a hundred."

"Oh, Jeez," he said. "That's a burn."

"They're super good. I've got them from him before; they're really not what you usually buy into. Take my word for it—they're worth it. Actually, I prefer to get them from him rather than from anybody else—when I can. He doesn't always have them. See, he just took a trip down south, I guess. He just got back. He picked them up himself, so I know they're good for sure. And you don't have to pay me in advance. When I get them. Okay? I trust you."

"I never front," he said.

"Sometimes you have to."

"Okay," he said. "Then can you get me at least a hundred?" He tried to figure, rapidly, how many he could get; in two days he probably could raise one hundred twenty dollars and get two hundred tabs from her. And if he ran across a better deal in the meantime, from other people who were holding, he could forget her deal and buy from them. That was the advantage of never fronting, that plus never being burned.

"It's lucky for you that you ran into me," Donna said as he started up his car and backed out into traffic. "I'm supposed to see this one dude in about an hour, and he'd probably take all I could get . . . you'd have been out of luck. This was your day." She smiled, and he did too.

"I wish you could get them sooner," he said.

"If I do . . ." Opening her purse, she got out a little note pad and a pen that had SPARKS BATTERY TUNE-UP stamped on it. "How do I get hold of you, and I forget your name."

"Charles B. Freck," he said. He told her his phone number—not his, really, but the one he made use of at a straight friend's house, for messages like this—and laboriously she wrote it down. What difficulty she had writing, he thought. Peering and slowly scrawling . . . They don't teach the chicks jack shit in school any more, he thought. Flat-out illiterate. But foxy. So she can't hardly read or write; so what? What matters with a fox is nice tits.

"I think I remember you," Donna said. "Sort of. It's all hazy, that night; I was really out of it. All I definitely remember was getting the powder into those little caps—Librium caps—we dumped the original contents. I must have dropped half. I mean, on the floor." She gazed at him meditatively as he drove. "You seem like a mellow dude," she said. "And you'll be in the market later on? After a while you'll want more?"

"Sure," he said, wondering to himself if he could beat her price by the time he saw her again; he felt he could, most likely. Either way he won. That is, either way he scored.

Happiness, he thought, is knowing you got some pills.

The day outside the car, and all the busy people, the sunlight and activity, streamed past unnoticed; he was happy.

Look what he had found by chance—because, in fact, a black-

and-white had accidentally paced him. An unexpected new supply of
Substance D. What more could he ask out of life? He could probably
now count on two weeks lying ahead of him, nearly *half a month,*
before he croaked or nearly croaked—withdrawing from Substance
D made the two the same. Two weeks! His heart soared, and he
smelled, for a moment, coming in from the open windows of the car,
the brief excitement of spring.

"Want to go with me to see Jerry Fabin?" he asked the girl. "I'm
taking a load of his things over to him at the Number Three Federal
Clinic, where they took him last night. I'm just carting over a little at
a time, because there's a chance he might get back out and I don't
want to have to drag it all back."

"I'd better not see him," Donna said.

"You know him? Jerry Fabin?"

"Jerry Fabin thinks I contaminated him orginally with those bugs."

"Aphids."

"Well, *then* he didn't know what they were. I better stay away.
Last time I saw him he got really hostile. It's his receptor sites, in his
brain, at least I think so. It seems like it, from what the government
pamphlets say now."

"That can't be restored, can it?" he said.

"No," Donna said. "That's irreversible."

"The clinic people said they'd let me see him, and they said they
believed he could work some, you know——" He gestured. "Not
be——" Again he gestured; it was hard to find words for that, what he
was trying to say about his friend.

Glancing at him, Donna said, "You don't have speech-center damage, do you? In your—what is it called?—occipital lobe."

"No," he said. Vigorously.

"Do you have any kind of damage?" She tapped her head.

"No, its just . . . you know. I have trouble saying it about those
fucking clinics; I hate the Neural-Aphasia Clinics. One time I was
there visiting a guy, he was trying to wax a floor—they said he
couldn't wax the floor, I mean he couldn't figure out how to do it
. . . What got me was he kept trying. I mean not just for like an
hour; he was still trying a month later when I came back. Just like he
had been, over and over again, when I first saw him there, when I
first went to visit him. He couldn't figure out why he couldn't get it
right. I remember the look on his face. He was sure he'd get it right
if he kept trying to flash on what he was doing wrong. 'What am I
doing wrong?' he kept asking them. There was no way to tell him. I
mean, they told him—hell, I told him—but he still couldn't figure it
out."

"The receptor sites in his brain are what I've read usually goes first," Donna said placidly. "Someone's brain where he's gotten a bad hit or like that, like too heavy." She was watching the cars ahead. "Look, there's one of those new Porsches with two engines." She pointed excitedly. "Wow."

"I knew a guy who hot-wired one of those new Porsches," he said, "and got it out on the Riverside Freeway and pushed it up to one seventy-five—wipe-out." He gestured. "Right into the ass of a semi. Never saw it, I guess." In his head he ran a fantasy number: himself at the wheel of a Porsche, but noticing the semi, all the semis. And everyone on the freeway—the Hollywood Freeway at rush hour—noticing him. Noticing him for sure, the lanky big-shouldered good-looking dude in the new Porsche going two hundred miles an hour, and all the cops' faces hanging open helplessly.

"You're shaking," Donna said. She reached over and put her hand on his arm. A quiet hand that he at once responded to. "Slow down."

"I'm tired," he said. "I was up two nights and two days counting bugs. Counting them and putting them in bottles. And finally when we crashed and got up and got ready the next morning to put the bottles in the car, to take to the doctor to show him, there was nothing in the bottles. Empty." He could feel the shaking now himself, and see it in his hands, on the wheel, the shaking hands on the steering wheel, at twenty miles an hour. "Every fucking one," he said. "Nothing. No bugs. And then I realized, I fucking realized. It came to me, about his brain, Jerry's brain."

The air no longer smelled of spring and he thought, abruptly, that he urgently needed a hit of Substance D; it was later in the day than he had realized, or else he had taken less than he thought. Fortunately, he had his portable supply with him, in the glove compartment, way back. He began searching for a vacant parking slot, to pull over.

"Your mind plays tricks," Donna said remotely; she seemed to have withdrawn into herself, gone far away. He wondered if his erratic driving was bumming her. Probably so.

Another fantasy film rolled suddenly into his head, without his consent: He saw, first, a big parked Pontiac with a bumper jack on the back of it that was slipping and a kid around thirteen with long thatched hair struggling to hold the car from rolling, meanwhile yelling for assistance. He saw himself and Jerry Fabin running out of the house together, Jerry's house, down the beer-can-littered drive-way to the car. Himself, he grabbed at the car door on the driver's side to open it, to stomp the brake pedal. But Jerry Fabin, wearing only his pants, without even shoes, his hair all disarranged and streaming—he had been sleeping—Jerry ran past the car to the back and knocked, with his bare pale shoulder that never saw the light of day, the boy entirely away from the car. The jack bent and fell, the rear of the car crashed down, the tire and wheel rolled away, and the boy was okay.

"Too late for the brake," Jerry panted, trying to get his ugly greasy hair from his eyes and blinking. "No time."

"'S he okay?" Charles Freck yelled. His heart still pounded.

"Yeah." Jerry stood by the boy, gasping. "Shit!" he yelled at the boy in fury. "Didn't I tell you to wait until we were doing it with you? And when a bumper jack slips—shit, man, you can't hold back five thousand pounds!" His face writhed. The boy, little Ratass, looked miserable and twitched guiltily. "I repeatedly and repeatedly told you!"

"I went for the brake," Charles Freck explained, knowing his idiocy, his own equal fuckup, great as the boy's and equally lethal. His failure as a full-grown man to respond right. But he wanted to justify it anyhow, as the boy did, in words. "But now I realize—" he yammered on, and then the fantasy number broke off; it was a documentary rerun, actually, because he remembered the day when this had happened, back when they were all living together. Jerry's good instinct—otherwise Ratass would have been under the back of the Pontiac, his spine smashed.

The three of them plodded gloomily back toward the house, not even chasing the tire and wheel, which was still rolling off.

"I was asleep," Jerry muttered as they entered the dark interior of the house. "It's the first time in a couple weeks the bugs let up enough so I could. I haven't got any sleep at all for five days—I been runnin' and runnin'. I thought they were maybe gone; they've *been* gone. I thought they finally gave up and went somewhere else, like next door and out of the house entirely. Now I can feel them again. That tenth No Pest Strip I got, or maybe it's the eleventh—they cheated me again, like they did with all the others." But his voice was subdued now, not angry, just low and perplexed. He put his hand on Ratass's head and gave him a sharp smack. "You dumb kid —when a bumper jack slips get the hell out of there. Forget the car. Don't ever get behind it and try to push back against all that mass and block it with your body."

"But, Jerry, I was afraid the axle—"

"Fuck the axle. Fuck the car. It's your life." They passed on through the dark living room, the three of them, and the rerun of a now gone moment winked out and died forever.

CHAPTER TWO

"Gentlemen of the Anaheim Lions Club," the man at the microphone said, "we have a wonderful opportunity this afternoon, for, you see, the County of Orange has provided us with the chance to hear from—and then put questions to and of—an undercover narcotics agent from the Orange County Sheriff's Department." He beamed, this man wearing his pink waffle-fiber suit and wide plastic yellow tie and blue shirt and fake leather shoes; he was an overweight man, overaged as well, overhappy even when there was little or nothing to be happy about.

Watching him, the undercover narcotics agent felt nausea.

"Now, you will notice," the Lions Club host said, "that you can barely see this individual, who is seated directly to my right, because he is wearing what is called a scramble suit, which is the exact same suit he wears—and in fact must wear—during certain parts, in fact most, of his daily activities of law enforcement. Later he will explain why."

The audience, which mirrored the qualities of the host in every possible way, regarded the individual in his scramble suit.

"This man," the host declared, "whom we will call Fred, because this is the code name under which he reports the information he gathers, once within the scramble suit, cannot be identified by voice, or by even technological voiceprint, or by appearance. He looks, does he not, like a vague blur and nothing more? Am I right?" He let loose a great smile. His audience, appreciating that this was indeed funny, did a little smiling on their own.

The scramble suit was an invention of the Bell Laboratories, conjured up by accident by an employee named S. A. Powers. He had, a few years ago, been experimenting with disinhibiting substances affecting neural tissue, and one night, having administered to himself an IV injection considered safe and mildly euphoric, had experienced a disastrous drop in the GABA fluid of his brain. Subjectively, he had then witnessed lurid phosphene activity projected on the far wall of his bedroom, a frantically progressing montage of what, at the time, he imagined to be modern-day abstract paintings.

For about six hours, entranced, S. A. Powers had watched thousands of Picasso paintings replace one another at flash-cut speed, and then he had been treated to Paul Klees, more than the painter had painted during his entire lifetime. S. A. Powers, now viewing Modigliani paintings replace themselves at furious velocity, had conjectured (one needs a theory for everything) that the Rosicrucians were telepathically beaming pictures at him, probably boosted by microrelay systems of an advanced order; but then, when Kandinsky paintings began to harass him, he recalled that the main art museum at Leningrad specialized in just such nonobjective moderns, and he decided that the Soviets were attempting telepathically to contact him.

In the morning he remembered that a drastic drop in the GABA fluid of the brain normally produced such phosphene activity; nobody was trying telepathically, with or without microwave boosting, to contact him. But it did give him the idea for the scramble suit. Basically, his design consisted of a multifaced quartz lens hooked to a miniaturized computer whose memory banks held up to a million and a half physiognomic fraction-representations of various people: men and women, children, with every variant encoded and then projected outward in all directions equally onto a superthin shroudlike membrane large enough to fit around an average human.

As the computer looped through its banks, it projected every conceivable eye color, hair color, shape and type of nose, formation of teeth, configuration of facial bone structure—the entire shroudlike membrane took on whatever physical characteristics were projected at any nanosecond, and then switched to the next. Just to make his scramble suit more effective, S. A. Powers programmed the computer to randomize the sequence of characteristics within each set. And to bring the cost down (the federal people always liked that), he found the source for the material of the membrane in a by-product of a large industrial firm already doing business with Washington.

In any case, the wearer of a scramble suit was Everyman and in every combination (up to combinations of a million and a half subbits) during the course of each hour. Hence, any description of him —or her—was meaningless. Needless to say, S. A. Powers had fed his own personal physiognomic characteristics into the computer units, so that, buried in the frantic permutation of qualities, his own surfaced and combined . . . on an average, he had calculated, of once each fifty years per suit, served up and reassembled, given enough time per suit. It was his closest claim to immortality.

"Let's hear it for the vague blur!" the host said loudly, and there was mass clapping.

In his scramble suit, Fred, who was also Robert Arctor, groaned and thought: This is terrible.

Once a month an undercover narcotics agent of the county was assigned at random to speak before bubblehead gatherings such as this. Today was his turn. Looking at his audience, he realized how much he detested straights. They thought this was all great. They were smiling. They were being entertained.

Maybe at this moment the virtually countless components of his scramble suit had served up S. A. Powers.

"But to be serious for just a moment," the host said, "this man here . . ." He paused, trying to remember.

"Fred," Bob Arctor said. S. A. Fred.

"Fred, yes." The host, invigorated, resumed, booming in the direction of his audience, "You see, Fred's voice is like one of those robot computer voices down in San Diego at the bank when you drive in, perfectly toneless and artificial. It leaves in our minds no characteristics, exactly as when he reports to his superiors in the Orange County Drug Abuse, ah, Program." He paused meaningfully. "You see, there is a dire risk for these police officers because the forces of dope, as we know, have penetrated with amazing skill into the various law-enforcement apparatuses throughout our nation, or may well have, according to most informed experts. So for the protection of these dedicated men, this scramble suit is necessary."

Slight applause for the scramble suit. And then expectant gazes at Fred, lurking within its membrane.

"But in his line of work in the field," the host added finally, as he moved away from the microphone to make room for Fred, "he, of course, does not wear this. He dresses like you or I, although, of course, in the hippie garb of those of the various subculture groups within which he bores in tireless fashion."

He motioned to Fred to rise and approach the microphone. Fred, Robert Arctor, had done this six times before, and he knew what to say and what was in store for him: the assorted degrees and kinds of asshole questions and opaque stupidity. The waste of time for him out of this, plus anger on his part, and a sense of futility each time, and always more so.

"If you saw me on the street," he said into the microphone, after the applause had died out, "you'd say, 'There goes a weirdo freak doper.' And you'd feel aversion and walk away."

Silence.

"I don't look like you," he said. "I can't afford to. My life depends on it." Actually, he did not look that different from them. And anyhow, he would have worn what he wore daily anyhow, job or not, life or not. He liked what he wore. But what he was saying had, by and large, been written by others and put before him to memorize. He could depart some, but they all had a standard format they used. Introduced a couple of years ago by a gung-ho division chief, it had by now become writ.

He waited while that sank in.

"I am not going to tell you first," he said, "what I am attempting to do as an undercover officer engaged in tracking down dealers and most of all the source of their illegal drugs in the streets of our cities and corridors of our schools, here in Orange County. I am going to tell you"—he paused, as they had trained him to do in PR class at the academy—"what I am afraid of," he finished.

That gaffed them; they had become all eyes.

"What I fear," he said, "night and day, is that our children, your children and my children . . ." Again he paused. "I have two," he said. Then, extra quietly, "Little ones, very little." And then he raised his voice emphatically. "But not too little to be addicted, calculatedly addicted, for profit, by those who would destroy this society." Another pause. "We do not know as yet," he continued presently, more calmly, "specifically who these men—or rather animals—are who prey on our young, as if in a wild jungle abroad, as in some foreign country, not ours. The identity of the purveyors of the poisons concocted of brain-destructive filth shot daily, orally taken daily, smoked daily by several million men and women—or rather, that were once men and women—is gradually being unraveled. But finally we will, before God, know for sure."

A voice from the audience: "Sock it to 'em!"

Another voice, equally enthusiastic: "Get the commies!"

Applause and reprise severally.

Robert Arctor halted. Stared at them, at the straights in their fat suits, their fat ties, their fat shoes, and he thought, Substance D can't destroy their brains; they have none.

"Tell it like it is," a slightly less emphatic voice called up, a woman's voice. Searching, Arctor made out a middle-aged lady, not so fat, her hands clasped anxiously.

"Each day," Fred, Robert Arctor, whatever, said, "this disease takes its toll of us. By the end of each passing day the flow of profits —and where they go we—" He broke off. For the life of him he could not dredge up the rest of the sentence, even though he had repeated it a million times, both in class and at previous lectures.

All in the large room had fallen silent.

"Well," he said, "it isn't the profits anyhow. It's something else. What you see happen."

They didn't notice any difference, he noticed, even though he had dropped the prepared speech and was wandering on, by himself, without help from the PR boys back at the Orange County Civic Center. What difference anyhow? he thought. So what? What, really, do they know or care? The straights, he thought, live in their fortified huge apartment complexes guarded by their guards, ready to open fire on any and every doper who scales the wall with an empty pillowcase to rip off their piano and electric clock and razor and stereo that they haven't paid for anyhow, so he can get his fix, get the shit that if he doesn't he maybe dies, outright flat-out dies, of the pain and shock of withdrawal. But, he thought, when you're living inside looking safely out, and your wall is electrified and your guard is armed, why think about that?

"If you were a diabetic," he said, "and you didn't have money for a hit of insulin, would you steal to get the money? Or just die?"

Silence.

In the headphone of his scramble suit a tinny voice said, "I think you'd better go back to the prepared text, Fred. I really do advise it."

Into his throat mike, Fred, Robert Arctor, whatever, said, "I forget it." Only his superior at Orange County GHQ, which was not Mr. F., that is to say, Hank, could hear this. This was an anonymous superior, assigned to him only for this occasion.

"Riiiight," the official tinny prompter said in his earphone. "I'll read it to you. Repeat it after me, but try to get it to sound casual." Slight hesitation, riffling of pages. "Let's see . . . 'Each day the profits flow—where they go we—' That's about where you stopped."

"I've got a block against this stuff," Arctor said.

"'—will soon determine,'" his official prompter said, unheeding, "'and then retribution will swiftly follow. And at that moment I would not for the life of me be in their shoes.'"

"Do you know why I've got a block against this stuff?" Arctor said. "Because this is what gets people on dope." He thought, This is why you lurch off and become a doper, this sort of stuff. This is why you give up and leave. In disgust.

But then he looked once more out at his audience and realized that for them this was not so. This was the only way they could be reached. He was talking to nitwits. Mental simps. It had to be put in the same way it had been put in first grade: *A* is for Apple and the Apple is Round.

"*D*," he said aloud to his audience, "is for Substance D. Which is for Dumbness and Despair and Desertion, the desertion of your friends from you, you from them, everyone from everyone, isolation and loneliness and hating and suspecting each other. *D*," he said then, "is finally Death. Slow Death, we—" He halted. "We, the dopers," he said, "call it." His voice rasped and faltered. "As you probably know. Slow Death. From the head on down. Well, that's it." He walked back to his chair and reseated himself. In silence.

"You blew it," his superior the prompter said. "See me in my office when you get back. Room 430."

"Yes," Arctor said. "I blew it."

They were looking at him as if he had pissed on the stage before their eyes. Although he was not sure just why.

Striding to the mike, the Lions Club host said, "Fred asked me in advance of this lecture to make it primarily a question-and-answer forum, with only a short introductory statement by him. I forgot to mention that. All right"—he raised his right hand—"who first, people?"

Arctor suddenly got to his feet again, clumsily.

"It would appear that Fred has something more to add," the host said, beckoning to him.

Going slowly back over to the microphone, Arctor said, his head down, speaking with precision, "Just this. Don't kick their asses after they're on it. The users, the addicts. Half of them, most of them, especially the girls, didn't know what they were getting on or even that they were getting on anything at all. Just try to keep them, the people, any of us, from getting on it." He looked up briefly. "See, they dissolve some reds in a glass of wine, the pushers, I mean—they give the booze to a chick, an underage little chick, with eight to ten reds in it, and she passes out, and then they inject her with a mex hit, which is half heroin and half Substance D—" He broke off. "Thank you," he said.

A man called up, "How do we stop them, sir?"

"Kill the pushers," Arctor said, and walked back to his chair.

He did not feel like returning right away to the Orange County Civic Center and Room 430, so he wandered down one of the commercial streets of Anaheim, inspecting the McDonaldburger stands and car washes and gas stations and Pizza Huts and other marvels.

Roaming aimlessly along like this on the public street with all kinds of people, he always had a strange feeling as to who he was. As he had said to the Lions types there in the hall, he looked like a doper when out of his scramble suit; he conversed like a doper; those around him now no doubt took him to be a doper and reacted accordingly. Other dopers—See there, he thought; "other," for instance —gave him a "peace, brother" look, and the straights didn't.

You put on a bishop's robe and miter, he pondered, and walk

around in that, and people bow and genuflect and like that, and try to kiss your ring, if not your ass, and pretty soon you're a bishop. So to speak. What is identity? he asked himself. Where does the act end? Nobody knows.

What really fouled up his sense of who and what he was came when the Man hassled him. When harness bulls, beat cops, or cops in general, any and all, for example, came cruising up slowly to the curb near him in an intimidating manner as he walked, scrutinized him at length with an intense, keen, metallic, blank stare, and then, often as not, evidently on whim, parked and beckoned him over.

"Okay, let's see your I.D.," the cop would say, reaching out; and then, as Arctor-Fred-Whatever-Godknew fumbled in his wallet pocket, the cop would yell at him, "Ever been ARRESTED?" Or, as a variant on that, adding, "BEFORE?" As if he were about to go into the bucket right then.

"What's the beef?" he usually said, if he said anything at all. A crowd naturally gathered. Most of them assumed he'd been nailed dealing on the corner. They grinned uneasily and waited to see what happened, although some of them, usually Chicanos or blacks or obvious heads, looked angry. And those that looked angry began after a short interval to be aware that they looked angry, and they changed that swiftly to impassive. Because everybody knew that anyone looking angry or uneasy—it didn't matter which—around cops must have something to hide. The cops especially knew that, legend had it, and they hassled such persons automatically.

This time, however, no one bothered him. Many heads were in evidence; he was only one of many.

What am I actually? he asked himself. He wished, momentarily, for his scramble suit. Then, he thought, I could go on being a vague blur and passers-by, street people in general, would applaud. Let's hear it for the vague blur, he thought, doing a short rerun. What a way to get recognition. How, for instance, could they be sure it wasn't some other vague blur and not the right one? It could be somebody other than Fred inside, or another Fred, and they'd never know, not even when Fred opened his mouth and talked. They wouldn't really know then. They'd never know. It could be Al pretending to be Fred, for example. It could be anyone in there, it could even be empty. Down at Orange County GHQ they could be piping a voice to the scramble suit, animating it from the sheriff's office. Fred could in that case be anybody who happened to be at his desk that day and happened to pick up the script and the mike, or a composite of all sorts of guys at their desks.

But I guess what I said at the end, he thought, finishes off that.

That wasn't anybody back in the office. The guys back in the office want to talk to me about that, as a matter of fact.

He didn't look forward to that, so he continued to loiter and delay, going nowhere, going everywhere. In Southern California it didn't make any difference anyhow where you went; there was always the same McDonaldburger place over and over, like a circular strip that turned past you as you pretended to go somewhere. And when finally you got hungry and went to the McDonaldburger place and bought a McDonald's hamburger, it was the one they sold you last time and the time before that and so forth, back to before you were born, and in addition bad people—liars—said it was made out of turkey gizzards anyhow.

They had by now, according to their sign, sold the same original burger fifty billion times. He wondered if it was to the same person. Life in Anaheim, California, was a commercial for itself, endlessly replayed. Nothing changed; it just spread out farther and farther in the form of neon ooze. What there was always more of had been congealed into permanence long ago, as if the automatic factory that cranked out these objects had jammed in the *on* position. How the land became plastic, he thought, remembering the fairy tale "How the Sea Became Salt." Someday, he thought, it'll be mandatory that we all sell the McDonald's hamburger as well as buy it; we'll sell it back and forth to each other forever from our living rooms. That way we won't even have to go outside.

He looked at his watch. Two-thirty: time to make a buy call. According to Donna, he could score, through her, on perhaps a thousand tabs of Substance D cut with meth.

Naturally, once he got it, he would turn it over to County Drug Abuse to be analyzed and then destroyed, or whatever they did with it. Dropped it themselves, maybe, or so another legend went. Or sold it. But his purchase from her was not to bust her for dealing; he had bought many times from her and had never arrested her. That was not what it was all about, busting a small-time local dealer, a chick who considered it cool and far-out to deal dope. Half the narcotics agents in Orange County were aware that Donna dealt, and recognized her on sight. Donna even dealt sometimes in the parking lot of the 7-11 store, in front of the automatic holo-scanner the police kept going there, and got away with it. In a sense, Donna could never be busted no matter what she did and in front of whom.

What his transaction with Donna, like all those before, added up to was an attempt to thread a path upward via Donna to the supplier she bought from. So his purchases from her gradually grew in quantity. Originally he had coaxed her—if that was the word—into laying

ten tabs on him, as a favor: friend-to-friend stuff. Then, later on, he
had wangled a bag of a hundred for recompense, then three bags.
Now, if he lucked out, he could score a thousand, which was ten
bags. Eventually, he would be buying in a quantity which would be
beyond her economic capacity; she could not front enough bread to
her supplier to secure the stuff at her end. Therefore, she would lose
instead of getting a big profit. They would haggle; she would insist
that he front at least part of it; he would refuse; she couldn't front it
herself to her source; time would run out—even in a deal that small
a certain amount of tension would grow; everyone would be getting
impatient; her supplier, whoever he was, would be holding and mad
because she hadn't shown. So eventually, if it worked out right, she
would give up and say to him and to her supplier, "Look, you better
deal direct with each other. I know you both; you're both cool. I'll
vouch for both of you. I'll set a place and a time and you two can
meet. So from now on, Bob, you can start buying direct, if you're
going to buy in this quantity." Because in that quantity he was for all
intents and purposes a dealer; these were approaching dealer's quantities. Donna would assume he was reselling at a profit per hundred,
since he was buying a thousand at a time at least. This way he could
travel up the ladder and come to the next person in line, become a
dealer like her, and then later on maybe get another step up and another as the quantities he bought grew.

Eventually—this was the name of the project—he would meet
someone high enough to be worth busting. That meant someone who
knew something, which meant someone either in contact with those
who manufactured or someone who ran it in from the supplier who
himself knew the source.

Unlike other drugs, Substance D had—apparently—only one
source. It was synthetic, not organic; therefore, it came from a lab. It
could be synthesized, and already had been in federal experiments.
But the constituents were themselves derived from complex substances almost equally difficult to synthesize. Theoretically it could
be manufactured by anyone who had, first, the formula and, second,
the technological capacity to set up a factory. But in practice the cost
was out of reach. Also, those who had invented it and were making it
available sold it too cheaply for effective competition. And the wide
distribution suggested that even though a sole source existed, it had a
diversified layout, probably a series of labs in several key areas, perhaps one near each major urban drug-using spot in North America
and Europe. Why none of these had been found was a mystery; but
the implication was, both publicly and no doubt under official wraps,
that the S. D. Agency—as the authorities arbitrarily termed it—had

penetrated so far up into law-enforcement groups, both local and na-
tional, that those who found out anything usable about its operations
soon either didn't care or didn't exist.

He had, naturally, several other leads at present besides Donna.
Other dealers he pressured progressively for larger quantities. But
because she was his chick—or anyhow he had hopes in that direction
—she was for him the easiest. Visiting her, talking to her on the
phone, taking her out or having her over—that was a personal pleasure as well. It was, in a sense, the line of least resistance. If you had
to spy on and report about someone, it might as well be people you'd
see anyhow; that was less suspicious and less of a drag. And if you
did not see them frequently before you began surveillance, you
would have to eventually anyhow; it worked out the same in the end.

Entering the phone booth, he did a phone thing.

Ring-ring-ring.

"Hello," Donna said.

Every pay phone in the world was tapped. Or if it wasn't, some
crew somewhere just hadn't gotten around to it. The taps fed electronically onto storage reels at a central point, and about once every
second day a print-out was obtained by an officer who listened to
many phones without having to leave his office. He merely rang up
the storage drums and, on signal, they played back, skipping all dead
tape. Most calls were harmless. The officer could identify ones that
weren't fairly readily. That was his skill. That was what he got paid
for. Some officers were better at it than others.

As he and Donna talked, therefore, no one was listening. The
playback would come maybe the next day at the earliest. If they
discussed anything strikingly illegal, and the monitoring officer
caught it, then voiceprints would be made. But all he and she had to
do was keep it mild. The dialogue could still be recognizable as a
dope deal. A certain governmental economy came into play here—it
wasn't worth going through the hassle of voiceprints and track-down
for routine illegal transactions. There were too many each day of the
week, over too many phones. Both Donna and he knew this.

"How you doin'?" he asked.

"Okay." Pause in her warm, husky voice.

"How's your head today?"

"Sort of in a bad space. Sort of down." Pause. "I was bum-tripped
this A.M. by my boss at the shop." Donna worked behind the counter
of a little perfume shop in Gateside Mall in Costa Mesa, to which
she drove every morning in her MG. "You know what he said? He
said this customer, this old guy, gray hair, who bilked us out of ten
bucks—he said it was my fault and I've got to make it good. It's

coming out of my paycheck. So I'm out ten bucks through no fuck-ing—excuse me—fault of my own."

Arctor said, "Hey, can I get anything from you?"

She sounded sullen now. As if she didn't want to. Which was a shuck. "How—much do you want? I don't know."

"Ten of them," he said. The way they had it set up, one was a hundred; this was a request for a thousand, then.

Among fronts, if transactions had to take place over public com-munications, a fairly good try consisted of masking a large one by an apparently small one. They could deal and deal forever, in fact, in these quantities, without the authorities taking any interest; other-wise, the narcotics teams would be raiding apartments and houses up and down each street each hour of the day, and achieving little.

" 'Ten,' " Donna muttered, irritably.

"I'm really hurting," he said, like a user. Rather than a dealer. "I'll pay you back later, when I've scored."

"No," she said woodenly. "I'll lay them on you gratis. Ten." Now, undoubtedly, she was speculating whether he was dealing. Probably he was. "Ten. Why not? Say, three days from now?"

"No sooner?"

"These are—"

"Okay," he said.

"I'll drop over."

"What time?"

She calculated. "Say around eight in the P.M. Hey, I want to show you a book I got, somebody left it at the shop. It's cool. It has to do with wolves. You know what wolves do? The male wolf? When he defeats his foe, he doesn't snuff him—he pees on him. Really! He stands there and pees on his defeated foe and then he splits. That's it. Territory is what they mostly fight over. And the right to screw. You know."

Arctor said, "I peed on some people a little while ago."

"No kidding? How come?"

"Metaphorically," he said.

"Not the usual way?"

"I mean," he said, "I told them—" He broke off. Talking too much; a fuckup. Jesus, he thought. "These dudes," he said, "like biker types, you dig? Around the Foster's Freeze? I was cruising by and they said something raunchy. So I turned around and said some-thing like—" He couldn't think of anything for a moment.

"You can tell me," Donna said, "even if it's super gross. You gotta be super gross with biker types or they won't understand."

Arctor said, "I told them I'd rather ride a pig than a hog. Any time."

"I don't get it."

"Well, a pig is a chick that—"

"Oh yeah. Okay, well I get it. Barf."

"I'll see you at my place like you said," he said. "Good-by." He started to hang up.

"Can I bring the wolf book and show you? It's by Konrad Lorenz. The back cover, where they tell, says he was the foremost authority on wolves on earth. Oh yeah, one more thing. Your roommates both came into the shop today, Ernie what's-his-name and that Barris. Looking for you, if you might have—"

"What about?" Arctor said.

"Your cephalochromoscope that cost you nine hundred dollars, that you always turn on and play when you get home—Ernie and Barris were babbling away about it. They tried to use it today and it wouldn't work. No colors and no ceph patterns, neither one. So they got Barris's tool kit and unscrewed the bottom plate."

"The hell you say!" he said, indignant.

"And they say it's been fucked over. Sabotaged. Cut wires, and like sort of weird stuff—you know, freaky things. Shorts and broken parts. Barris said he'd try to—"

"I'm going right home," Arctor said, and hung up. My primo possession, he thought bitterly. And that fool Barris tinkering with it. But I can't go home right now, he realized. I've got to go over to New-Path to check on what they're up to.

It was his assignment: mandatory.

CHAPTER THREE

Charles Freck, too, had been thinking about visiting New-Path. The freakout of Jerry Fabin had gotten to him that much.

Seated with Jim Barris in the Fiddler's Three coffee shop in Santa Ana, he fooled around with his sugar-glazed doughnut morosely. "It's a heavy decision," he said. "That's cold turkey they do. They just keep with you night and day so you don't snuff yourself or bite off your arm, but they never give you anything. Like, a doctor will prescribe. Valium, for instance."

Chuckling, Barris inspected his patty melt, which was melted imitation cheese and fake ground beef on special organic bread. "What kind of bread is this?" he asked.

"Look on the menu," Charles Freck said. "It explains."

"If you go in," Barris said, "you'll experience symptoms that emanate up from the basic fluids of the body, specifically those located in the brain. By that I refer to the catecholamines, such as noradrenalin and seratonin. You see, it functions this way: Substance D, in fact all addictive dope, but Substance D most of all, interacts with the catecholamines in such a fashion that involvement is locked in place at a subcellular level. Biological counter-adaptation has occurred, and in a sense forever." He ate a huge bite of the right half of his patty melt. "They used to believe this occurred only with the alkaloid narcotics, such as heroin."

"I never shot smack. It's a downer."

The waitress, foxy and nice in her yellow uniform, with pert boobs and blond hair, came over to their table. "Hi," she said. "Is everything all right?"

Charles Freck gazed up in fear.

"Is your name Patty?" Barris asked her, signaling to Charles Freck that it was cool.

"No." She pointed to the name badge on her right boob. "It's Beth."

I wonder what the left one's called, Charles Freck thought.

"The waitress we had last time was named Patty," Barris said, eying the waitress grossly. "Same as the sandwich."

"That must have been a different Patty from the sandwich. I think she spells it with an *i*."

"Everything is super good," Barris said. Over his head Charles Freck could see a thought balloon in which Beth was stripping off her clothes and moaning to be banged.

"Not with me," Charles Freck said. "I got a lot of problems nobody else has."

In a somber voice, Barris said, "More people than you'd think. And more each day. This is a world of illness, and getting progressively worse." Above his head, the thought balloon got worse too.

"Would you like to order dessert?" Beth asked, smiling down at them.

"What like?" Charles Freck said with suspicion.

"We have fresh strawberry pie and fresh peach pie," Beth said smiling, "that we make here ourselves."

"No, we don't want any dessert," Charles Freck said. The waitress left. "That's for old ladies," he said to Barris, "those fruit pies."

"The idea of turning yourself over for rehabilitation," Barris said, "certainly makes you apprehensive. That's a manifestation of purposeful negative symptoms, your fear. It's the drug talking, to keep you out of New-Path and keep you from getting off it. You see, all symptoms are purposeful, whether they are positive or negative."

"No shit," Charles Freck muttered.

"The negative ones show up as the cravings, which are deliberately generated by the total body to force its owner—which in this case is you—to search frantically—"

"The first thing they do to you when you go into New-Path," Charles Freck said, "is they cut off your pecker. As an object lesson. And then they fan out in all directions from there."

"Your spleen next," Barris said.

"They what, they cut— What does that do, a spleen?"

"Helps you digest your food."

"How?"

"By removing the cellulose from it."

"Then I guess after that—"

"Just noncellulose foods. No leaves or alfalfa."

"How long can you live that way?"

Barris said, "It depends on your attitude."

"How many spleens does the average person have?" He knew there usually were two kidneys.

"Depends on his weight and age."

"Why?" Charles Freck felt keen suspicion.

"A person grows more spleens over the years. By the time he's eighty"—

"You're shitting me."

Barris laughed. Always he had been a strange laugher, Charles Freck thought. An unreal laugh, like something breaking. "Why your decision," Barris said presently, "to turn yourself in for residence therapy at a drug rehab center?"

"Jerry Fabin," he said.

With a gesture of easy dismissal, Barris said, "Jerry was a special case. I once watched Jerry Fabin staggering around and falling down, shitting all over himself, not knowing where he was, trying to get me to look up and research what poison he'd got hold of, thallium sulfate most likely . . . it's used in insecticides and to snuff rats. It was a burn, somebody paying him back. I could think of ten different toxins and poisons that might"—

"There's another reason," Charles Freck said. "I'm running low again in my supply, and I can't stand it, this always running low and not knowing if I'm fucking ever going to see any more."

"Well, we can't even be sure we'll see another sunrise."

"But shit—I'm down so low now that it's like a matter of days. And also . . . I think I'm being ripped off. I can't be taking them that fast; somebody must be pilfering from my fucking stash."

"How many tabs do you drop a day?"

"That's very difficult to determine. But not that many."

"A tolerance builds up, you know."

"Sure, right, but not like that. I can't stand running out and like that. On the other hand . . ." He reflected. "I think I got a new source. That chick, Donna. Donna something."

"Oh, Bob's girl."

"His old lady," Charles Freck said, nodding.

"No, he never got into her pants. He tries to."

"Is she reliable?"

"Which way? As a lay or—" Barris gestured: hand to mouth and swallowing.

"What kind of sex is that?" Then he flashed on it. "Oh, yeah, the latter."

"Fairly reliable. Scatterbrained, somewhat. Like you'd expect with a chick, especially the darker ones. Has her brain between her legs, like most of them. Probably keeps her stash there too." He chuckled. "Her whole dealer's stash."

Charles Freck leaned toward him. "Arctor never balled Donna? He talks about her like he did."

Barris said, "That's Bob Arctor. Talks like he did many things. Not the same, not at all."

"Well, how come he never laid her? Can't he get it on?"

Barris reflected wisely, still fiddling with his patty melt; he had now torn it into little bits. "Donna has problems. Possibly she's on junk. Her aversion to bodily contact in general—junkies lose interest in sex, you realize, due to their organs swelling up from vasoconstriction. And Donna, I've observed, shows an inordinate failure of sexual arousal, to an unnatural degree. Not just toward Arctor but toward . . ." He paused grumpily. "Other males as well."

"Shit, you just mean she won't come across."

"She would," Barris said, "if she were handled right. For instance . . ." He glanced up in a mysterious fashion. "I can show you how to lay her for ninety-eight cents."

"I don't want to lay her. I just want to buy from her." He felt uneasy. There was perpetually something about Barris that made his stomach uncomfortable. "Why ninety-eight cents?" he said. "She wouldn't take money; she's not turning tricks. Anyhow, she's Bob's chick."

"The money wouldn't be paid directly to her," Barris said in his precise, educated way. He leaned toward Charley Freck, pleasure and guile quivering amid his hairy nostrils. And not only that, the green tint of his shades had steamed up. "Donna does coke. Anybody who would give her a gram of coke she'd undoubtedly spread her legs for, especially if certain rare chemicals were added in strictly scientific fashion that I've done painstaking original research on."

"I wish you wouldn't talk that way," Charles Freck said. "About her. Anyhow, a gram of coke's selling now for over a hundred dollars. Who's got that?"

Half sneezing, Barris declared, "I can derive a gram of pure cocaine at a total cost to me, for the ingredients from which I get it, not including my labor, of less than a dollar."

"Bullshit."

"I'll give you a demonstration."

"Where do these ingredients come from?"

"The 7-11 store," Barris said, and stumbled to his feet, discarding bits of patty melt in his excitement. "Get the check," he said, "and I'll show you. I've got a temporary lab set up at the house, until I can create a better one. You can watch me extract a gram of cocaine from common legal materials purchased openly at the 7-11 food store for under a dollar total cost." He started down the aisle. "Come on." His voice was urgent.

"Sure," Charles Freck said, picking up the check and following.

The mother's dingey, he thought. Or maybe he isn't. With all those chemistry experiments he does, and reading and reading at the county library . . . maybe there's something to it. Think of the profit, he thought. Think what we could clear!

He hurried after Barris, who was getting out the keys to his Karmann Ghia as he strode, in his surplus flier's jump suit, past the cashier.

They parked in the lot of the 7-11, got out and walked inside. As usual, a huge dumb cop stood pretending to read a stroke-book magazine at the front counter; in actuality, Charles Freck knew, he was checking out everyone who entered, to see if they were intending to hit the place.

"What do we pick up here?" he asked Barris, who was casually strolling about the aisles of stacks of food.

"A spray can," Barris said. "Of Solarcaine."

"Sunburn spray?" Charles Freck did not really believe this was happening, but on the other hand, who knew? Who could be sure? He followed Barris to the counter; this time Barris paid.

They purchased the can of Solarcaine and then made it past the cop and back to their car. Barris drove rapidly from the lot, down the street, on and on at high speed, ignoring posted speed-limit signs, until finally he rolled to a halt before Bob Arctor's house, with all the old unopened newspapers in the tall grass of the front yard.

Stepping out, Barris lifted some items with wires dangling from the back seat to carry indoors. Voltmeter, Charles Freck saw. And other electronic testing gear, and a soldering gun. "What's that for?" he asked.

"I've got a long and arduous job to do," Barris said, carrying the various items, plus the Solarcaine, up the walk to the front door. He handed Charles Freck the door key. "And I'm probably not getting paid. As is customary."

Charles Freck unlocked the door, and they entered the house. Two cats and a dog rattled at them, making hopeful noises; he and Barris carefully edged them aside with their boots.

At the rear of the dinette Barris had, over the weeks, laid out a funky lab of sorts, bottles and bits of trash here and there, worthless-looking objects he had filched from different sources. Barris, Charles Freck knew, from having to hear about it, believed not so much in thrift as in ingenuity. You should be able to use the first thing that came to hand to achieve your objective, Barris preached. A thumb-tack, a paper clip, part of an assembly the other part of which was broken or lost . . . It looked to Charles Freck as if a rat had set up shop here, was performing experiments with what a rat prized.

The first move in Barris's scheme was to get a plastic bag from the roll by the sink and squirt the contents of the spray can into it, on and on until the can or at least the gas was exhausted.

"This is unreal," Charles Freck said. "Super unreal."

"What they have deliberately done," Barris said cheerfully as he labored, "is mix the cocaine with oil so it can't be extracted. But my knowledge of chemistry is such that I know precisely how to separate the coke from the oil." He had begun vigorously shaking salt into the gummy slime in the bag. Now he poured it all into a glass jar. "I'm freezing it," he announced, grinning, "which causes the cocaine crystals to rise to the top, since they are lighter than air. Than the oil, I mean. And then the terminal step, of course, I keep to myself, but it involves an intricate methodological process of filtering." He opened the freezer above the refrigerator and carefully placed the jar inside.

"How long will it be in there?" Charles Freck asked.

"Half an hour." Barris got out one of his hand-rolled cigarettes, lit it, then strolled over to the heap of electronic testing equipment. He stood there meditating, rubbing his bearded chin.

"Yeah," Charles Freck said, "but I mean, so even if you get a whole gram of pure coke out of this, I can't use it on Donna to . . . you know, get into her pants in exchange. It's like buying her; that's what it amounts to."

"Exchange," Barris corrected. "You give her a gift, she gives you one. The most precious gift a woman has."

"She'd know she was being bought." He had seen enough of Donna to flash on that; Donna would make out the shuck right off.

"Cocaine is an aphrodisiac," Barris muttered, half to himself; he was setting up the testing equipment beside Bob Arctor's cephalochromoscope, which was Bob's most expensive possession. "After she's snorted a good part of it she'll be happy to uncork herself."

"Shit, man," Charles Freck protested. "You're talking about Bob Arctor's girl. He's my friend, and the guy you and Luckman live with."

Barris momentarily raised his shaggy head; he scrutinized Charles Freck for a time. "There's a great deal about Bob Arctor you're not aware of," he said. "That none of us are. Your view is simplistic and naïve, and you believe about him what he wants you to."

"He's an all-right guy."

"Certainly," Barris said, nodding and grinning. "Beyond a doubt. One of the world's best. But I have come—we have come, those of us who have observed Arctor acutely and perceptively—to distinguish in him certain contradictions. Both in terms of personality structure and in behavior. In his total relatedness to life. In, so to speak, his innate style."

"You have anything specific?"

Barris's eyes, behind his green shades, danced.

"Your eyes dancing don't mean nothing to me," Charles Freck said. "What's wrong with the cephscope that you're working on it?" He moved in closer to look for himself.

Tilting the central chassis on end, Barris said, "Tell me what you observe there with the wiring underneath."

"I see cut wires," Charles Freck said. "And a bunch of what look like deliberate shorts. Who did it?"

Still Barris's merry knowing eyes danced with special delight.

"This crummy significant crud doesn't go down with me worth shit," Charles Freck said. "Who damaged this cephscope? When did it happen? You just find out recently? Arctor didn't say anything the last time I saw him, which was the day before yesterday."

Barris said, "Perhaps he wasn't prepared to talk about it yet."

"Well," Charles Freck said, "as far as I'm concerned, you're talking in spaced-out riddles. I think I'll go over to one of the New-Path residences and turn myself in and go through withdrawal cold turkey and get therapy, the destruct game they play, and be with those guys day and night, and not have to be around mysterious nuts like yourself that don't make sense and I can't understand. I can see this cephscope has been fucked over, but you're not telling me anything. Are you trying to allege that Bob Arctor did it, to his own expensive equipment, or are you not? What are you saying? I wish I was living over at New-Path, where I wouldn't have to go through this meaningful shit I don't dig day after day, if not with you then with some burned-out freak like you, equally spaced." He glared.

"I did not damage this transmitting unit," Barris said speculatively, his whiskers twitching, "and doubt seriously that Ernie Luckman did."

"I doubt seriously if Ernie Luckman ever damaged anything in his life, except that time he flipped out on bad acid and threw the living-room coffee table and everything else besides out through the window of that apartment they had, him and that Joan chick, onto the parking area. That's different. Normally Ernie's got it all together more than the rest of us. No, Ernie wouldn't sabotage somebody else's cephscope. And Bob Arctor—it's his, isn't it? What'd he do, get up secretly in the middle of the night without his knowledge and do this, burn himself like this? This was done by somebody out to burn him. That's what this was." You probably did it, you gunjy motherfucker, he thought. You got the technical know-how and your mind's weird. "The person that did this," he said, "ought to be either in a federal Neural-Aphasia Clinic or the marble orchard. Preferaably, in my opinion, the latter. Bob always really got off on this Altec cephscope; I musta seen him put it on, put it on, every time as soon as he gets home from work at night, soon as he steps in the door. Every guy has one thing he treasures. This was his. So I say, this is shit to do to him, man, shit."

"That's what I mean."

"What's what you mean?"

" 'As soon as he gets home from work at night,' " Barris repeated. "I have been for some time conjecturing as to who Bob Arctor is really employed by, what specific actual organization it is that he can't tell us."

"It's the fucking Blue Chip Redemption Stamp Center in Placentia," Charles Freck said. "He told me once."

"I wonder what he does there."

Charles Freck sighed. "Colors the stamps blue." He did not like Barris, really. Freck wished he were elsewhere, maybe scoring from the first person he ran into or called. Maybe I should split, he said to himself, but then he recalled the jar of oil and cocaine cooling in the freezer, one hundred dollars' worth for ninety-eight cents. "Listen," he said, "when will that stuff be ready? I think you're shucking me. How could the Solarcaine people sell it for that little if it has a gram of pure coke in it? How could they make a profit?"

"They buy," Barris declared, "in large quantities."

In his head, Charles Freck rolled an instant fantasy: dump trucks full of cocaine backing up to the Solarcaine factory, wherever it was, Cleveland maybe, dumping tons and tons of pure, unstepped-on, uncut, high-grade cocaine into one end of the factory, where it was mixed with oil and inert gas and other garbage and then stuck in little bright-colored spray cans to be stacked up by the thousands in 7-11 stores and drugstores and supermarkets. What we ought to do, he ruminated, is knock over one of those dump trucks; take the whole load, maybe seven or eight hundred pounds—hell, lots more. What does a dump truck hold?

Barris brought him the now empty Solarcaine spray can for his inspection; he showed him the label, on which were listed all the contents. "See? Benzocaine. Which only certain gifted people know is a trade name for cocaine. If they said cocaine on the label people would flash on it and they'd eventually do what I do. People just don't have the education to realize. The scientific training, such as I went through."

"What are you going to do with this knowledge?" Charles Freck asked. "Besides making Donna Hawthorne horny?"

"I plan to write a best-seller eventually," Barris said. "A text for the average person about how to manufacture safe dope in his kitchen without breaking the law. You see, this does not break the law. Benzocaine is legal. I phoned a pharmacy and asked them. It's in a lot of things."

"Gee," Charles Freck said, impressed. He examined his wristwatch, to see how much longer they had to wait.

Bob Arctor had been told by Hank, who was Mr. F., to check out the local New-Path residence centers in order to locate a major dealer, whom he had been watching, but who had abruptly dropped from sight.

Now and then a dealer, realizing he was about to be busted, took refuge in one of the drug-rehabilitation places, like Synanon and Center Point and X-Kalay and New-Path, posing as an addict seeking help. Once inside, his wallet, his name, everything that identified him, was stripped away in preparation for building up a new personality not drug-oriented. In this stripping-away process, much that the law-enforcement people needed in order to locate their suspect disappeared. Then, later on, when the pressure was off, the dealer emerged and resumed his usual activity outside.

How often this happened nobody knew. The drug-rehab outfits tried to discern when they were being so used, but not always successfully. A dealer in fear of forty years' imprisonment had motivation to spin a good story to the rehab staff that had the power to admit or refuse him. His agony at that point was mainly real.

Driving slowly up Katella Boulevard, Bob Arctor searched for the New-Path sign and the wooden building, formerly a private dwelling, that the energetic rehab people operated in this area. He did not enjoy shucking his way into a rehab place posing as a prospective resident in need of help, but this was the only way to do it. If he identified himself as a narcotics agent in search of somebody, the rehab people—most of them usually, anyhow—would begin evasive action as a matter of course. They did not want their family hassled by the Man, and he could get his head into that space, appreciate the validity of that. These ex-addicts were supposed to be safe at last; in fact, the rehab staff customarily officially guaranteed their safety on entering. On the other hand, the dealer he sought was a mother of the first water, and to use the rehab places this way ran contrary to every good interest for everyone. He saw no other choice for himself, or for Mr. F., who had originally put him onto Spade Weeks. Weeks had been Arctor's main subject for an interminable time, without result. And now, for ten whole days, he had been unfindable.

He made out the bold sign, parked in their little lot, which this particular branch of New-Path shared with a bakery, and walked in an uneven manner up the path to the front door, hands stuffed in his pockets, doing his loaded-and-miserable number.

At least the department didn't hold it against him for losing Spade Weeks. In their estimation, officially, it just proved how slick Weeks was. Technically Weeks was a runner rather than a dealer: he brought shipments of hard dope up from Mexico at irregular intervals, to somewhere short of L.A., where the buyers met and split it up. Weeks's method of sneaking the shipment across the border was a neat one: He taped it on the underside of the car of some straight type ahead of him at the crossing, then tracked the dude down on the U.S. side and shot him at the first convenient opportunity. If the U.S. border patrol discovered the dope taped on the underside of the straight's vehicle, then the straight got sent up, not Weeks. Possession was prima facie in California. Too bad for the straight, his wife and kids.

Better than anyone else in Orange County undercover work, he recognized Weeks on sight: fat black dude, in his thirties, with a unique slow and elegant speech pattern, as if memorized at some phony English school. Actually, Weeks came from the slums of L.A. He'd learned his diction, most likely, from edutapes loaned by some college library.

Weeks liked to dress in a subdued but classy way, as if he were a doctor or a lawyer. Often he carried an expensive alligator-hide attaché case and wore horn-rimmed glasses. Also, he usually was armed, with a shotgun for which he had commissioned a custom-made pistol grip from Italy, very posh and stylish. But at New-Path his assorted shucks would have been stripped away; they would have dressed him like everyone else, in random, donated clothes, and stuck his attaché case in the closet.

Opening the solid wood door, Arctor entered.

Gloomy hall, lounge to his left, with guys reading. A ping-pong table at the far end, then a kitchen. Slogans on the walls, some hand-done and some printed: THE ONLY REAL FAILURE IS TO FAIL OTHERS and so forth. Little noise, little activity. New-Path maintained assorted retail industries; probably most of the residents, guys and chicks alike, were at work, at their hair shops and gas stations and ballpoint-pen works. He stood there, waiting in a weary way.

"Yes?" A girl appeared, pretty, wearing an extremely short blue

cotton skirt and T-shirt with NEW-PATH dyed across it from nipple to
nipple.

He said, in a thick, croaking, humiliated voice, "I'm—in a bad
space. Can't get it together any more. Can I sit down?"

"Sure." The girl waved, and two guys, mediocre in appearance,
showed up, looking impassive. "Take him where he can sit down and
get him some coffee."

What a drag, Arctor thought as he let the two guys coerce him to a
seedy-looking overstuffed couch. Dismal walls, he noticed. Dismal
low-quality donated paint. They subsisted, though, on contributions;
difficulty in getting funded. "Thanks," he grated shakily, as if it was
an overwhelming relief to be there and sit. "Wow," he said, attempting to smooth his hair; he made it seem that he couldn't, and gave
up.

The girl, directly before him, said firmly, "You look like hell,
mister."

"Yeah," both guys agreed, in a surprisingly snappy tone. "Like
real shit. What you been doing, lying in your own crap?"

Arctor blinked.

"Who are you?" one guy demanded.

"You can see what he is," the other said. "Some scum from the
fucking garbage pail. Look." He pointed at Arctor's hair. "Lice.
That's why you itch, Jack."

The girl, calm and above it, but not in any way friendly, said,
"Why did you come in here, mister?"

To himself Arctor thought, Because you have a big-time runner in
here somewhere. And I'm the Man. And you're stupid, all of you.
But instead he muttered cringingly, which was evidently what was
expected, "Did you say—"

"Yes, mister, you can have some coffee." The girl jerked her head,
and one of the guys obediently strode off to the kitchen.

A pause. Then the girl bent down and touched his knee. "You feel
pretty bad, don't you?" she said softly.

He could only nod.

"Shame and a sense of disgust at the thing you are," she said.

"Yeah," he agreed.

"At the pollution you've made of yourself. A cesspool. Sticking
that spike up your ass day after day, injecting your body with—"

"I couldn't go on any more," Arctor said. "This place is the only
hope I could think of. I had a friend come in here, I think, he said he
was going to. A black dude, in his thirties, educated, very polite
and—"

"You'll meet the family later," the girl said. "If you qualify. You have to pass our requirements, you realize. And the first one is sincere need."

"I have that," Arctor said. "Sincere need."

"You've got to be bad off to be let in here."

"I am," he said.

"How strung out are you? What's your habit up to?"

"Ounce a day," Arctor said.

"Pure?"

"Yeah." He nodded. "I keep a sugar bowl of it on the table."

"It's going to be super rough. You'll gnaw your pillow into feathers all night; there'll be feathers everywhere when you wake up. And you'll have seizures and foam at the mouth. And dirty yourself the way sick animals do. Are you ready for that? You realize we don't give you anything here."

"There isn't anything," he said. This was a drag, and he felt restless and irritable. "My buddy," he said, "the black guy. Did he make it here? I sure hope he didn't get picked up by the pigs on the way—he was so out of it, man, he could hardly navigate. He thought—"

"There are no one-to-one relationships at New-Path," the girl said. "You'll learn that."

"Yeah, but did he make it here?" Arctor said. He could see he was wasting his time. Jesus, he thought; this is worse than we do downtown, this hassling. And she won't tell me jack shit. Policy, he realized. Like an iron wall. Once you go into one of these places you're dead to the world. Spade Weeks could be sitting beyond the partition, listening and laughing his ass off, or not be here at all, or anything in between. Even with a warrant—that never worked. The rehab outfits knew how to drag their feet, stall around until anyone living there sought by the police had zipped out a side door or bolted himself inside the furnace. After all, the staff here were all ex-addicts themselves. And no law-enforcement agency liked the idea of rousting a rehab place: the yells from the public never ceased.

Time to give up on Spade Weeks, he decided, and extricate myself. No wonder they never sent me around here before; these guys are not nice. And then he thought, So as far as I'm concerned, I've indefinitely lost my main assignment; Spade Weeks no longer exists.

I'll report back to Mr. F., he said to himself, and await reassignment. The hell with it. He rose to his feet stiffly and said, "I'm splitting." The two guys had now returned, one of them with a mug of coffee, the other with literature, apparently of an instructional kind.

"You're chickening out?" the girl said, haughtily, with contempt. "You don't have it at gut level to stick with a decision? To get off the filth? You're going to crawl back out of here on your belly?" All three of them glared at him with anger.

"Later," Arctor said, and moved toward the front door, the way out.

"Fucking doper," the girl said from behind him. "No guts, brain fried, nothing. Creep out, creep; it's your decision."

"I'll be back," Arctor said, nettled. The mood here oppressed him, and it had intensified now that he was leaving.

"We may not want you back, gutless," one of the guys said.

"You'll have to plead," the other said. "You may have to do a lot of heavy pleading. And even then we may not want you."

"In fact, we don't want you now," the girl said.

At the door Arctor paused and turned to face his accusers. He wanted to say something, but for the life of him he couldn't think of anything. They had blanked out his mind.

His brain would not function. No thoughts, no response, no answer to them, even a lousy and feeble one, came to him at all.

Strange, he thought, and was perplexed.

And passed on out of the building to his parked car.

As far as I'm concerned, he thought, Spade Weeks has disappeared forever. I ain't going back inside one of those places.

Time, he decided queasily, to ask to be reassigned. To go after somebody else.

They're tougher than we are.

CHAPTER FOUR

From within his scramble suit the nebulous blur who signed in as Fred faced another nebulous blur representing himself as Hank.

"So much for Donna, for Charley Freck, and—let's see . . ." Hank's metallic monotone clicked off for a second. "All right, you've covered Jim Barris." Hank made an annotation on the pad before him. "Doug Weeks, you think, is probably dead or out of this area."

"Or hiding and inactive," Fred said.

"Have you heard anyone mention this name: Earl or Art De Winter?"

"No."

"How about a woman named Molly? Large woman."

"No."

"How about a pair of spades, brothers, about twenty, named something like Hatfield? Possibly dealing in pound bags of heroin."

"Pounds? *Pound* bags of heroin?"

"That's right."

"No," Fred said. "I'd remember that."

"A Swedish person, tall, Swedish name. Male. Served time, wry sense of humor. Big man but thin, carrying a great deal of cash, probably from the split of a shipment earlier this month."

"I'll watch for him," Fred said. "Pounds." He shook his head, or rather the nebulous blur wobbled.

Hank sorted among his holographic notes. "Well, this one is in jail." He held up a picture briefly, then read the reverse. "No, this one's dead; they've got the body downstairs." He sorted on. Time passed. "Do you think the Jora girl is turning tricks?"

"I doubt it." Jora Kajas was only fifteen. Strung out on injectable Substance D already, she lived in a slum room in Brea, upstairs, the only heat radiating from a water heater, her source of income a State of California tuition scholarship she had won. She had not attended classes, so far as he knew, in six months.

"When she does, let me know. Then we can go after the parents."

"Okay." Fred nodded.

"Boy, the bubblegummers go downhill fast. We had one in here the other day—she looked fifty. Wispy gray hair, missing teeth, eyes sunk in, arms like pipe cleaners . . . We asked her what her age was and she said, 'Nineteen.' We double-checked. 'You know how old you look?' this one matron said to her. 'Look in the mirror.' So she looked in the mirror. She started to cry. I asked her how long she'd been shooting up."

"A year," Fred said.

"Four months."

"The street stuff is bad right now," Fred said, not trying to imagine the girl, nineteen, with her hair falling out. "Cut with worse garbage than usual."

"You know how she got strung out? Her brothers, both of them, who were dealing, went in her bedroom one night, held her down and shot her up, then balled her. Both of them. To break her in to her new life, I guess. She'd been on the corner several months when we hauled her in here."

"Where are they now?" He thought he might run into them.

"Serving a six-month sentence for possession. The girl's also got the clap, now, and didn't realize it. So it's gone up deep inside her, the way it does. Her brothers thought that was funny."

"Nice guys," Fred said.

"I'll tell you one that'll get you for sure. You're aware of the three babies over at Fairfield Hospital that they have to give hits of smack to every day, that are too young to withdraw yet? A nurse tried to—"

"It gets me," Fred said in his mechanical monotone. "I heard enough, thanks."

Hank continued, "When you think of newborn babies being heroin addicts because—"

"Thanks," the nebulous blur called Fred repeated.

"What do you figure the bust should be for a mother that gives a newborn baby a joypop of heroin to pacify it, to keep it from crying? Overnight in the county farm?"

"Something like that," Fred said tonelessly. "Maybe a weekend, like they do the drunks. Sometimes I wish I knew how to go crazy. I forget how."

"It's a lost art," Hank said. "Maybe there's an instruction manual on it."

"There was this flick back around 1970," Fred said, "called *The French Connection,* about a two-man team of heroin narks, and when they made their hit one of them went totally bananas and started shooting everyone in sight, including his superiors. It made no difference."

"It's maybe better you don't know who I am, then," Hank said. "You could only get me by accident."

"Somebody," Fred said, "will get us all anyhow eventually."

"It'll be a relief. A distinct relief." Going farther into his pile of notes, Hank said, "Jerry Fabin. Well, we'll write him off. N.A.C. The boys down the hall say Fabin told the responding officers on the way to the clinic that a little contract man three feet high, legless, on a cart, had been rolling after him day and night. But he never told anybody because if he did they'd freak and get the hell out and then he'd have no friends, nobody to talk to."

"Yeah," Fred said stoically. "Fabin has had it. I read the EEG analysis from the clinic. We can forget about him."

Whenever he sat facing Hank and did his reporting thing, he experienced a certain deep change in himself. Afterward was when he usually noticed it, although at the time he sensed that for a reason he assumed a measured and uninvolved attitude. Whatever came up and whoever it was about possessed no emotional significance to him during these sessions.

At first he had believed it to be the scramble suits that both of them wore; they could not physically sense each other. Later on he conjectured that the suits made no actual difference; it was the situation itself. Hank, for professional reasons, purposefully played down the usual warmth, the usual arousal in all directions; no anger, no love, no strong emotions of any sort would help either of them. How could intense natural involvement be of use when they were discussing crimes, serious crimes, committed by persons close to Fred and even, as in the case of Luckman and Donna, dear to him? He had to neutralize himself; they both did, him more so than Hank. They became neutral; they spoke in a neutral fashion; they looked neutral. Gradually it became easy to do so, without prearrangement.

And then afterward all his feelings seeped back.

Indignation at many of the events he had seen, even horror, in retrospect: shock. Great overpowering runs for which there had been no previews. With the audio always up too loud inside his head.

But while he sat across the table from Hank he felt none of these. Theoretically, he could describe anything he had witnessed in an impassive way. Or hear anything from Hank.

For example, he could offhandedly say "Donna is dying of hep and using her needle to wipe out as many of her friends as she can. Best thing here would be to pistol-whip her until she knocks it off." His own chick . . . *if* he had observed that or knew it for a fact. Or "Donna suffered a massive vasoconstriction from a mickey-mouse LSD analogue the other day and half the blood vessels in her brain

shut down." Or "Donna is dead." And Hank would note that down
and maybe say "Who sold her the stuff and where's it made?" or
"Where's the funeral, and we should get license numbers and
names," and he'd discuss that without feeling.

This was Fred. But then later on Fred evolved into Bob Arctor,
somewhere along the sidewalk between the Pizza Hut and the Arco
gas station (regular now a dollar two cents a gallon), and the terrible
colors seeped back into him whether he liked it or not.

This change in him as Fred was an economy of the passions.
Firemen and doctors and morticians did the same trip in their work.
None of them could leap up and exclaim each few moments; they
would first wear themselves out and be worthless and then wear out
everyone else, both as technicians on the job and as humans off. An
individual had just so much energy.

Hank did not force this dispassion on him; he *allowed* him to be
like this. For his own sake. Fred appreciated it.

"What about Arctor?" Hank asked.

In addition to everyone else, Fred in his scramble suit naturally reported on himself. If he did not, his superior—and through him the
whole law-enforcement apparatus—would become aware of who
Fred was, suit or not. The agency plants would report back, and very
soon he as Bob Arctor, sitting in his living room smoking dope and
dropping dope with the other dopers, would find he had a little three-
foot-high contract man on a cart coasting after him, too. And he
would not be hallucinating, as had been Jerry Fabin.

"Arctor's not doing anything much," Fred said, as he always did.
"Works at his nowhere Blue Chip Stamp job, drops a few tabs of
death cut with meth during the day—"

"I'm not sure." Hank fiddled with one particular sheet of paper.
"We have a tip here from an informant whose tips generally pan out
that Arctor has funds above and beyond what the Blue Chip Redemption Center pays him. We called them and asked what his take-
home pay is. It's not much. And then we inquired into that, why that
is, and we found he isn't employed there full time throughout the
week."

"No shit," Fred said dismally, realizing that the "above-and-
beyond" funds were of course those provided him for his narking.
Every week small-denomination bills were dispensed to him by a
machine masquerading as a Dr. Pepper source at a Mexican bar and
restaurant in Placentia. This was in essence payoffs on information
he gave that resulted in convictions. Sometimes this sum became ex-
ceptionally great, as when a major heroin seizure occurred.

Hank read on reflectively, "And according to this informant, Arctor comes and goes mysteriously, especially around sunset. After he arrives home he eats, then on what may be pretexts takes off again. Sometimes very fast. But he's never gone for long." He glanced up—the scramble suit glanced up—at Fred. "Have you observed any of this? Can you verify? Does it amount to anything?"

"Most likely his chick, Donna," Fred said.

"Well, 'most likely.' You're supposed to know."

"It's Donna. He's over there banging her night and day." He felt acutely uncomfortable. "But I'll check into it and let you know. Who's this informant? Might be a burn toward Arctor."

"Hell, we don't know. On the phone. No print—he used some sort of rinky-dink electronic grid." Hank chuckled; it sounded odd, coming out metallically as it did. "But it worked. Enough."

"Christ," Fred protested, "it's that burned-out acid head Jim Barris doing a schizy grudge number on Arctor's head! Barris took endless electronic-repair courses in the Service, plus heavy-machinery maintenance. I wouldn't give him the time of day as an informant."

Hank said, "We don't know it's Barris, and anyhow there may be more to Barris than 'burned-out acid head.' We've got several people looking into it. Nothing I feel would be of use to you, at least so far."

"Anyhow, it's one of Arctor's friends," Fred said.

"Yes, it's undoubtedly a vengeance burn trip. These dopers—phoning in on each other every time they get sore. As a matter of fact, he did seem to know Arctor from a close standpoint."

"Nice guy," Fred said bitterly.

"Well, that's how we find out," Hank said. "What's the difference between that and what you're doing?"

"I'm not doing it for a grudge," Fred said.

"Why are you doing it, actually?"

Fred, after an interval said, "Damned if I know."

"You're off Weeks. I think for the time being I'll assign you primarily to observe Bob Arctor. Does he have a middle name? He uses the initial—"

Fred made a strangled, robotlike noise. "Why Arctor?"

"Covertly funded, covertly engaged, making enemies by his activities. What's Arctor's middle name?" Hank's pen poised patiently. He waited to hear.

"Postlethwaite."

"How do you spell that?"

"I don't know, I don't fucking know," Fred said.

"Postlethwaite," Hank said, writing a few letters. "What nationality is that?"

"Welsh," Fred said curtly. He could barely hear; his ears had blurred out, and one by one his other senses as well.

"Are those the people who sing about the men of Harlech? What is 'Harlech'? A town somewhere?"

"Harlech is where the heroic defense against the Yorkists in 1468—" Fred broke off. Shit, he thought. This is terrible.

"Wait, I want to get this down," Hank was saying, writing away with his pen.

Fred said, "Does this mean you'll be bugging Arctor's house and car?"

"Yes, with the new holographic system; it's better, and we currently have a number of them unrequisitioned. You'll want storage and printout on everything, I would assume." Hank noted that too.

"I'll take what I can get," Fred said. He felt totally spaced from all this; he wished the debriefing session would end and he thought: If only I could drop a couple tabs—

Across from him the other formless blur wrote and wrote, filling in all the inventory ident numbers for all the technological gadgetry that would, if approval came through, soon be available to him, by which to set up a constant monitoring system of the latest design, on his own house, on himself.

For over an hour Barris had been attempting to perfect a silencer made from ordinary household materials costing no more than eleven cents. He had almost done so, with aluminum foil and a piece of foam rubber.

In the night darkness of Bob Arctor's back yard, among the heaps of weeds and rubbish, he was preparing to fire his pistol with the homemade silencer on it.

"The neighbors will hear," Charles Freck said uneasily. He could see lit windows all over, many people probably watching TV or rolling joints.

Luckman, lounging out of sight but able to watch, said, "They only call in murders in this neighborhood."

"Why do you need a silencer?" Charles Freck asked Barris. "I mean, they're illegal."

Barris said moodily, "In this day and age, with the kind of degenerate society we live in and the depravity of the individual, every person of worth needs a gun at all times. To protect himself." He half shut his eyes, and fired his pistol with its homemade silencer. An enormous report sounded, temporarily deafening the three of them. Dogs in far-off yards barked.

Smiling, Barris began unwrapping the aluminum foil from the foam rubber. He appeared to be amused.

"That's sure some silencer," Charles Freck said, wondering when the police would appear. A whole bunch of cars.

"What it did," Barris explained, showing him and Luckman black-seared passages burned through the foam rubber, "is augment the sound rather than dampen it. But I almost have it right. I have it in principle, anyhow."

"How much is that gun worth?" Charles Freck asked. He had never owned a gun. Several times he had owned a knife, but somebody always stole it from him. One time a chick had done that, while he was in the bathroom.

"Not much," Barris said. "About thirty dollars used, which this is." He held it out to Freck, who backed away apprehensively. "I'll sell it to you," Barris said. "You really ought to have one, to guard yourself against those who would harm you."

"There's a lot of those," Luckman said in his ironic way, with a grin. "I saw in the L. A. *Times* the other day, they're giving away a free transistor radio to those who would harm Freck most successfully."

"I'll trade you a Borg-Warner tach for it," Freck said.

"That you stole from the guy's garage across the street," Luckman said.

"Well, probably the gun's stolen, too," Charles Freck said. Most everything that was worth something was originally ripped off anyhow; it indicated the piece had value. "As a matter of fact," he said, "the guy across the street ripped the tach off in the first place. It's probably changed hands like fifteen times. I mean, it's a really cool tach."

"How do you know he ripped it off?" Luckman asked him.

"Hell, man, he's got eight tachs there in his garage, all dangling cut wires. What else would he be doing with them, that many, I mean? Who goes out and buys eight tachs?"

To Barris, Luckman said, "I thought you were busy working on the cephscope. You finished already?"

"I cannot continually work on that night and day, because it is so extensive," Barris said. "I've got to knock off." He cut, with a complicated pocketknife, another section of foam rubber. "This one will be totally soundless."

"Bob thinks you're at work on the cephscope," Luckman said. "He's lying there in his bed in his room imagining that, while you're out here firing off your pistol. Didn't you agree with Bob that the back rent you owe would be compensated by your—"

"Like good beer," Barris said, "an intricate, painstaking reconstruction of a damaged electronic assembly—"

"Just fire off the great eleven-cent silencer of our times," Luckman said, and belched.

I've had it, Robert Arctor thought.

He lay alone in the dim light of his bedroom, on his back, staring grimly at nothing. Under his pillow he had his .32 police-special revolver; at the sound of Barris's .22 being fired in the back yard he had reflexively gotten his own gun from beneath the bed and placed it within easier reach. A safety move, against any and all dangers; he hadn't even thought it out consciously.

But his .32 under his pillow wouldn't be much good against anything so indirect as sabotage of his most precious and expensive possession. As soon as he had gotten home from the debriefing with Hank he had checked out all the other appliances, and found them okay—especially the car—always the car first, in a situation like this. Whatever was going on, whoever it was by, it was going to be chickenshit and devious: some freak without integrity or guts lurking on the periphery of his life, taking indirect potshots at him from a position of concealed safety. Not a person but more a sort of walking, hiding symptom of their way of life.

There had been a time, once, when he had not lived like this, a .32 under his pillow, a lunatic in the back yard firing off a pistol for God knew what purpose, some other nut or perhaps the same one imposing a brain-print of his own shorted-out upstairs on an incredibly expensive and valued cephscope that everyone in the house, plus all their friends, loved and enjoyed. In former days Bob Arctor had run his affairs differently: there had been a wife much like other wives, two small daughters, a stable household that got swept and cleaned and emptied out daily, the dead newspapers not even opened carried from the front walk to the garbage pail, or even, sometimes, read. But then one day, while lifting out an electric corn popper from under the sink, Arctor had hit his head on the corner of a kitchen cabinet directly above him. The pain, the cut in his scalp, so unexpected and undeserved, had for some reason cleared away the cobwebs. It flashed on him instantly that he didn't hate the kitchen cabinet: he hated his wife, his two daughters, his whole house, the back yard with its power mower, the garage, the radiant heating system, the front yard, the fence, the whole fucking place and everyone in it. He wanted a divorce; he wanted to split. And so he had, very soon. And entered, by degrees, a new and somber life, lacking all of that.

Probably he should have regretted his decision. He had not. That life had been one without excitement, with no adventure. It had been too safe. All the elements that made it up were right there before his eyes, and nothing new could ever be expected. It was like, he had once thought, a little plastic boat that would sail on forever, without incident, until it finally sank, which would be a secret relief to all.

But in this dark world where he now dwelt, ugly things and surprising things and once in a long while a tiny wonderous thing spilled out at him constantly; he could count on nothing. Like the deliberate, evil damage to his Altec cephalochromoscope, around which he had built the pleasure part of his schedule, the segment of the day in which they all relaxed and got mellow. For someone to damage that made no sense, viewed rationally. But not much among these long dark evening shadows here was truly rational, at least in the strict sense. The enigmatic act could have been done by anyone for almost any reason. By any person he knew or had ever encountered. Any one of eight dozen weird heads, assorted freaks, burned-out dopers, psychotic paranoids with hallucinatory grudges acted out in reality, not fantasy. Somebody, in fact, he'd *never* met, who'd picked him at random from the phonebook.

Or his closest friend.

Maybe Jerry Fabin, he thought, before they carted him off. There was a burned-out, poisoned husk. Him and his billions of aphids. Blaming Donna—blaming all chicks, in fact—for "contaminating" him. The queer. But, he thought, if Jerry had gone out to get anybody it'd have been Donna, not me. He thought, And I doubt if Jerry could figure out how to remove the bottom plate from the unit; he might try, but he'd still be there now, screwing and unscrewing the same screw. Or he'd try to get the plate off with a hammer. Anyhow, if Jerry Fabin had done it, the unit would be full of bug eggs that dropped off him. Inside his head Bob Arctor grinned wryly.

Poor fucker, he thought, and his inner grin departed. Poor nowhere mother: once the trace amounts of complex heavy metals got carried to his brain—well, that was it. One more in a long line, a dreary entity among many others like him, an almost endless number of brain-damaged retards. Biological life goes on, he thought. But the soul, the mind—everything else is dead. A reflex machine. Like some insect. Repeating doomed patterns, a single pattern, over and over now. Appropriate or not.

Wonder what he used to be like, he mused. He had not known Jerry that long. Charles Freck claimed that once Jerry had functioned fairly well. I'd have to see that, Arctor thought, to believe it.

Maybe I should tell Hank about the sabotage of my cephscope, he thought. They'd know immediately what it implies. But what can they do for me anyhow? This is the risk you run when you do this kind of work.

It isn't worth it, this work, he thought. There isn't that much money on the fucking planet. But it wasn't the money anyhow. "How come you do this stuff?" Hank had asked him. What did any man, doing any kind of work, know about his actual motives? Boredom, maybe; the desire for a little action. Secret hostility toward every person around him, all his friends, even toward chicks. Or a horrible positive reason: to have watched a human being you loved deeply, that you had gotten real close to, held and slept with and kissed and worried about and befriended and most of all *admired*—to see that warm living person burn out from the inside, burn from the heart outward. Until it clicked and clacked like an insect, repeating one sentence again and again. A *recording*. A closed loop of tape.

". . . I know if I just had another hit . . ."

I'd be okay, he thought. And still saying that, like Jerry Fabin, when three quarters of the brain was mush.

". . . I know, if I just had another hit, that my brain would repair itself."

He had a flash then: Jerry Fabin's brain as the fucked-over wiring of the cephalochromoscope: wires cut, shorts, wires twisted, parts overloaded and no good, line surges, smoke, and a bad smell. And somebody sitting there with a voltmeter, tracing the circuit and muttering, "My, my, a lot of resistors and condensers need to be replaced," and so forth. And then finally from Jerry Fabin would come only a sixty-cycle hum. And they'd give up.

And in Bob Arctor's living room his thousand-dollar custom-quality cephscope crafted by Altec would, after supposedly being repaired, cast onto the wall in dull gray on one small spot:

I KNOW IF I JUST HAD ANOTHER HIT . . .

After that they'd throw the cephscope, damaged beyond repair, and Jerry Fabin, damaged beyond repair, into the same ash can.

Oh well, he thought. Who needs Jerry Fabin? Except maybe Jerry Fabin, who had once envisioned designing and building a nine-foot-long quad-and-TV console system as a present for a friend, and when asked how he would get it from his garage to the friend's house, it being so huge when built and weighing so much, had replied, "No problem, man, I'll just fold it up—I've got the hinges bought already—fold it up, see, fold the whole thing up and put it in an envelope and mail it to him."

Anyhow, Bob Arctor thought, we won't have to keep sweeping aphids out of the house after Jerry's been by to visit. He felt like

laughing, thinking about it; they had, once, invented a routine—
mostly Luckman had, because he was good at that, funny and clever
—about a psychiatric explanation for Jerry's aphid trip. It had to do,
naturally, with Jerry Fabin as a small child. Jerry Fabin, see, comes
home from first grade one day, with his little books under his arm,
whistling merrily, and there, sitting in the dining room beside his
mother, is this great aphid, about four feet high. His mother is gazing
at it fondly.

"What's happening?" little Jerry Fabin inquires.

"This here is your older brother," his mother says, "who you've
never met before. He's come to live with us. I like him better than
you. He can do a lot of things you can't."

And from then on, Jerry Fabin's mother and father continually
compare him unfavorably with his older brother, who is an aphid. As
the two of them grow up, Jerry progressively gets more and more of
an inferiority complex—naturally. After high school his brother re-
ceives a scholarship to college, while Jerry goes to work in a gas station. After that this brother the aphid becomes a famous doctor or
scientist; he wins the Nobel Prize; Jerry's still rotating tires at the gas
station, earning a dollar-fifty an hour. His mother and father never
cease reminding him of this. They keep saying,

"If only you could have turned out like your brother,"

Finally Jerry runs away from home. But he still subconsciously be-
lieves aphids to be superior to him. At first he imagines he is safe,
but then he starts seeing aphids everywhere, in his hair and around
the house, because his inferiority complex has turned into some kind
of sexual guilt, and the aphids are a punishment he inflicts on himself, etc.

It did not seem funny now. Now that Jerry had been lugged off in
the middle of the night at the request of his own friends. They themselves, all of them present with Jerry that night, had decided to do it;
it couldn't be either postponed or avoided. Jerry, that night, had
piled every goddamn object in his house against the front door, like
maybe nine hundred pounds of assorted crap, including couches
and chairs and the refrigerator and TV set, and then told everybody
that a giant superintelligent aphid from another planet was out there
preparing to break in and git him. And more would be landing later
on, even if he got this one. These extraterrestrial aphids were smarter
by far than any humans, and would come directly through the walls
if necessary, revealing their actual secret powers in such ways. To
save himself as long as possible, he had to flood the house with cyanide gas, which he was prepared to do. How was he prepared to do
this? He had already taped all the windows and doors airtight. He

then proposed to turn on the water faucets in the kitchen and bathroom, flooding the house, saying that the hot-water tank in the garage was filled with cyanide, not water. He had known this for a long time and was saving it for last, as a final defense. They would all die themselves, but at least it would keep the super-intelligent aphids out.

His friends phoned the police, and the police broke down the front door and dragged Jerry off to the N.A. Clinic. The last thing Jerry said to them all was "Bring my things later on—bring my new jacket with the beads on the back." He had just bought it. He liked it a lot. It was about all he liked any more; he considered everything else he owned contaminated.

No, Bob Arctor thought, it doesn't seem funny now, and he wondered why it ever had. Maybe it had stemmed from fear, the dreadful fear they had all felt during the last weeks being around Jerry. Sometimes in the night, Jerry had told them, he prowled his house with a shotgun, sensing the presence of an enemy. Preparing to shoot first, before being shot. That is, both of them.

And now, Bob Arctor thought, I've got an enemy. Or anyhow I've come onto his trail: signs of him. Another slushed creep in his final stages, like Jerry. And when the final stages of that shit hits, he thought, it really does hit. Better than any special Ford or GM ever sponsored on prime-time TV.

A knock at his bedroom door.

Touching the gun beneath his pillow, he said, "Yeah?"

Mubble-mubble. Barris's voice.

"Come in," Arctor said. He reached to snap on a bedside lamp.

Barris entered, eyes twinkling. "Still awake?"

"A dream woke me," Arctor said. "A religious dream. In it there was this huge clap of thunder, and all of a sudden the heavens rolled aside and God appeared and His voice rumbled at me—what the hell did He say?—oh yeah. 'I am vexed with you, my son,' He said. He was scowling. I was shaking, in the dream, and looking up, and I said, 'What'd I do now, Lord?' And He said, 'You left the cap off the toothpaste tube again.' And then I realized it was my ex-wife."

Seating himself, Barris placed a hand on each of his leather-covered knees, smoothed himself, shook his head, and confronted Arctor. He seemed in an extremely good mood. "Well," he said briskly, "I've got an initial theoretical view as to who might have systematically damaged with malice your cephscope and may do it again."

"If you're going to say it was Luckman—"

"Listen," Barris said, rocking back and forth in agitation. "W-w-what if I told you I've anticipated for weeks a serious malfunction in one of the household appliances, especially an expensive one difficult to repair? My theory *called* for this to happen! This is a confirmation of my over-all theory!"

Arctor eyed him.

Slowly sinking back down, Barris resumed his calm and bright smiling. "You," he said, pointing.

"You think I did it," Arctor said. "Screwed up my own cephscope, with no insurance." Disgust and rage swelled through him. And it was late at night; he needed his sleep.

"No, no," Barris said rapidly, looking distressed. "You are *looking* at the person who did it. Buggered your cephscope. That was my complete intended statement, which I was not allowed to utter."

"You did it?" Mystified, he stared at Barris, whose eyes were murky with a sort of dim triumph. "Why?"

"I mean, it's my theory that I did it," Barris said. "Under posthypnotic suggestion, evidently. With an amnesia block so I wouldn't remember." He began to laugh.

"Later," Arctor said, and snapped off his bedside lamp. "Much later."

Barris rose, dithering. "Hey, but don't you see—I've got the advanced specialized electronic technical skills, and I have access to it —I live here. What I can't figure out, though, is my motive."

"You did it because you're nuts," Arctor said.

"Maybe I was hired by secret forces," Barris muttered in perplexity. "But what would their motives be? Possibly to start suspicion and trouble among us, to cause dissension to break out, causing us to be pitted against one another, all of us, uncertain of whom we can trust, who is our enemy, and like that."

"Then they've succeeded," Arctor said.

"But why would they want to do that?" Barris was saying as he moved toward the door; his hands flapped urgently. "So much trouble—removing that plate on the bottom, getting a passkey to the front door—"

I'll be glad, Bob Arctor thought, when we get in the holo-scanners and have them set up all over this house. He touched his gun, felt reassured, then wondered if he should make certain it was still full of shells. But then, he realized, I'll wonder if the firing pin is gone or if the powder has been removed from the shells and so forth, on and on, obsessively, like a little boy counting cracks in the sidewalk to reduce his fear. Little Bobby Arctor, coming home from the first grade with his little schoolbooks, frightened at the unknown lying ahead.

Reaching down, he fumbled at the bed frame, along and along

until his fingers touched Scotch tape. Pulling it loose, he tore from it, with Barris still in the room and watching, two tabs of Substance D mixed with quaak. Lifting them to his mouth, he tossed them down his throat, without water, and then lay back, sighing.

"Get lost," he said to Barris.

And slept.

CHAPTER FIVE

It was necessary for Bob Arctor to be out of his house for a period of time in order that it be properly (which meant unerringly) bugged, phone included, even though the phone line was tapped elsewhere. Usually the practice consisted of observing the house involved until everyone was seen to leave it in such a fashion as to suggest they were not going to return soon. The authorities sometimes had to wait for days or even several weeks. Finally, if nothing else worked, a pretext was arranged: the residents were informed that a fumigator or some such shuck personality was going to be coming in for a whole afternoon and everybody had to get lost until, say, six P.M.

But in this case the suspect Robert Arctor obligingly left his house, taking his two roommates with him, to go check out a cephalochromoscope they could use on loan until Barris had his working again. The three of them were seen to drive off in Arctor's car, looking serious and determined. Then later on, at a convenient point, which was a pay phone at a gas station, using the audio grid of his scramble suit, Fred called in to report that definitely nobody would be home the rest of that day. He'd overheard the three men deciding to cruise down all the way to San Diego in search of a cheap, ripped-off cephscope that some dude had for sale for around fifty bucks. A smack-freak price. At that price it was worth the long drive and all that time.

Also, this gave the authorities the opportunity to do a little illegal searching above and beyond what their undercover people did when no one was looking. They got to pull out bureau drawers to see what was taped to the backs. They got to pull apart pole lamps to see if hundreds of tabs sprang out. They got to look down inside toilet bowls to see what sort of little packets in toilet paper were lodged out of sight where the running water would automatically flush them. They got to look in the freezer compartment of the refrigerator to see if any of the packages of frozen peas and beans actually contained frozen dope, slyly mismarked. Meanwhile, the complicated holoscanners were mounted, with officers seating themselves in various places to test the scanners out. The same with the audio ones. But the video part was more important and took more time. And of course the scanners should never be visible. It took skill to so mount them. A number of locations had to be tried. The technicians who did this got paid well, because if they screwed up and a holo-scanner got detected later on by an occupant of the premises, then the occupants, all of them, would know they had been penetrated and were under scrutiny, and cool their activities. And in addition they would sometimes tear off the whole scanning system and sell it.

It had proven difficult in the courts, Bob Arctor reflected as he drove along the San Diego Freeway south, to get convictions on theft and sale of electronic detection devices illegally installed in someone's residence. The police could only tack the bust on somewhere else, under another statute violation. However, the pushers, in an analogous situation, reacted directly. He recalled a case in which a heroin dealer, out to burn a chick, had planted two packets of heroin in the handle of her iron, then phoned in an anonymous tip on her to *WE TIP*. Before the tip could be acted on, the chick found the heroin, but instead of flushing it she had sold it. The police came, found nothing, then made a voiceprint on the phone tip, and arrested the pusher for giving false information to the authorities. While out on bail, the pusher visited the chick late one night and beat her almost to death. When caught and asked why he'd put out one of her eyes and broken both her arms and several ribs, he explained that the chick had come across two packets of high-grade heroin belonging to him, sold them for a good profit, and not cut him in. Such, Arctor reflected, went the pusher mentality.

He dumped off Luckman and Barris to do a scrounging number for the cephscope; this not only stranded both men and kept them from getting back to the house while the bugging installation was going on, but permitted him to check up on an individual he hadn't seen for over a month. He seldom got down this way, and the chick seemed to be doing nothing more than shooting meth two or three times a day and turning tricks to pay for it. She lived with her dealer, who was therefore also her old man. Usually Dan Mancher was gone during the day, which was good. The dealer was an addict, too, but Arctor had not been able to figure out to what. Evidently a variety of drugs. Anyhow, whatever it was, Dan had become weird and vicious, unpredictable and violent. It was a wonder the local police hadn't picked him up long ago on local disturbance-of-the-peace infractions. Maybe they were paid off. Or, most likely, they just didn't care; these people lived in a slum-housing area among senior citizens and the other poor. Only for major crimes did the police enter the Cromwell

Village series of buildings and related garbage dump, parking lots, and rubbled roads.

There seemed to be nothing that contributed more to squalor than a bunch of basalt-block structures designed to lift people out of squalor. He parked, found the right urine-smelling stairs, ascended into darkness, found the door of Building 4 marked *G*. A full can of Drāno lay before the door, and he picked it up automatically, wondering how many kids played here and remembering, for a moment, his own kids and the protective moves he had made on their behalf over the years. This was one now, picking up this can. He rapped against the door with it.

Presently the door lock rattled and the door opened, chained inside; the girl, Kimberly Hawkins, peered out. "Yes?"

"Hey, man," he said. "It's me, Bob."

"What do you have there?"

"Can of Drāno," he said.

"No kidding." She unchained the door in a listless way; her voice, too, was listless. Kimberly was down, he could see: very down. Also, the girl had a black eye and a split lip. And as he looked around he saw that the windows of the small, untidy apartment were broken. Shards of glass lay on the floor, along with overturned ashtrays and Coke bottles.

"Are you alone?" he asked.

"Yeah. Dan and I had a fight and he split." The girl, half Chicano, small and not too pretty, with the sallow complexion of a crystal freak, gazed down sightlessly, and he realized that her voice rasped when she spoke. Some drugs did that. Also, so did strep throat. The apartment probably couldn't be heated, not with the broken windows.

"He beat you up." Arctor set the can of Drāno down on a high shelf, over some paperback porn novels, most of them out of date.

"Well, he didn't have his knife, thank God. His Case knife that he carries on his belt in a sheath now." Kimberly seated herself in an overstuffed chair out of which springs stuck. "What do you want, Bob? I'm bummed, I really am."

"You want him back?"

"Well—" She shrugged a little. "Who knows?"

Arctor walked to the window and looked out. Dan Mancher would no doubt be showing up sooner or later: the girl was a source of money, and Dan knew she'd need her regular hits once her supply had run out. "How long can you go?" he asked.

"Another day."

"Can you get it anywhere else?"

"Yeah, but not so cheap."

"What's wrong with your throat?"

"A cold," she said. "From the wind coming in."

"You should——"

"If I go to a doctor," she said, "then he'll see I'm on crystal. I can't go."

"A doctor wouldn't care."

"Sure he would." She listened then: the sound of car pipes, irregular and loud. "Is that Dan's car? Red Ford 'seventy-nine Torino?"

At the window Arctor looked out onto the rubbishy lot, saw a battered red Torino stopping, its twin exhausts exhaling dark smoke, the driver's door opening. "Yes."

Kimberly locked the door: two extra locks. "He probably has his knife."

"You have a phone?"

"No," she said.

"You should get a phone."

The girl shrugged.

"He'll kill you," Arctor said.

"Not now. You're here."

"But later, after I'm gone."

Kimberly reseated herself and shrugged again.

After a few moments they could hear steps outside, and then a knock on the door. Then Dan yelling for her to open the door. She yelled back no and that someone was with her. "Okay," Dan yelled, in a high-pitched voice, "I'll slash your tires." He ran downstairs, and Arctor and the girl watched through the broken window together as Dan Mancher, a skinny, short-haired, homosexual-looking dude waving a knife, approached her car, still yelling up at her, his words audible to everyone else in the housing area. "I'll slash your tires, your fucking tires! And then I'll fucking kill you!" He bent down and slashed first one tire and then another on the girl's old Dodge.

Kimberly suddenly aroused, sprang to the door of the apartment and frantically began unlocking the various locks. "I got to stop him! He's slashing all my tires! I don't have insurance!"

Arctor stopped her. "My car's there too." He did not have his gun with him, of course, and Dan had the Case knife and was out of control. "Tires aren't——"

"My tires!" Shrieking, the girl struggled to open the door.

"That's what he wants you to do," Arctor said.

"Downstairs," Kimberly panted. "We can phone the police—they have a phone. Let me go!" She fought him off with tremendous strength and managed to get the door open. "I'm going to call the police. My tires! One of them is new!"

"I'll go with you." He grabbed her by the shoulder; she tumbled ahead of him down the steps, and he barely managed to catch up. Already she had reached the next apartment and was pounding on its door. "Open, please?" she called. "Please, I want to call the police! Please let me call the police!"

Arctor got up beside her and knocked. "We need to use your phone," he said. "It's an emergency."

An elderly man, wearing a gray sweater and creased formal slacks and a tie, opened the door.

"Thanks," Arctor said.

Kimberly pushed inside, ran to the phone, and dialed the operator. Arctor stood facing the door, waiting for Dan to show up. There was no sound now, except for Kimberly babbling at the operator: a garbled account, something about a quarrel about a pair of boots worth seven dollars. "He said they were his because I got them for him for Christmas," she was babbling, "but they were mine because I paid for them, and then he started to take them and I ripped the backs of them with a can opener, so he——" She paused; then, nodding: "All right, thank you. Yes, I'll hold on."

The elderly man gazed at Arctor, who gazed back. In the next room an elderly lady in a print dress watched silently, her face stiff with fear.

"This must be bad on you," Arctor said to the two elderly people.

"It goes on all the time," the elderly man said. "We hear them all night, night after night, fighting, and him saying all the time he'll kill her."

"We should have gone back to Denver," the elderly lady said. "I told you that, we should have moved back."

"These terrible fights," the elderly man said. "And smashing things, and the noise." He gazed at Arctor, stricken, appealing for help maybe, or maybe understanding. "On and on, it never does stop, and then, what is worse, do you know that every time——"

"Yes, tell him that," the elderly lady urged.

"What is worse," the elderly man said with dignity, "is that every time we go outdoors, we go outside to shop or mail a letter, we step in . . . you know, what the dogs leave."

"Dog do," the elderly lady said, with indignation.

The local police car showed up. Arctor gave him deposition as a witness without identifying himself as a law-enforcement officer. The cop took down his statement and tried to take one from Kimberly, as the complaining party, but what she said made no sense: she rambled on and on about the pair of boots and why she had gotten them, how much they meant to her. The cop, sitting with his clipboard and sheet, glanced up once at Arctor and regarded him with a cold expression that Arctor could not read but did not like anyhow. The cop finally advised Kimberly to get a phone and to call if the suspect returned and made any more trouble.

"Did you note the slashed tires?" Arctor said as the cop started to leave. "Did you examine her vehicle out there on the lot and note personally the number of tires slashed, casing slashes with a sharp instrument, recently made—there is still some air leaking out?"

The cop glanced at him again with the same expression and left with no further comment.

"You better not stay here," Arctor said to Kimberly. "He should have advised you to clear out. Asked if there was some other place you could stay."

Kimberly sat on her seedy couch in her debris-littered living room, her eyes lusterless again now that she had ceased the futile effort of trying to explain her situation to the investigating officer. She shrugged.

"I'll drive you somewhere," Arctor said. "Do you know some friend you could—"

"Get the fuck out!" Kimberly said abruptly, with venom, in a voice much like Dan Mancher's but more raspy. "Get the fuck out of here, Bob Arctor—get lost, get lost, goddammit. Will you get lost?" Her voice rose shrilly and then broke in despair.

He left and walked slowly back down the stairs, step by step. When he reached the bottom step something banged and rolled down after him: it was the can of Drāno. He heard her door lock, one bolt after another. Futile locks, he thought. Futile everything. The investigating officer advises her to call if the suspect returns. How can she, without going out of her apartment? And there Dan Mancher will stab her like he did the tires. And—remembering the complaint of the old folks downstairs—she will probably first step on and then fall dead into dog shit. He felt like laughing hysterically at the old folks' priorities: not only did a burned-out freak upstairs night after night beat up and threaten to kill and probably would soon kill a young girl addict turning tricks who no doubt had strep throat if not much else besides, but *in addition to that—*

As he drove Luckman and Barris back north, he chuckled aloud. "Dog shit," he said. "Dog shit." Humor in dog shit, he thought, if you can flash on it. Funny dog shit.

"Better change lanes and pass that Safeway truck," Luckman said. "The humper's hardly moving."

He moved into the lane to the left and picked up speed. But then, when he took his foot off the throttle, the pedal all at once fell to the floor mat, and at the same time the engine roared all the way up furiously and the car shot forward at enormous, wild speed.

"Slow down!" both Luckman and Barris said together.

By now the car had reached almost one hundred; ahead, a VW van loomed. His gas pedal was dead: it did not return and it did nothing. Both Luckman, who sat next to him, and Barris, beyond him, threw up their arms instinctively. Arctor twisted the wheel and shot by the VW van, to its left, where a limited space remained before a fast-moving 'Vet filled it up. The Corvette honked, and they heard its brakes screech. Now Luckman and Barris were yelling; Luckman suddenly reached and shut off the ignition; meanwhile, Arctor shifted out of gear into neutral. The car slowed, and he braked it down, moved into the right-hand lane and then, with the engine finally dead and the transmission out of gear, rolled off onto the emergency strip and came by degrees to a stop.

The Corvette, long gone down the freeway, still honked its indignation. And now the giant Safeway truck rolled by them and for a deafening moment sounded its own warning air horn.

"What the hell happened?" Barris said.

Arctor, his hands and voice and the rest of him shaking, said, "The return spring on the throttle cable—the gas. Must have caught or broken." He pointed down. They all peered at the pedal, which lay still flat against the floor. The engine had revved up to its entire maximum rpm, which for his car was considerable. He had not clocked their final highest road speed, probably well over one hundred. And, he realized, though he had been reflexively pushing down on the power brakes, the car had only slowed.

Silently the three of them got out onto the emergency pavement and raised the hood. White smoke drifted up from the oil caps and from underneath as well. And near-boiling water fizzled from the overflow spout of the radiator.

Luckman reached over the hot engine and pointed. "Not the spring," he said. "It's the linkage from the pedal to the carb. See? It fell apart." The long rod lay aimlessly against the block, hanging impotently and uselessly down with its locking ring still in place. "So the gas pedal didn't push back up when you took your foot off. But —" He inspected the carb for a time, his face wrinkled.

"There's a safety override on the carb," Barris said, grinning and showing his syntheticlike teeth. "This system when the linkage parts—"

"Why'd it part?" Arctor broke in. "Shouldn't this locking ring hold the nut in place?" He stroked along the rod. "How could it just fall off like that?"

As if not hearing him, Barris continued, "If for any reason the linkage gives, then the engine should drop down to idle. As a safety factor. But it revved up all the way instead." He bent his body around to get a better look at the carb. "This screw has been turned all the way out," he said. "The idle screw. So that when the linkage parted the override went the other way, up instead of down."

"How could that happen?" Luckman said loudly. "Could it screw itself all the way out like that accidentally?"

Without answering, Barris got out his pocketknife, opened the small blade, and began slowly screwing the idle-adjustment screw back in. He counted aloud. Twenty turns of the screw to get it in. "To loosen the lock ring and nut assembly that holds the accelerator-linkage rods together," he said, "a special tool would be needed. A couple, in fact. I'd estimate it'll take about half an hour to get this back together. I have the tools, though, in my toolbox."

"Your toolbox is back at the house," Luckman said.

"Yes." Barris nodded. "Then we'll have to get to a gas station and either borrow theirs or get their tow truck out here. I suggest we get them out here to look it over before we drive it again."

"Hey, man," Luckman said loudly, "did this happen by accident or was this done deliberately? Like the cephscope?"

Barris pondered, still smiling his wily, rueful smile. "I couldn't say for sure about this. Normally, sabotage on a car, malicious damage to cause an accident . . ." He glanced at Arctor, his eyes invisible behind his green shades. "We almost piled up. If that 'Vet had been coming any faster . . . There was almost no ditch to head for. You should have cut the ignition as soon as you realized what happened."

"I got it out of gear," Arctor said. "When I realized. For a second I couldn't figure it out." He thought, If it had been the brakes, if the brake pedal had gone to the floor, I'd have flashed on it sooner, known better what to do. This was so—weird.

"Someone deliberately did it," Luckman said loudly. He spun around in a circle of fury, lashing out with both fists. "MOTHER-FUCKER! We almost bought it! They fucking almost got us!"

Barris, standing visible by the side of the freeway with all its heavy traffic whizzing by, got out a little horn snuffbox of death tabs and took several. He passed the snuffbox to Luckman, who took a few, then passed it to Arctor.

"Maybe that's what's fucking us up," Arctor said, declining irritably. "Messing up our brains."

"Dope can't screw up an accelerator linkage and carb-idle adjustment," Barris said, still holding the snuffbox out to Arctor. "You'd better drop at least three of these—they're Primo, but mild. Cut with a little meth."

"Put the damn snuffbox away," Arctor said. He felt, in his head, loud voices singing: terrible music, as if the reality around him had gone sour. Everything now—the fast-moving cars, the two men, his own car with its hood up, the smell of smog, the bright, hot light of midday—it all had a rancid quality, as if, throughout, his world had putrefied, rather than anything else. Not so much become all at once, because of this, dangerous, not frightening, but more as if rotting away, stinking in sight and sound and odor. It made him sick, and he shut his eyes and shuddered.

"What do you smell?" Luckman asked. "A clue, man? Some engine smell that—"

"Dog shit," Arctor said. He could smell it, from within the engine area. Bending, he sniffed, smelled it distinctly and more strongly. Weird, he thought. Freaky and fucking weird. "Do you smell dog shit?" he asked Barris and Luckman.

"No," Luckman said, eying him. To Barris he said, "Were there any psychedelics in that dope?"

Barris, smiling, shook his head.

As he bent over the hot engine, smelling dog shit, Arctor knew to himself that it was an illusion; there was no dog-shit smell. But still he smelled it. And now he saw, smeared across the motor block, especially down low by the plugs, dark-brown stains, an ugly substance. Oil, he thought. Spilled oil, thrown oil: I may have a leaky head gasket. But he needed to reach down and touch to be sure, to fortify his rational conviction. His fingers met the sticky brown smears, and his fingers leaped back. He had run his fingers into dog shit. There was a coating of dog shit all over the block, on the wires. Then he realized it was on the fire wall as well. Looking up, he saw it on the soundproofing underneath the hood. The stink overpowered him, and he shut his eyes, shuddering.

"Hey, man," Luckman said acutely, taking hold of Arctor by the shoulder. "You're getting a flashback, aren't you?"

"Free theater tickets," Barris agreed, and chuckled.

"You better sit down," Luckman said; he guided Arctor back to the driver's seat and got him seated there. "Man, you're really freaked. Just sit there. Take it easy. Nobody got killed, and now we're warned." He shut the car door beside Arctor. "We're okay now, dig?"

Barris appeared at the window and said, "Want a lump of dog shit, Bob? To chew on?"

Opening his eyes, chilled, Arctor stared at him. Barris's dead green-glass eyes gave nothing back, no clue. Did he really say that? Arctor wondered. Or did my head make that up? "What, Jim?" he said.

Barris began to laugh. And laugh and laugh.

"Leave him alone, man," Luckman said, punching Barris on the back. "Fuck off, Barris!"

Arctor said to Luckman, "What did he say just now? What the hell exactly did he say to me?"

"I don't know," Luckman said. "I can't figure out half the things Barris lays on people."

Barris still smiled, but had become silent.

"You goddamn Barris," Arctor said to him. "I know you did it, screwed over the cephscope and now the car. You fucking did it, you kinky freak mother bastard." His voice was hardly audible to him, but as he yelled that out at smiling Barris, the dreadful stench of dog shit grew. He gave up trying to speak and sat there at the useless wheel of his car trying not to throw up. Thank God Luckman came along, he thought. Or it'd be all over for me this day. It'd all fucking be over, at the hands of this burned-out fucking creep, this mother living right in the same house with me.

"Take it easy, Bob," Luckman's voice filtered to him through the waves of nausea.

"I know it's him," Arctor said.

"Hell, why?" Luckman seemed to be saying, or trying to say. "He'd of snuffed himself too this way. Why, man? Why?"

The smell of Barris still smiling overpowered Bob Arctor, and he heaved onto the dashboard of his own car. A thousand little voices tinkled up, shining at him, and the smell receded finally. A thousand little voices crying out their strangeness; he did not understand them, but at least he could see, and the smell was going away. He trembled, and reached for his handkerchief from his pocket.

"What was in those tabs you gave us?" Luckman demanded at smiling Barris.

"Hell, I dropped some too," Barris said, "and so did you. And it didn't give us a bad trip. So it wasn't the dope. And it was too soon. How could it have been the dope? The stomach can't absorb—"

"You poisoned me," Arctor said savagely, his vision almost clear, his mind clearing, except for the fear. Now fear had begun, a rational response instead of insanity. Fear about what had almost happened, what it signified, fear fear terrible fear of smiling Barris and his fucking snuffbox and his explanations and his creepy sayings and ways and habits and customs and comings and goings. And his anonymous phoned-in tip to the police about Robert Arctor, his mickeymouse grid to conceal his real voice that had pretty well worked. Except that it had to have been Barris.

Bob Arctor thought, *The fucker is on to me.*

"I never saw anybody space out as fast," Barris was saying, "but then—"

"You okay now, Bob?" Luckman said. "We'll clean up the barf, no trouble. Better get in the back seat." Both he and Barris opened the car door; Arctor slid dizzily out. To Barris, Luckman said, "You sure you didn't slip him anything?"

Barris waved his hands up high, protesting.

CHAPTER SIX

Item. What an undercover narcotics agent fears most is not that he will be shot or beaten up but that he will be slipped a great hit of some psychedelic that will roll an endless horror feature film in his head for the remainder of his life, or that he will be shot up with a mex hit, half heroin and half Substance D, or both of the above plus a poison such as strychnine, which will nearly kill him but not completely, so that the above can occur: lifelong addiction, lifelong horror film. He will sink into a needle-and-a-spoon existence, or bounce off the walls in a psychiatric hospital or, worst of all, a federal clinic. He will try to shake the aphids off him day and night or puzzle forever over why he cannot any longer wax a floor. And all this will occur deliberately. Someone figured out what he was doing and then got him. And they got him this way. The worst way of all: with the stuff they sell that he was after them for selling.

Which, Bob Arctor considered as he cautiously drove home, meant that both the dealers and the narks knew what the street drugs did to people. On that they agreed.

A Union station near where they had parked had driven out and gone over the car and finally fixed it up at a cost of thirty dollars. Nothing else seemed wrong, except that the mechanic had examined the left front suspension for quite a while.

"Anything wrong there?" Arctor had asked.

"Seems like you should be experiencing trouble when you corner sharply," the mechanic had said. "Does it yaw at all?"

The car didn't yaw, not that Arctor had noticed. But the mechanic refused to say more; he just kept poking at the coil spring and ball joint and oil-filled shock. Arctor paid him, and the tow truck drove off. He then got back into his own car, along with Luckman and Barris—both of whom now rode in back—and started north toward Orange County.

As he drove, Arctor ruminated about other ironic agreements in the minds of narcotics agents and dealers. Several narcotics agents that he had known had posed as dealers in their undercover work and wound up selling like hash and then, sometimes, even smack. This was a good cover, but it also brought the nark a gradually increasing profit over and above his official salary plus what he made when he helped bust and seize a good-sized shipment. Also, the agents got deeper and deeper into using their own stuff, the whole way of life, as a matter of course; they became rich dealer addicts as well as narks, and after a time some of them began to phase out their law-enforcement activities in favor of full-time dealing. But then, too, certain dealers, to burn their enemies or when expecting imminent busts, began narking and went that route, winding up as sort of unofficial undercover narks. It all got murky. The drug world was a murky world for everyone anyhow. For Bob Arctor, for example, it had become murky now: during this afternoon along the San Diego Freeway, while he and his two buddies had been within foot-seconds of being wiped out, the authorities, on his behalf, had been—he hoped—properly bugging their house, and if this had been done, then possibly he would be safe from now on from the kind of thing that had happened today. It was a piece of luck that ultimately might mean the difference between him winding up poisoned or shot or addicted or dead compared to nailing his enemy, nailing whoever was after him and who today had in fact almost gotten him. Once the holo-scanners were mounted in place, he ruminated, there would be very little sabotage or attacks against him. Or anyhow successful sabotage or successful attacks.

This was about the only thought that reassured him. The guilty, he reflected as he drove amid the heavy late-afternoon traffic as carefully as possible, may flee when no one pursues—he had heard that, and maybe that was true. What for a certainty was true, however, was that the guilty fled, fled like hell and took plenty of swift precautions, when someone did pursue: someone real and expert and at the same time hidden. And very close by. As close, he thought, as the back seat of this car. Where, if he has his funky .22 single-action German-made nowhere pistol with him and his equally funky rinky-dink laughable alleged silencer on it, and Luckman has gone to sleep as usual, he can put a hollow-nose bullet through the back of my skull and I will be as dead as Bobby Kennedy, who died from gunshot wounds of the same caliber—a bore that small.

And not only today but every day. And every night.

Except that in the house, when I check the storage drums of the holo-scanners, I'll pretty well know pretty soon what everyone in my house is doing and when they do it and probably even why, myself included. I will watch my own self, he thought, get up in the night to pee. I will watch all the rooms on a twenty-four-hour basis

. . . although there will be a lag. It won't help me much if the holo-scanners pick up me being given a hotshot of some disorientation drug ripped off by the Hell's Angels from a military arsenal and dumped in my coffee; someone else from the academy who goes over the storage drums will have to watch my thrashing around, unable to see or know where or what I am any more. It will be a hindsight I won't even get to have. Somebody else will have to have it for me.

Luckman said, "I wonder what's been going on back at the house while we've been gone all day. You know, this proves you got some-body out to burn you real bad, Bob. I hope when we get back the house is still there."

"Yeah," Arctor said. "I didn't think of that. And we didn't get a loan cephscope anyhow." He made his voice sound leaden with res-ignation.

Barris said, in a surprisingly cheerful voice, "I wouldn't worry too much."

With anger, Luckman said, "You wouldn't? Christ, they may have broken in and ripped off all we got. All Bob's got, anyhow. And killed or stomped the animals. Or—"

"I left a little surprise," Barris said, "for anybody entering the house while we're gone today. I perfected it early this morning . . . I worked until I got it. An electronic surprise."

Sharply, concealing his concern, Arctor said, "What kind of elec-tronic surprise? It's my house, Jim, you can't start rigging up—"

"Easy, easy," Barris said. "As our German friends would say, *leise*. Which means be cool."

"What is it?"

"If the front door is opened," Barris said, "during our absence, my cassette tape recorder starts recording. It's under the couch. It has a two-hour tape. I placed three omnidirectional Sony mikes at three different—"

"You should have told me," Arctor said.

"What if they come in through the windows?" Luckman said. "Or the back door?"

"To increase the chances of their making their entry via the front door," Barris continued, "rather than in other less usual ways, I providentially left the front door unlocked."

After a pause, Luckman began to snigger.

"Suppose they don't know it's unlocked?" Arctor said.

"I put a note on it," Barris said.

"You're jiving me!"

"Yes," Barris said, presently.

"Are you fucking jiving us or not?" Luckman said. "I can't tell with you. Is he jiving, Bob?"

"We'll see when we get back," Arctor said. "If there's a note on the door and it's unlocked we'll know he isn't jiving us."

"They probably would take the note down," Luckman said, "after ripping off and vandalizing the house, and then lock the door. So we won't know. We'll never know. For sure. It's that gray area again."

"Of course I'm kidding!" Barris said, with vigor. "Only a psychotic would do that, leave the front door of his house unlocked and a note on the door."

Turning, Arctor said to him, "What did you write on the note, Jim?"

"Who's the note to?" Luckman chimed in. "I didn't even know you knew how to write."

With condescension, Barris said, "I wrote: 'Donna, come on inside; door's unlocked. We—'" Barris broke off. "It's to Donna," he finished, but not smoothly.

"He did do that," Luckman said. "He really did. All of it."

"That way," Barris said, smoothly again, "we'll know who had been doing this, Bob. And that's of prime importance."

"Unless they rip off the tape recorder when they rip off the couch and everything else," Arctor said. He was thinking rapidly as to how much of a problem this really was, this additional example of Barris's messed-up electronic nowhere genius of a kindergarten sort. Hell, he concluded, they'll find the mikes in the first ten minutes and trace them back to the recorder. They'll know exactly what to do. They'll erase the tape, rewind it, leave it as it was, leave the door unlocked and the note on it. In fact, maybe the unlocked door will make their job easier. Fucking Barris, he thought. Great genius plans which will work out so as to screw up the universe. He probably forgot to plug the recorder into the wall outlet anyhow. Of course, if he finds it unplugged—

He'll reason that proves someone was there, he realized. He'll flash on that and rap at us for days. Somebody got in who was hip to his device and cleverly unplugged it. So, he decided, if they find it unplugged I hope they think to plug it in, and not only that, make it run right. In fact, what they really should do is test out his whole detection system, run it through its cycle as thoroughly as they do their own, be absolutely certain it functions perfectly, and then wind it back to a blank state, a tablet on which nothing is inscribed but on which something would for sure be had anyone—themselves, for example—entered the house. Otherwise, Barris's suspicions will be aroused forever.

As he drove, he continued his theoretical analysis of his situation by means of a second well-established example. They had brought it up and drilled it into his own memory banks during his police training at the academy. Or else he had read it in the newspapers.

Item. One of the most effective forms of industrial or military sabotage limits itself to damage that can never be thoroughly proven—or even proven at all—to be anything deliberate. It is like an invisible political movement; perhaps it isn't there at all. If a bomb is wired to a car's ignition, then obviously there is an enemy; if a public building or a political headquarters is blown up, then there is a political enemy. But if an accident, or a series of accidents, occurs, if equipment merely fails to function, if it appears faulty, especially in a slow fashion, over a period of natural time, with numerous small failures and misfirings—then the victim, whether a person or a party or a country, can never marshal itself to defend itself.

In fact, Arctor speculated as he drove along the freeway very slowly, the person begins to assume he's paranoid and has no enemy; he doubts himself. His car broke down normally; his luck has just become bad. And his friends agree. It's in his head. And this wipes him out more thoroughly than anything that can be traced. However, it takes longer. The person or persons doing him in must tinker and putter and make use of chance over a long interval. Meanwhile, if the victim can figure out who they are, he has a better chance of getting them—certainly better than if, say, they shoot him with a scopesight rifle. That is *his* advantage.

Every nation in the world, he knew, trains and sends out a mass of agents to loosen bolts here, strip threads there, break wires and start little fires, lose documents—little misadventures. A wad of gum inside a Xerox copying machine in a government office can destroy an irreplaceable—and vital—document: instead of a copy coming out, the original is wiped out. Too much soap and toilet paper, as the Yippies of the sixties knew, can screw up the entire sewage of an office building and force all the employees out for a week. A mothball in a car's gas tank wears out the engine two weeks later, when it's in another town, and leaves no fuel contaminants to be analyzed. Any radio or TV station can be put off the air by a pile driver accidentally cutting a microwave cable or a power cable. And so forth.

Many of the previous aristocratic social class knew about maids and gardeners and other serf-type help: a broken vase here, a dropped priceless heirloom that slips out of a sullen hand . . .

"Why'd you do that, Rastus Brown?"

"Oh, Ah jes' fogot ta—" and there was no recourse, or very little. By a rich homeowner, by a political writer unpopular with the regime, a small new nation shaking its fist at the U.S. or at the U.S.S.R.—

Once, an American ambassador to Guatemala had had a wife who had publicly boasted that her "pistol-packin'" husband had overthrown that little nation's left-wing government. After its abrupt fall, the ambassador, his job done, had been transferred to a small Asian nation, and while driving his sports car he had suddenly discovered a slow-moving hay truck pulling out of a side road directly ahead of him. A moment later nothing remained of the ambassador except a bunch of splatted bits. Packing a pistol, and having at his call an entire CIA raised private army, had done him no good. His wife wrote no proud poetry about that.

"Uh, do what?" the owner of the hay truck had probably said to the local authorities. "Do what, massah? Ah jes'—" .

Or like his own ex-wife, Arctor remembered. At that time he had worked for an insurance firm as an investigator ("Do your neighbors across the hall drink a lot?"), and she had objected to his filling out his reports late at night instead of thrilling at the very sight of her. Toward the end of their marriage she had learned to do such things during his late-night work period as burn her hand while lighting a cigarette, get something in her eye, dust his office, or search forever throughout or around his typewriter for some little object. At first he had resentfully stopped work and succumbed to thrilling at the very sight of her; but then he had hit his head in the kitchen while getting out the corn popper and had found a better solution.

"If they kill our animals," Luckman was saying, "I'll fire bomb them. I'll get all of them. I'll hire a professional down from L.A., like a bunch of Panthers."

"They won't," Barris said. "There's nothing to be gained by injuring animals. The animals haven't done anything."

"Have I?" Arctor said.

"Evidently they think so," Barris said.

Luckman said, *"If I had known it was harmless I would have killed it myself.* Remember?"

"But she was a straight," Barris said. "That girl never turned on, and she had heavy bread. Remember her apartment? The rich never understand the value of life. That's something else. Remember Thelma Kornford, Bob? The short girl with the huge breasts—she never wore a bra and we used to just sit and look at her nipples? She came over to our place to get us to kill that mosquito hawk for her? And when we explained—"

At the wheel of his slow car, Bob Arctor forgot theoretical matters and did a rerun of a moment that had impressed them all: the dainty

and elegant straight girl in her turtleneck sweater and bell-bottoms
and trippy boobs who wanted them to murder a great harmless bug
that in fact did good by wiping out mosquitoes—and in a year in
which an outbreak of encephalitis had been anticipated in Orange
County—and when they saw what it was and explained, she had said
words that became for them their parody evil-wall-motto, to be
feared and despised:

IF I HAD KNOWN IT WAS HARMLESS
I WOULD HAVE KILLED IT MYSELF.

That had summed up to them (and still did) what they distrusted
in their straight foes, assuming they had foes; anyhow, a person like
well-educated-with-all-the-financial-advantages Thelma Kornford became at once a foe by uttering that, from which they had run that
day, pouring out of her apartment and back to their own littered pad,
to her perplexity. The gulf between their world and hers had
manifested itself, however much they'd meditated on how to ball her,
and remained. Her heart, Bob Arctor reflected, was an empty
kitchen: floor tile and water pipes and a drainboard with pale
scrubbed surfaces, and one abandoned glass on the edge of the sink
that nobody cared about.

One time before he got solely into undercover work he had taken a
deposition from a pair of upper-class well-off straights whose furniture had been ripped off during their absence, evidently by junkies;
in those days such people still lived in areas where roving rip-off
bands stole what they could, leaving little. Professional bands, with
walkie-talkies in the hands of spotters who watched a couple miles
down the street for the marks' return. He remembered the man and
his wife saying, "People who would burglarize your house and take
your color TV are the same kind of criminals who slaughter animals
or vandalize priceless works of art." No, Bob Arctor had explained,
pausing in writing down their deposition, what makes you believe
that? Addicts, in his experience anyhow, rarely hurt animals. He had
witnessed junkies feeding and caring for injured animals over long
periods of time, where straights probably would have had the animals "put to sleep," a straight-type term if there ever was one—and
also an old Syndicate term as well, for murder. Once he had assisted
two totally spaced-out heads in the sad ordeal of unscrewing a cat
which had impaled herself within a broken window. The heads,
hardly able to see or understand anything any more, had over almost
an entire hour deftly and patiently worked the cat loose until she was
free, bleeding a little, all of them, heads and cat alike, with the cat

calm in their hands, one dude inside the house with Arctor, the other outdoors, where the ass and tail were. The cat had come free at last with no real injury, and then they had fed her. They did not know whose cat she was; evidently she had been hungry and smelled food through their broken window and finally, unable to rouse them, had tried to leap in. They hadn't noticed her until her shriek, and then they had forgotten their various trips and dreams for a while in her behalf.

As to "priceless works of art" he wasn't too sure, because he didn't exactly understand what that meant. At My Lai during the Viet Nam War, four hundred and fifty priceless works of art had been vandalized to death at the orders of the CIA—priceless works of art plus oxen and chickens and other animals not listed. When he thought about that he always got a little dingey and was hard to reason with about paintings in museums and like that.

"Do you think," he said aloud as he painstakingly drove, "that when we die and appear before God on Judgment Day, that our sins will be listed in chronological order or in order of severity, which could be ascending or descending, or alphabetically? Because I don't want to have God boom out at me when I die at the age of eighty-six, 'So you're the little boy who stole the three Coke bottles off the Coca-Cola truck when it was parked in the 7-11 lot back in 1962, and you've got a lot of fast talking to do.'"

"I think they're cross-referenced," Luckman said. "And they just hand you a computer printout that's the total of a long column that's been added up already."

"Sin," Barris said, chuckling, "is a Jewish-Christian myth that is outdated."

Arctor said, "Maybe they've got all your sins in one big pickle barrel"—he turned to glare at Barris the anti-Semite—"a kosher pickle barrel, and they just hoist it up and throw the whole contents all at once in your face, and you just stand there dripping sins. Your own sins, plus maybe a few of somebody else's that got in by mistake."

"Somebody else by the same name," Luckman said. "Another Robert Arctor. How many Robert Arctors do you think there are, Barris?" He nudged Barris. "Could the Cal Tech computers tell us that? And cross-file all the Jim Barrises too while they're doing it?"

To himself, Bob Arctor thought, *How many Bob Arctors are there?* A weird and fucked-up thought. Two that I can think of, he thought. The one called Fred, who will be watching the other one, called Bob. The same person. Or is it? Is Fred actually the same as Bob? Does anybody know? I would know, if anyone did, because

I'm the only person in the world that knows that Fred is Bob Arctor. *But,* he thought, *who am I? Which of them is me?*

When they rolled to a stop in the driveway, parked, and walked warily toward the front door, they found Barris's note and the door unlocked, but when they cautiously opened the door everything appeared as it had been when they left.

Barris's suspicions surfaced instantly. "Ah," he murmured, entering. He swiftly reached to the top of the bookshelf by the door and brought down his .22 pistol, which he gripped as the other men moved about. The animals approached them as usual, clamoring to be fed.

"Well, Barris," Luckman said, "I can see you're right. There definitely was someone here, because you see—you see, too, don't you, Bob?—the scrupulous covering-over of all the signs they would have otherwise left testifies to their—" He farted then, in disgust, and wandered into the kitchen to look in the refrigerator for a can of beer. "Barris," he said, "you're fucked."

Still moving about alertly with his gun, Barris ignored him as he sought to discover telltale traces. Arctor, watching, thought, Maybe he will. They may have left some. And he thought, Strange how paranoia can link up with reality now and then, briefly. Under very specialized conditions, such as today. Next thing, Barris will be reasoning that I lured everyone out of the house deliberately to permit secret intruders to accomplish their thing here. And later on he will discern why and who and everything else, and in fact maybe he already has. Had a while ago, in fact; long-enough ago to initiate sabotage and destruct actions on the cephscope, car, and God knows what else. Maybe when I turn on the garage light the house will burn down. But the main things is, did the bugging crew arrive and get all the monitors in and finish up? He would not know until he talked to Hank and Hank gave him a proof-positive layout of the monitors and where their storage drums could be serviced. And whatever additional information the bugging crew's boss, plus other experts involved in this operation, wanted to dump on him. In their concerted play against Bob Arctor, the suspect.

"Look at this!" Barris said. He bent over an ashtray on the coffee table. "Come here!" he called sharply to both of them, and both men responded.

Reaching down, Arctor felt heat rising from the ashtray.

"A still-hot cigarette butt," Luckman said, marveling. "It sure is."

Jesus, Arctor thought. They did screw up. One of the crew smoked and then reflexively put the butt here. So they must just have gone.

The ashtray, as always, overflowed; the crewman probably assumed no one would notice the addition, and in another few moments it would have cooled.

"Wait a second," Luckman said, examining the ashtray. He fished out, from among the tobacco butts, a roach. "This is what's hot, this roach. They lit up a joint while they were here. But what did they do? What the hell did they do?" He scowled and peered about, angry and baffled. "Bob, fuck it—Barris was right. *There was somebody here!* This roach is still hot, and you can smell it if you hold it—" He held it under Arctor's nose. "Yeah, it's still burning a little down inside. Probably a seed. They didn't manicure it too good before they rolled it."

"That roach," Barris said, equally grim, "may not have been left here by accident. This evidence may not be a slip-up."

"What now?" Arctor said, wondering what kind of police bugging crew would have a member who smoked a joint in front of the others while on the job.

"Maybe they were here specifically to plant dope in this house," Barris said. "Setting us up, then phone in a tip later . . . Maybe there's dope hidden like this in the phone, for example, and the wall outlets. We're going to have to go through the whole house and get it absolutely clean before they phone the tip in. And we've probably got only hours."

"You check the wall sockets," Luckman said. "I'll take the phone apart."

"Wait," Barris said, holding up his hand. "If they see us scrambling around just before the raid—"

"What raid?" Arctor said.

"If we're running frantically around flushing dope," Barris said, "then we can't allege, even though it's true, that we didn't know the dope was there. They'll catch us actually holding it. And maybe that, too, is part of their plan."

"Aw shit," Luckman said in disgust. He threw himself down on the couch. "Shit shit shit. We can't do anything. There's probably dope hidden in a thousand places we'll never find. We've had it." He glared up at Arctor in baffled fury. *"We've had it!"*

Arctor said to Barris, "What about your electronic cassette thing rigged to the front door?" He had forgotten about it. So had Barris, evidently. Luckman, too.

"Yes, this should be extremely informational at this point," Barris said. He knelt down by the couch, reached underneath, grunted, then hauled forth a small plastic cassette tape recorder. "This should tell us a great deal," he began, and then his face sank. "Well, it probably wouldn't ultimately have proven that important." He pulled out the power plug from the back and set the casette down on the coffee table. "We know the main fact—that they did enter during our absence. That was its main task."

Silence.

"I'll bet I can guess," Arctor said.

Barris said, "The first thing they did when they entered was switch it to the *off* position. I left it set to *on,* but look—now it's turned to *off.* So although I—"

"It didn't record?" Luckman said, disappointed.

"They made their move swiftly," Barris said. "Before so much as an inch of tape passed through the recording head. This, by the way, is a neat little job, a Sony. It has a separate head for playback, erase and record, and the Dolby noise-reduction system. I got it cheap. At a swap meet. And it's never given me any trouble."

Arctor said, "Mandatory soul time."

"Absolutely," Barris agreed as he seated himself in a chair and leaned back, removing his shades. "At this point we have no other recourse in view of their evasive tactics. You know, Bob, there is one thing you could do, although it would take time."

"Sell the house and move out," Arctor said.

Barris nodded.

"But hell," Luckman protested. "This is our *home.*"

"What are houses like this in this area worth now?" Barris asked, hands behind his head. "On the market? I wonder, too, what interest rates are up to. Maybe you could make a considerable profit, Bob. On the other hand, you might have to take a loss on a quick sale. But, Bob, my God, you're up against professionals."

"Do you know a good realtor?" Luckman asked both of them.

Arctor said, "What reason should we give for selling? They always ask."

"Yeah, we can't tell the realtor the truth," Luckman agreed. "We could say . . ." He pondered as he moodily drank his beer. "I can't think of a reason. Barris, what's a reason, a shuck we could give?"

Arctor said, "We'll just say flat-out there's narcotics planted all over the house and since we don't know where it is we decided to move out and let the new owner get busted instead of us."

"No," Barris disagreed, "I don't think we can afford to be up front like that. I'd suggest you say, Bob, you say that you got a job transfer."

"Where to?" Luckman said.

"Cleveland," Barris said.

"I think we should tell them the truth," Arctor said. "In fact, we could put an ad in the L. A. *Times:* 'Modern three-bedroom tract house with two bathrooms for easy and fast flushing, high-grade dope stashed throughout all rooms; dope included in sale price."

"But they'd be calling asking what kind of dope," Luckman said. "And we don't know; it could be anything."

"And how much there is," Barris murmured. "Prospective buyers might inquire about the quantity."

"Like," Luckman said, "it could be an ounce of roachweed, just shit like that, or it could be pounds of heroin."

"What I suggest," Barris said, "is that we phone county drug abuse and inform them of the situation and ask them to come in and remove the dope. Search the house, find it, dispose of it. Because, to be realistic, there really isn't time to sell the house. I researched the legal situation once for this type of bind, and most lawbooks agree—"

"You're crazy," Luckman said, staring at him as if he were one of Jerry's aphids. "Phone *drug abuse?* There'll be narks in here within less time than—"

"That's the best hope," Barris continued smoothly, "and we can all take lie-detector tests to prove we didn't know where it was or what it was or even put it there. It is there without our knowledge or permission. If you tell them that, Bob, they'll exonerate you." After a pause he admitted, "Eventually. When all the facts are known in open court."

"But on the other hand," Luckman said, "we've got our own stashes. We *do* know where they are and like that. Does this mean we've got to flush all our stashes? And suppose we miss some? Even one? Christ, this is awful!"

"There is no way out," Arctor said. "They appear to have us."

From one of the bedrooms Donna Hawthorne appeared, wearing a funny little knee-pants outfit, hair tumbled in disarray, her face puffy with sleep.

"I came on in," she said, "like the note said. And I sat around for a while and then crashed. The note didn't say when you'd be back. Why were you yelling? God, you're uptight. You woke me."

"You smoked a joint just now?" Arctor asked her. "Before you crashed?"

"Sure," she said. "Otherwise I can't ever sleep."

"It's Donna's roach," Luckman said. "Give it to her."

My God, Bob Arctor thought. I was into that trip as much as they were. We all got into it together that deep. He shook himself, shuddered, and blinked. Knowing what I know, I still stepped across into that freaked-out paranoid space with them, viewed it as they viewed it—muddled, he thought. Murky again; the same murk that covers them covers me; the murk of this dreary dream world we float around in.

"You got us out of it," he said to Donna.

"Out of what?" Donna said, puzzled and sleepy.

Not what I am, he thought, or what I know was supposed to take place here today, but this chick—*she* put my head back together, got all three of us out. A little black-haired chick wearing a funky outfit who I report on and am shucking and hopefully will be fucking . . . another shuck-and-fuck reality world, he thought, with this foxy girl the center of it: a rational point that unwired us abruptly. Otherwise where would our heads finally have gone? We, all three of us, had gotten out of it entirely.

But not for the first time, he thought. Not even today.

"You shouldn't leave your place unlocked like that," Donna said. "You could get ripped off and it'd be your own fault. Even the giant capitalist insurance companies say that if you leave a door or window unlocked they won't pay. That's the main reason I came in when I saw the note. Somebody ought to be here if it's unlocked like that."

"How long have you been here?" Arctor asked her. Maybe she had aborted the bugging; maybe not. Probably not.

Donna consulted her twenty-dollar electric Timex wristwatch, which he had given her. "About thirty-eight minutes. Hey." Her face brightened. "Bob, I got the wolf book with me—you want to look at it now? It's got a lot of heavy shit in it, if you can dig it."

"Life," Barris said, as if to himself, "is only heavy and none else; there is only the one trip, all heavy. Heavy that leads to the grave. For everyone and everything."

"Did I hear you say you're going to sell your house?" Donna asked him. "Or was that—you know, me dreaming? I couldn't tell; what I heard sounded spaced out and weird."

"We're all dreaming," Arctor said. If the last to know he's an addict is the addict, then maybe the last to know when a man means what he says is the man himself, he reflected. He wondered how much of the garbage that Donna had overheard he had seriously meant. He wondered how much of the insanity of the day—his insanity—had been real, or just induced as a contact lunacy, by the situation. Donna, always, was a pivot point of reality for him; for her this was the basic, natural question. He wished he could answer.

CHAPTER SEVEN

The next day Fred showed up in his scramble suit to hear about the bugging installation.

"The six holo-scanners now operating within the premises—six should be sufficient for now, we feel—transmit to a safe apartment down the street in the same block as Arctor's house," Hank explained, laying out a floor plan of Bob Arctor's house on the metal table between them. It chilled Fred to see this, but not overly much. He picked the sheet up and studied the locations of the various scanners, in the various rooms, here and there so that everything fell under constant video scrutiny, as well as audio.

"So I do the playback at that apartment," Fred said.

"We use it as a playback-monitor spot for about eight—or perhaps it's nine, now—houses or apartments under scrutiny in that particular neighborhood. So you'll be bumping into other undercover people doing their playbacks. *Always have your suit on then.*"

"I'll be seen going into the apartment. It's too close."

"Guess so, but it's an enormous complex, hundreds of units, and it's the only one we've found electronically feasible. It'll have to do, at least until we get legal eviction on another unit elsewhere. We're working on it . . . two blocks farther away, where you'll be less conspicuous. Week or so, I'd guess. If holo-scans could be transmitted with acceptable resolution along micro-relay cables and ITT lines like the older—"

"I'll just use the shuck that I'm balling some broad in that complex, if Arctor or Luckman or any of those heads see me entering." It really didn't complicate matters that much; in fact, it would cut down his in-transit unpaid time, which was an important factor. He could easily truck on over to the safe apartment, do the scanning replay, determine what was relevant to his reports and what could be discarded, and then return very soon to—"

To my own house, he thought. Arctor's house. Up the street at the house I am Bob Arctor, the heavy doper suspect being scanned without his knowledge, and then every couple of days I find a pretext to slip down the street and into the apartment where I am Fred replaying miles and miles of tape to see what I did, and this whole business, he thought, depresses me. Except for the protection—and valuable personal information—it will give me.

Probably whoever's hunting me will be caught by the holoscanners within the first week.

Realizing that, he felt mellow.

"Fine," he said to Hank.

"So you see where the holos are placed. If they need servicing, you probably can do it yourself while you're in Arctor's house and no one else is around. You do get into his house, normally, don't you?"

Well shit, Fred thought. If I do that, then I will be on the holoreplays. So when I turn them over to Hank I have to be, obviously, one of the individuals visible on them, and that cuts it down.

Up to now he had never actually laid it on Hank as to how he knew what he knew about his suspects; he himself as Fred the effective screening device carried the information. But now: audio- and holo-scanners, which did not automatically edit out as did his verbal report all identifying mention of himself. There would be Robert Arctor tinkering with the holos when they malfunctioned, his face mushrooming up to fill the screen. But on the other hand *he* would be the first to replay the storage tapes; he could still edit. Except that it would take time and care.

But edit out *what*? Edit out Arctor—entirely? Arctor was the suspect. Just Arctor when he went to fiddle with the holos.

"I'll edit myself out," he said. "So you won't see me. As a matter of conventional protection."

"Of course. You haven't done this before?" Hank reached to show him a couple of pictures. "You use a bulk erasing device that wipes out any section where you as the informant appear. That's the holos, of course; for audio, there's no set policy followed. You won't have any real trouble, though. We take it for granted that you're one of the individuals in Arctor's circle of friends who frequent that house—you are either Jim Barris or Ernie Luckman or Charles Freck or Donna Hawthorne—"

"Donna?" He laughed. The suit laughed, actually. In its way.

"Or Bob Arctor," Hank continued, studying his list of suspects.

"I report on myself all the time," Fred said.

"So you will have to include yourself from time to time in the holo-tapes you turn over to us, because if you systematically edit yourself out then we can deduce who you are by a process of elimination, whether we want to or not. What you must do, really, is edit yourself out in—what should I call it?—an inventive, artistic . . . Hell, the word is, *creative* way . . . as for instance during the brief intervals when you're in the house alone and doing research, going through papers and drawers, or servicing a scanner within view of another scanner, or—"

"You should just send someone to the house once a month in a uniform," Fred said. "And have him say, 'Good morning! I'm here to service the monitoring devices covertly installed on your premises, in your phone, and in your car.' Maybe Arctor would pick up the bill."

"Arctor would probably off him and then disappear."

The scramble suit Fred said, "If Arctor is hiding that much. That's not been proved."

"Arctor may be hiding a great deal. We've got more recent information on him gathered and analyzed. There is no substantial doubt of it: he is a ringer, a three-dollar bill. He is *phony*. So keep on him until he drops, until we have enough to arrest him and make it stick."

"You want stuff planted?"

"We'll discuss that later."

"You think he's up high in the, you know, the S. D. Agency?"

"What we *think* isn't of any importance in your work," Hank said. "We evaluate; *you* report with your own limited conclusions. This is not a put-down of you, but we have information, lots of it, not available to you. The broad picture. The computerized picture."

"Arctor is doomed," Fred said. "If he's up to anything. And I have a hunch from what you say that he is."

"We should have a case on him this way soon," Hank said. "And then we can close the book on him, which will please us all."

Fred stoically memorized the address and number of the apartment and suddenly recalled that he had seen a young head-type couple who had recently abruptly disappeared now and then entering and leaving the building. Busted, and their apartment taken over for this. He had liked them. The girl had long flaxen hair, wore no bra. One time he had driven past as she was lugging groceries and offered her a lift; they had talked. She was an organic type, into megavitamins and kelp and sunlight, nice, shy, but she'd declined. Now he could see why. Evidently the two of them had been holding. Or, more likely, dealing. On the other hand, if the apartment was needed, a possession rap would do, and you could always get that.

What, he wondered, would Bob Arctor's littered but large house be used for by the authorities when Arctor had been hauled off? An even vaster intelligence-processing center, most likely.

"You'd like Arctor's house," he said aloud. "It's run-down and typically doper dirty, but it's big. Nice yard. Lots of shrubs."

"That's what the installation crew reported back. Some excellent possibilities."

"They *what?* They reported it had 'plenty of possibilities,' did they?" The scramble suit voice clacked out maddeningly without tone or resonance, which made him even angrier. "Like what?"

"Well, one obvious possibility: its living room gives a view of an intersection, so passing vehicles could be graphed and their license plates . . ." Hank studied his many, many papers. "But Burt What's-his-face, who headed the crew, felt the house had been allowed to deteriorate so badly that it wouldn't be worth our taking over. As an investment."

"In what way? In what fashion deteriorated?"

"The roof."

"The roof's perfect."

"The interior and exterior paint. The condition of the floors. The kitchen cabinets—"

"Bullshit," Fred said, or anyhow the suit droned. "Arctor may have let dishes pile up and the garbage and not dusted, but after all, three dudes living there with no chicks? His wife left him; women are supposed to do all that. If Donna Hawthorne had moved in like Arctor wanted her to, begged her to, she would have kept it up. Anyhow, any professional janitorial service could put the whole house in top shape as far as cleaning goes in a half a day. Regarding the roof, that really makes me mad, because—"

"Then you recommend we acquire it after Arctor's been arrested and loses title."

Fred, the suit, stared at him.

"Well?" Hank said impassively, ballpoint pen ready.

"I have no opinion. One way or another." Fred rose from his chair to leave.

"You're not splitting yet," Hank said, motioning him to reseat himself. He fished among the papers on his desk. "I have a memo here—"

"You always have memos," Fred said. "For everybody."

"This memo," Hank said, "instructs me to send you over to Room 203 before you leave today."

"If it's about that anti-drug speech I gave at the Lion's Club, I've already had my ass chewed about it."

"No, this isn't that." Hank tossed him the fluttery note. "This is something different. I'm finished with you, so why don't you head right over there now and get it done with."

He found himself confronting an all-white room with steel fixtures and steel chairs and steel desk, all bolted down, a hospital-like room, purified and sterile and cold, with the light too bright. In fact, to the right stood a weighing scale with a sign HAVE TECHNICIAN ONLY ADJUST. Two deputies regarded him, both in full uniform of the Orange County Sheriff's Office, but with medical stripes.

"You are Officer Fred?" one of them, with a handle-bar mustache, said.

"Yes, sir," Fred said. He felt scared.

"All right, Fred, first let me state that, as you undoubtedly are aware, your briefings and debriefings are monitored and later played back for study, in case anything was missed at the original sessions. This is SOP, of course, and applies to all officers reporting in orally, not you alone."

The other medical deputy said, "Plus all other contacts you maintain with the department, such as phone contacts, and additional activities, such as your recent public speech in Anaheim to the Rotary Club boys."

"Lions," Fred said.

"Do you take Substance D?" the left-hand medical deputy said.

"That question," the other said, "is moot because it's taken for granted that in your work you're compelled to. So don't answer. Not that it would be incriminating, but it's simply moot." He indicated a table on which a bunch of blocks and other riff-raff colorful plastic objects lay, plus peculiar items that Officer Fred could not identify. "Step over here and be seated, Officer Fred. We are going to administer, briefly, several easy tests. This won't consume much of your time, and there will be no physical discomfort involved."

"About that speech I gave——" Fred said.

"What this is about," the left-hand medical deputy said, as he seated himself and produced a pen and some forms, "stems from a recent departmental survey showing that several undercover agents working in this area have been admitted to Neural Aphasia Clinics during the past month."

"You're conscious of the high factor of addictiveness of Substance D?" the other deputy said to Fred.

"Sure," Fred said. "Of course I am."

"We're going to give you these tests now," the seated deputy said, "in this order, starting with what we call the BG or——"

"You think I'm an addict?" Fred said.

"Whether you are an addict or not isn't a prime issue, since a blocking agent is expected from the Army Chemical Warfare Division sometime within the next five years."

"These tests do not pertain to the addictive properties of Substance D but to— Well, let me give you this Set-Ground Test first, which determines your ability readily to distinguish set from ground. See this geometric diagram?" He laid a drawn-on card before Fred, on the table. "Within the apparently meaningless lines is a familiar object that we would all recognize. You are to tell me what the . . .

Item. In July 1969, Joseph E. Bogen published his revolutionary article "The Other Side of the Brain: An Appositional Mind." In this article he quoted an obscure Dr. A. L. Wigan, who in 1844 wrote:

> The mind is essentially dual, like the organs by which it is exercised. This idea has presented itself to me, and I have dwelt on it for more than a quarter of a century, without being able to find a single valid or even plausible objection. I believe myself then able to prove—(1) That each cerebrum is a distinct and perfect whole as an organ of thought. (2) That a separate and distinct process of thinking or ratiocination may be carried on in each cerebrum simultaneously.

In his article, Bogen concluded: "I believe [with Wigan] that each of us has two minds in one person. There is a host of detail to be marshaled in this case. But we must eventually confront directly the principal resistance to the Wigan view: that is, the subjective feeling possessed by each of us that we are One. This inner conviction of Oneness is a most cherished opinion of Western Man. . . ."

". . . object is and point to it in the total field."

I'm being Mutt-and-Jeffed, Fred thought. "What is all this?" he said, gazing at the deputy and not the diagram. "I'll bet it's the Lion Club speech," he said. He was positive.

The seated deputy said, "In many of those taking Substance D, a split between the right hemisphere and the left hemisphere of the brain occurs. There is a loss of proper gestalting, which is a defect within both the percept and cognitive systems, although *apparently* the cognitive system continues to function normally. But what is now received from the percept system is contaminated by being split, so it too, therefore, fails gradually to function, progressively deteriorating. Have you located the familiar object in this line drawing? Can you find it for me?"

Fred said, "You're not talking about heavy metals trace deposits in the neuroreceptor sites, are you? Irreversible—"

"No," the standing deputy said. "This is not brain damage but a form of toxicity, brain toxicity. It's a toxic brain psychosis affecting the percept system by splitting it. What you have before you, this BG test, measures the accuracy of your percept system to act as a unified whole. Can you see the form here? It should jump right out at you."

"I see a Coke bottle," Fred said.

"A soda pop bottle is correct," the seated deputy said, and whipped the drawing away, replacing it with another.

"Have you noticed anything," Fred said, "in studying my briefings and like that? Anything slushed?" It's the speech, he thought. "What about the speech I gave?" he said. "Did I show bilateral dysfunction there? Is that why I've been hauled in here for these tests?" He had read about these split-brain tests, given by the department from time to time.

"No, this is routine," the seated deputy said. "We realize, Officer Fred, that undercover agents must of necessity take drugs in the line of duty; those who've had to go into federal—"

"Permanently?" Fred asked.

"Not many permanently. Again, this is percept contamination that could in the course of time rectify itself as—"

"Murky," Fred said. "It murks over everything."

"Are you getting any cross-chatter?" one of the deputies asked him suddenly.

"What?" he said uncertainly.

"Between hemispheres. If there's damage to the left hemisphere, where the linguistic skills are normally located, then sometimes the right hemisphere will fill in to the best of its ability."

"I don't know," he said. "Not that I'm aware of."

"Thoughts not your own. As if another person or mind were thinking. But different from the way you would think. Even foreign words that you don't know. That it's learned from peripheral perception sometime during your lifetime."

"Nothing like that. I'd notice that."

"You probably would. From people with left-hemisphere damage who've reported it, evidently it's a pretty shattering experience."

"Well, I guess I'd notice that."

"It used to be believed the right hemisphere had no linguistic faculties at all, but that was before so many people had screwed up their left hemispheres with drugs and gave it—the right—a chance to come on. To fill the vacuum."

"I'll certainly keep my eyes open for that," Fred said, and heard the mere mechanical quality of his voice, like that of a dutiful child in school. Agreeing to obey whatever dull order was imposed on him by those in authority. Those taller than he was, and in a position to impose their strength and will on him, whether it was reasonable or not.

Just agree, he thought. And do what you're told.

"What do you see in this second picture?"

"A sheep," Fred said.

"Show me the sheep." The seated deputy leaned forward and rotated the picture. "An impairment in set-background discrimination gets you into a heap of trouble—instead of perceiving no forms you perceive faulty forms."

Like dog shit, Fred thought. Dog shit certainly would be considered a faulty form. By any standard. He . . .

> The data indicate that the mute, minor hemisphere is specialized for Gestalt perception, being primarily a synthesist in dealing with information input. The speaking, major hemisphere, in contrast, seems to operate in a more logical, analytic, computerlike fashion and the findings suggest that a possible reason for cerebral lateralization in man is basic incompatibility of language functions on the one hand and synthetic perceptual functions on the other.

. . . felt ill and depressed, almost as much as he had during his Lions Club speech. "There's no sheep there, is there?" he said. "But was I close?"

"This is not a Rorschach test," the seated deputy said, "where a muddled blot can be interpreted many ways by many subjects. In this, one specific object, as such, has been delineated and one only. In this case it's a dog."

"A what?" Fred said.

"A dog."

"How can you tell it's a dog?" He saw no dog. "Show me." The deputy . . .

> This conclusion finds its experimental proof in the split-brain animal whose two hemispheres can be trained to perceive, consider, and act independently. In the hu-

man, where propositional thought is typically lateralized in one hemisphere, the other hemisphere evidently specializes in a different mode of thought, which may be called *appositional*. The rules or methods by which propositional thought is elaborated on "this" side of the brain (the side which speaks, reads, and writes) have been subjected to analyses of syntax, semantics, mathematical logic, etc. for many years. The rules by which appositional thought is elaborated on the other side of the brain will need study for many years to come.

. . . turned the card over; on the back the formal stark simple outline of A DOG had been inscribed, and now Fred recognized it as the shape drawn within the lines on the front side. In fact it was a specific type of dog: a greyhound, with drawn-in gut.

"What's that mean," he said, "that I saw a sheep instead?"

"Probably just a psychological block," the standing deputy said, shifting his weight about. "Only when the whole set of cards is run, and then we have the several other tests——"

"Why this is a superior test to the Rorschach," the seated deputy interrupted, producing the next drawing, "is that it is not interpretive; there are as many wrongs as you can think up, *but only one right*. The right object that the U. S. Department of Psych-Graphics drew into it and certified for it, for each card; that's what's right, because it is handed down from Washington. You either get it or you don't, and if you show a *run* of not getting it, then we have a fix on a functional impairment in perception and we dry you out for a while, until you test okay later on."

"A federal clinic?" Fred said.

"Yes. Now, what do you see in this drawing, among these particular black and white lines?"

Death City, Fred thought as he studied the drawing. That is what I see: death in pluriform, not in just the one correct form but throughout. Little three-foot-high contract men on carts.

"Just tell me," Fred said, "was it the Lions Club speech that alerted you?"

The two medical deputies exchanged glances.

"No," the standing one said finally. "It had to do with an exchange that was—actually—off the cuff, in fact just bullshitting between you and Hank. About two weeks ago . . . you realize, there's a technological lag in processing all this garbage, all this raw information that flows in. They haven't gotten to your speech yet. They won't in fact for another couple of days."

"What was this bullshitting?"

"Something about a stolen bicycle," the other deputy said. "A so-called seven-speed bicycle. You'd been trying to figure out where the missing three speeds had gone, was that it?" Again they glanced at each other, the two medical deputies. "You felt they had been left on the floor of the garage it was stolen from?"

"Hell," Fred protested. "That was Charles Freck's fault, not mine; he got everybody's ass in an uproar talking about it. I just thought it was funny."

BARRIS: (*Standing in the middle of the living room with a great big new shiny bike, very pleased*) Look what I got for twenty dollars.

FRECK: What is it?

BARRIS: A bike, a ten-speed racing bike, virtually brand new. I saw it in the neighbor's yard and asked about it and they had four of them so I made an offer of twenty dollars cash and they sold it to me. Colored people. They even hoisted it over the fence for me.

LUCKMAN: I didn't know you could get a ten-speed nearly new for twenty dollars. It's amazing what you can get for twenty dollars.

DONNA: It resembles the one the chick across the street from me had that got ripped off about a month ago. They probably ripped it off, those black guys.

ARCTOR: Sure they did, if they've got four. And selling it that cheap.

DONNA: You ought to give it back to the chick across the street from me, if it's hers. Anyhow you should let her look at it to see if it's hers.

BARRIS: It's a man's bike. So it can't be.

FRECK: Why do you say it's ten speeds when it's only got seven gears?

BARRIS: (*Astonished*) What?

FRECK: (*Going over to bike and pointing*) Look, five gears here, two gears here at the other end of the chain. Five and two . . .

When the optic chiasm of a cat or a monkey is divided sagittally, the input into the right eye goes only into the right hemisphere and similarly the left eye informs only the left hemisphere. If an animal with this operation is trained to choose between two symbols

while using only one eye, later tests show that it can
make the proper choice with the other eye. But if the
commissures, especially the corpus callosum, have been
severed before training, the initially covered eye and
its ipsilateral hemisphere must be trained from the
beginning. That is, the training does not transfer from
one hemisphere to the other if the commissures have
been cut. This is the fundamental split-brain experiment
of Myers and Sperry (1953; Sperry, 1961; Myers,
1965; Sperry, 1967).

. . . makes seven. So it's only a seven-speed bike.

LUCKMAN: Yeah, but even a seven-speed racing bike is worth
twenty dollars. He still got a good buy.

BARRIS: (*Nettled*) Those colored people told me it was ten
speeds. It's a rip-off.

(*Everyone gathers to examine bike. They count the gears again
and again.*)

FRECK: Now I count eight. Six in front, two in back. That makes
eight.

ARCTOR: (*Logically*) But it should be ten. There are no seven-
or eight-speed bikes. Not that I ever heard of. What do you suppose
happened to the missing gears?

BARRIS: Those colored guys must have been working on it, taking it apart with improper tools and no technical knowledge, and
when they reassembled it they left three gears lying on the floor of
their garage. They're probably still lying there.

LUCKMAN: Then we should go ask for the missing gears back.

BARRIS: (*Pondering angrily*) But that's where the rip-off is:
they'll probably offer to sell them to me, not give them to me as they
should. I wonder what else they've damaged. (*Inspects entire bike*)

LUCKMAN: If we all go together they'll give them to us; you can
bet on it, man. We'll all go, right? (*Looks around for agreement*)

DONNA: Are you positive there're only seven gears?

FRECK: Eight.

DONNA: Seven, eight. Anyhow, I mean, before you go over there,
ask somebody. I mean, it doesn't look to me like they've done anything to it like taking it apart. Before you go over there and lay
heavy shit on them, find out. Can you dig it?

ARCTOR: She's right.

LUCKMAN: Who should we ask? Who do we know that's an authority on racing bikes?

FRECK: Let's ask the first person we see. Let's wheel it out the door and when some freak comes along we'll ask him. That way we'll get a disheartened viewpoint.

(*They collectively wheel bike out front, right off encounter young black man parking his car. They point to the seven—eight?—gears questioningly and ask how many there are, although they can see— except for Charles Freck—that there are only seven: five at one end of the chain, two at the other. Five and two add up to seven. They can ascertain it with their own eyes. What's going on?*)

YOUNG BLACK MAN: (*Calmly*) What you have to do is multiply the number of gears in front by the number in the rear. It is not an adding but a multiplying, because, you see, the chain leaps across from gear to gear, and in terms of gear ratios you obtain five (*He indicates the five gears.*) times one of the two in front (*He points to that.*), which gives you one times five, which is five, and then when you shift with this lever on the handle-bar (*He demonstrates.*) the chain jumps to the other one of the two in front and interacts with the same five in the back all over again, which is an additional five. The addition involved is five plus five, which is ten. Do you see how that works? You see, gear ratios are always derived by—

(*They thank him and silently wheel the bike back inside the house. The young black man, whom they have never seen before and who is no more than seventeen and driving an incredibly beat- up old transportation-type car, goes on locking up, and they close the front door of the house and just stand there.*)

LUCKMAN: Anybody got any dope? "Where there's dope there's hope." (*No one . . .*

All the evidence indicates that separation of the hemispheres creates two independent spheres of consciousness within a single cranium, that is to say, within a single organism. This conclusion is disturbing to some people who view consciousness as an indivisible property of the human brain. It seems premature to others, who insist that the capacities revealed thus far for the right hemisphere are at the level of an automaton. There is, to be sure, hemispheric inequality in the present cases, but it may well be a characteristic of the individuals we have studied. It is entirely possible that if a human brain were divided in a very young person, both hemispheres could as a result separately and inde-

pendently develop mental functions of a high order at
the level attained only in the left hemisphere of normal
individuals.

. . . *laughs*.)
"We know you were one of the people in that group," the seated
medical deputy said. "It doesn't matter which one. None of you
could look at the bike and perceive the simple mathematical operation involved in determining the number of its very small system of
gear ratios." In the deputy's voice Fred heard a certain compassion,
a measure of being kind. "An operation like that constitutes a junior
high school aptitude test. Were you all stoned?"
"No," Fred said.
"They give aptitude tests like that to children," the other medical
deputy said.
"So what was wrong, Fred?" the first deputy asked.
"I forget," Fred said. He shut up now. And then he said, "It
sounds to me like a cognitive fuckup, rather than perceptive. Isn't
abstract thinking involved in a thing like that? Not—"
"You might imagine so," the seated deputy said. "But tests show
that the cognitive system fails because it isn't receiving accurate data.
In other words, the inputs are distorting in such a fashion that when
you go to reason about what you see you reason wrongly because
you don't—" The deputy gestured, trying to find a way to express it.
"But a ten-speed bike *has* seven gears," Fred said. "What we saw
was accurate. Two in front, five in back."
"But you didn't perceive, any of you, how they interact: five in
back with *each* of the two in front, as the black told you. Was he a
highly educated man?"
"Probably not," Fred said.
"What the black saw," the standing deputy said, "was different
from what all of you saw. He saw two separate connecting lines between the rear gear system and the front, two simultaneous different
lines perceptible to him between the gears in front running to each of
the five back ones in turn. . . . What you saw was *one* connective to
all back ones."
"But that would make six gears, then," Fred said. "Two front
gears but one connective."
"Which is inaccurate perception. Nobody taught that black boy
that; what they taught him to do, if anyone taught him at all, was to
figure out, cognitively, what the meaning of those two connectives
were. You missed one of them entirely, all of you. What you did was

that although you counted two front gears, you *perceived* them as a homogeneity."

"I'll do better next time," Fred said.

"Next time what? When you buy a ripped-off ten-speed bike? Or abstracting all daily percept input?"

Fred remained silent.

"Let's continue the test," the seated deputy said. "What do you see in this one, Fred?"

"Plastic dog shit," Fred said. "Like they sell here in the Los Angeles area. Can I go now?" It was the Lions Club speech all over again.

Both deputies, however, laughed.

"You know, Fred," the seated one said, "if you can keep your sense of humor like you do you'll perhaps make it."

"Make it?" Fred echoed. "Make what? The team? The chick? Make good? Make do? Make out? Make sense? Make money? Make time? Define your terms. The Latin for 'make' is *facere,* which always reminds me of *fuckere,* which is Latin for 'to fuck,' and I haven't . . .

> The brain of the higher animals, including man, is a double organ, consisting of right and left hemispheres connected by an isthmus of nerve tissue called the corpus callosum. Some 15 years ago Ronald E. Myers and R. W. Sperry, then at the University of Chicago, made a surprising discovery: when this connection between the two halves of the cerebrum was cut, each hemisphere functioned independently as if it were a complete brain.

. . . been getting it on worth jack shit lately, plastic shit or otherwise, any kind of shit. If you boys are psychologist types and you've been listening to my endless debriefings with Hank, what the hell is Donna's handle? How do I get next to her? I mean, how is it done? With that kind of sweet, unique, stubborn little chick?"

"Each girl is different," the seated deputy said.

"I mean approach her ethically," Fred said. "Not cram her with reds and booze and then stick it into her while she's lying on the living-room floor."

"Buy her flowers," the standing deputy said.

"What?" Fred said, his suit-filtered eyes opening wide.

"This time of year you can get little spring flowers. At the nursery departments of, say, Penney's or K Mart. Or an azalea."

"Flowers," Fred murmured. "You mean plastic flowers or real flowers? Real ones, I guess."

"The plastic ones are no good," the seated deputy said. "They look like they're . . . well, fake. Somehow fake."

"Can I leave now?" Fred asked.

After an exchange of glances, both deputies nodded. "We'll evaluate you some other time, Fred," the standing one said. "It's not that urgent. Hank will notify you of a later appointment time."

For some obscure reason Fred felt like shaking hands with them before he left, but he did not; he just left, saying nothing, a little down and a little bewildered, because, probably, of the way it had shot out of left field at him, so suddenly. They've been going over and over my material, he thought, trying to find signs of my being burned out, and they did find some. Enough, anyhow, to want to run these tests.

Spring flowers, he thought as he reached the elevator. Little ones; they probably grow close to the ground and a lot of people step on them. Do they grow wild? Or in special commercial vats or in huge enclosed farms? I wonder what the country is like. The fields and like that, the strange smells. And, he wondered, where do you find that? Where do you go and how do you get there and stay there? What kind of trip is that, and what kind of ticket does it take? And who do you buy the ticket from?

And, he thought, I would like to take someone with me when I go there, maybe Donna. But how do you ask that, ask a chick that, when you don't even know how to get next to her? When you've been scheming on her and achieving nothing—not even step one. We should hurry, he thought, because later on all the spring flowers like they told me about will be dead.

CHAPTER EIGHT

On his way over to Bob Arctor's house, where a bunch of heads could usually be found for a mellow turned-on time, Charles Freck worked out a gag to put ol' Barris on, to pay him back for the spleen jive at the Fiddler's Three restaurant that day. In his head, as he skillfully avoided the radar traps that the police kept everywhere (the police radar vans checking out drivers usually took the disguise of old raunchy VW vans, painted dull brown, driven by bearded freaks; when he saw such vans he slowed), he ran a preview fantasy number of his put-on:

FRECK: (*Casually*) I bought a methedrine plant today.
BARRIS: (*With a snotty expression on his face*) Methedrine is a benny, like speed; it's crank, it's crystal, it's amphetamine, it's made synthetically in a lab. So it isn't organic, like pot. There's no such thing as a methedrine plant like there is a pot plant.
FRECK: (*Springing the punch line on him*) I mean I inherited forty thousand from an old uncle and purchased a plant hidden in this dude's garage where he makes methedrine. I mean, he's got a factory there where he manufactures meth. Plant in the sense of—

He couldn't get it phrased exactly right as he drove, because part of his mind stayed on the vehicles around him and the lights; but he knew when he got to Bob's house he'd lay it on Barris super good. And, especially if a bunch of people were there, Barris would rise to the bait and be visible to everyone flat-out as a clear and evident asshole. And that would super pay him back, because Barris worse than anybody else couldn't stand to be made fun of.

When he pulled up he found Barris outdoors working on Bob Arctor's car. The hood was up, and both Barris and Arctor stood together with a pile of car tools.

"Hey, man," Freck said, slamming his door and sauntering casually over. "Barris," he said right off in a cool way, putting his hand on Barris's shoulder to attract his attention.

"Later," Barris growled. He had his repair clothes on; grease and like that covered the already dirty fabric.

Freck said, "I bought a methedrine plant today."

With an impatient scowl, Barris said, "How big?"

"What do you mean?"

"How big a plant?"

"Well," Freck said, wondering how to go on.

"How much'd you pay for it?" Arctor said, also greasy from the car repair. They had the carb off, Freck saw, air filter, hoses, and all.

Freck said, "About ten bucks."

"Jim could have gotten it for you cheaper," Arctor said, resuming his labors. "Couldn't you, Jim?"

"They're practically giving meth plants away," Barris said.

"This is a whole fucking garage!" Freck protested. "A factory! It turns out a million tabs a day—the pill-rolling machinery and everything. *Everything!*"

"All that cost ten dollars?" Barris said, grinning widely.

"Where's it located?" Arctor said.

"Not around here," Freck said uneasily. "Hey, fuck it, you guys."

Pausing in his work—Barris did a lot of pausing in his work, whether anyone was talking to him or not—Barris said, "You know, Freck, if you drop or shoot too much meth you start talking like Donald Duck."

"So?" Freck said.

"Then nobody can understand you," Barris said.

Arctor said, "What'd you say, Barris? I couldn't understand you."

His face dancing with merriment, Barris made his voice sound like Donald Duck's. Freck and Arctor grinned and enjoyed it. Barris went on and on, gesturing finally at the carburetor.

"What about the carburetor?" Arctor said, not smiling now.

Barris, in his regular voice, but still grinning widely, said, "You've got a bent choke shaft. The whole carb should be rebuilt. Otherwise the choke's going to shut on you while you're driving along the freeway and then you'll find your motor is flooded and dead and some asshole will rear-end you. And possibly in addition that raw gas washing down the cylinder walls—if it goes on long enough— will wash the lubrication away, so your cylinders will be scored and permanently damaged. And then you'll need them rebored."

"Why is the choke rod bent?" Arctor asked.

Shrugging, Barris resumed taking apart the carb, he did not answer. He left that up to Arctor and to Charles Freck, who knew nothing about engines, especially complex repairs like this.

Coming out of the house, Luckman, wearing a snazzy shirt and tight high-style Levi jeans, carrying a book and wearing shades, said, "I phoned and they're checking to see what a rebuilt carb will set you back for this car. They'll phone in a while, so I left the front door open."

Barris said, "You could put a four-barrel on instead of this two, while you're at it. But you'd have to put on a new manifold. We could pick up a used one for not very much."

"It would idle too high," Luckman said, "with like a Rochester four-barrel—is that what you mean? And it wouldn't shift properly. It wouldn't upshift."

"The idling jets could be replaced with smaller jets," Barris said, "that would compensate. And with a tach he could watch his rpms so it didn't over-rev. He'd know by the tach when it wasn't upshifting. Usually just backing off on the gas pedal causes it to upshift if the automatic linkage to the transmission doesn't do it. I know where we can get a tach, too. In fact, I have one."

"Yeah," Luckman said, "well, if he tromped down heavy on the step-down passing gear to get a lot of torque suddenly in an emergency on the freeway, it'd downshift and rev up so high it'd blow the head gasket or worse, a lot worse. Blow up the whole engine."

Barris, patiently, said, "He'd see the tach needle jump and he'd back right off."

"While passing?" Luckman said. "Halfway past a fucking big semi? Shit, he'd have to keep barreling on, high revs or not; he'd have to blow up the engine rather than back off, because if he backed off he'd never get around what he was trying to pass."

"Momentum," Barris said. "In a car this heavy, momentum would carry him on by even if he backed off."

"What about uphill?" Luckman said. "Momentum doesn't carry you very far uphill when you're passing."

To Arctor, Barris said, "What does this car . . ." He bent to see what make it was. "This . . ." His lips moved. "Olds."

"It weighs about a thousand pounds," Arctor said. Charles Freck saw him wink toward Luckman.

"You're right, then," Barris agreed. "There wouldn't be much inertia mass at that light weight. Or would there?" He groped for a pen and something to write on. "A thousand pounds traveling at eighty miles an hour builds up force equal to—"

"That's a thousand pounds," Arctor put in, "with the passengers in it and with a full tank of gas and a big carton of bricks in the trunk."

"How many passengers?" Luckman said, deadpan.

"Twelve."

"Is that six in back," Luckman said, "and six in—"

"No," Arctor said, "that's eleven in back and the driver sitting alone in front. So, you see, so there will be more weight on the rear wheels for more traction. So it won't fishtail."

Barris glanced alertly up. "This car fishtails?"

"Unless you get eleven people riding in the back," Arctor said.

"Be better, then, to load the trunk with sacks of sand," Barris said. "Three two-hundred-pound sacks of sand. Then the passengers could be distributed more evenly and they would be more comfortable."

"What about one six-hundred-pound box of gold in the trunk?" Luckman asked him. "Instead of three two-hundred—"

"Will you lay off?" Barris said. "I'm trying to calculate the inertial force of this car traveling at eighty miles an hour."

"It won't go eighty," Arctor said. "It's got a dead cyclinder. I meant to tell you. It threw a rod last night, on my way home from the 7-11."

"Then why are we pulling the carb?" Barris demanded. "We have to pull the whole head for that. In fact, much more. In fact, you may have a cracked block. Well, that's why it won't start."

"Won't your car start?" Freck asked Bob Arctor.

"It won't start," Luckman said, "because we pulled the carb off."

Puzzled, Barris said, "Why'd we pull the carb? I forget."

"To get all the springs and little dinky parts replaced," Arctor said. "So it won't fuck up again and nearly kill us. The Union station mechanic advised us to."

"If you bastards wouldn't rappity-rap on," Barris said, "like a lot of speed freaks, I could complete my computations and tell you how this particular car with its weight would handle with a four-barrel Rochester carb, modified naturally with smaller idling jets." He was genuinely sore now. "So SHUT UP!"

Luckman opened the book he was carrying. He puffed up, then, to much larger than usual; his great chest swelled, and so did his biceps. "Barris, I'm going to read to you." He began to read from the book, in a particularly fluent way. " 'He to whom it is given to see Christ *more real* than any other reality . . .' "

"What?" Barris said.

Luckman continued reading. " '. . . than any other reality in the World, Christ everywhere present and everywhere growing more great, Christ the final determination and plasmatic Principle of the Universe—' "

"What is that?" Arctor said.

"Chardin. Teilhard de Chardin."

"Jeez, Luckman," Arctor said.

" '. . . that man indeed lives in a zone where no multiplicity can distress him and which is nevertheless the most active workshop of universal fulfilment.'" Luckman shut the book.

With a high degree of apprehension, Charles Freck moved in between Barris and Luckman. "Cool it, you guys."

"Get out of the way, Freck," Luckman said, bringing back his right arm, low, for a vast sweeping haymaker at Barris. "Come on, Barris, I'm going to coldcock you into tomorrow, for talking to your betters like that."

With a bleat of wild, appealing terror, Barris dropped his felt pen and pad of paper and scuttled off erratically toward the open front door of the house, yelling back as he ran, "I hear the phone about the rebuilt carb."

They watched him go.

"I was just kidding him," Luckman said, rubbing his lower lip.

"What if he gets his gun and silencer?" Freck said, his nervousness off the scale entirely. He moved by degrees in the direction of his own parked car, to drop swiftly behind it if Barris reappeared firing.

"Come on," Arctor said to Luckman; they fell back together into their car work, while Freck loitered apprehensively by his own vehicle, wondering why he had decided to bop over here today. It had no mellow quality today, here, none at all, as it usually did. He had sensed the bad vibes under the kidding right from the start. What's the motherfuck wrong? he wondered, and got back somberly into his own car, to start it up.

Are things going to get heavy and bad here too, he wondered, like they did at Jerry Fabian's house during the last few weeks with him? It used to be mellow here, he thought, everybody kicking back and turning on, grooving to acid rock, especially the Stones. Donna sitting there in her leather jacket and boots, filling caps, Luckman rolling joints and telling about the seminar he planned to give at UCLA in dope-smoking and joint-rolling, and how someday he'd suddenly roll the perfect joint and it would be placed under glass and helium back at Constitution Hall, as part of American history with those other items of similar importance. When I look back, he thought, even to when Jim Barris and I were sitting at the Fiddler's, the other day . . . it was better even then. Jerry began it, he thought; that's what's coming down here, that there which carried off Jerry. How can days and happenings and moments so good become so quickly ugly, and for no reason, for no real reason? Just—change. With nothing causing it.

"I'm splitting," he said to Luckman and Arctor, who were watching him rev up.

"No, stay, hey, man," Luckman said with a warm smile. "We need you. You're a brother."

"Naw, I'm cutting out."

From the house Barris appeared cautiously. He carried a hammer. "It was a wrong number," he shouted, advancing with great caution, halting and peering like a crab-thing in a drive-in movie.

"What's the hammer for?" Luckman said.

Arctor said, "To fix the engine."

"Thought I would bring it with me," Barris explained as he returned gingerly to the Olds, "since I was indoors and noticed it."

"The most dangerous kind of person," Arctor said, "is one who is afraid of his own shadow." That was the last Freck heard as he drove away; he pondered over what Arctor meant, if he meant him, Charles Freck. He felt shame. But shit, he thought, why stick around when it's such a super bummer? Where's the chicken in that? Don't never participate in no bad scenes, he reminded himself; that was his motto in life. So he drove away now, without looking back. Let them snuff each other, he thought. Who needs them? But he felt bad, really bad, to leave them and to have witnessed the darkening change, and he wondered again why, and what it signified, but then it occurred to him that maybe things would go the other way again and get better, and that cheered him. In fact, it caused him to roll a short fantasy number in his head as he drove along avoiding invisible police cars:

THERE THEY ALL SAT AS BEFORE.

Even people who were either dead or burned out, like Jerry Fabin. They all sat here and there in a sort of clear white light, which wasn't daylight but better light than that, a kind of sea which lay beneath them and above them as well.

Donna and a couple other chicks looked so foxy—they had on halters and hot pants, or tank tops with no bras. He could hear music although he could not quite distinguish what track it was from what LP. Maybe Hendrix! he thought. Yeah, an old Hendrix track, or now all at once it was J.J. All of them: Jim Croce, and J.J., but especially Hendrix. "Before I die," Hendrix was murmuring, "let me live my life as I want to," and then immediately the fantasy number blew up because he had forgotten both that Hendrix was dead and how Hendrix and also Joplin had died, not to mention Croce. Hendrix and J.J. OD'ing on smack, both of them, two neat cool fine people like that, two outrageous humans, and he remembered how he'd heard that Janis's manager had only allowed her a couple hundred bucks now and then; she couldn't have the rest, all that she earned, because of her junk habit. And then he heard in his head her song "All Is Loneliness," and he began to cry. And in that condition drove on toward home.

In his living room, sitting with his friends and attempting to determine whether he needed a new carb, a rebuilt carb, or a modification carb-and-manifold, Robert Arctor sensed the silent constant scrutiny, the electronic presence, of the holo-scanners. And felt good about it.

"You look mellow," Luckman said. "Putting out a hundred bucks wouldn't make me mellow."

"I decided to cruise along the street until I come across an Olds like mine," Arctor explained, "and then unbolt their carb and pay nothing. Like everyone else we know."

"Especially Donna," Barris said in agreement. "I wish she hadn't been in here the other day while we were gone. Donna steals everything she can carry, and if she can't carry it she phones up her rip-off gang buddies and they show up and carry it off for her."

"I'll tell you a story I heard about Donna," Luckman said. "One time, see, Donna put a quarter into one of those automatic stamp machines that operate off a coil of stamps, and the machine was dingey and just kept cranking out stamps. Finally she had a market-basket full. It *still* kept cranking them out. Ultimately she had like— she and her rip-off friends counted them—over eighteen thousand U.S. fifteen-cent stamps. Well, that was cool, except what was Donna Hawthorne going to do with them? She never wrote a letter in her life, except to her lawyer to sue some guy who burned her in a dope deal."

"Donna does *that?*" Arctor said. "She has an attorney to use in a default on an illegal transaction? How can she do that?"

"She just probably says the dude owes her bread."

"Imagine getting an angry pay-up-or-go-to-court letter from an attorney about a dope deal," Arctor said, marveling at Donna, as he frequently did.

"Anyhow," Luckman continued, "there she was with a market-basket full of at least eighteen thousand U.S. fifteen-cent stamps, and what the hell to do with them? You can't sell them back to the Post Office. Anyhow, when the P.O. came to service the machine they'd know it went dingey, and anyone who showed up at a window with all those fifteen-cent stamps, especially a coil of them—shit, they'd flash on it; in fact, they'd be waiting for Donna, right? So she thought about it—after of course she'd loaded the coil of stamps into her MG and drove off—and then she phoned up more of those rip-

off freaks she works with and had them drive over with a jack-
hammer of some kind, water-cooled and water-silenced, a real kinky
special one which, Christ, they ripped off, too, and they dug the
stamp machine loose from the concrete in the middle of the night
and carried it to her place in the back of a Ford Ranchero. Which
they also probably ripped off. For the stamps."

"You mean she sold the stamps?" Arctor said, marveling. "From a
vending machine? One by one?"

"They remounted—this is what I heard, anyhow—they relocated
the U.S. stamp machine at a busy intersection where a lot of people
pass by, but back out of sight where no mail truck would spot it, and
they put it back in operation."

"They would have been wiser just to knock over the coin box,"
Barris said.

"So they were selling stamps, then," Luckman said, "for like a
few weeks until the machine ran out, like it naturally had to eventually. And what the fuck next? I can imagine Donna's brain working
on that during those weeks, that peasant-thrift brain . . . her family is
peasant stock from some European country. Anyhow, by the time it
ran out of its coil, Donna had decided to convert it over to soft
drinks, which are from the P.O.—they're really guarded. And you go
into the bucket forever for that."

"Is this true?" Barris said.

"Is what true?" Luckman said.

Barris said, "That girl is disturbed. She should be forcibly com-
mited. Do you realize that all our taxes were raised by her stealing
those stamps?" He sounded angry again.

"Write the government and tell them," Luckman said, his face
cold with distaste for Barris. "Ask Donna for a stamp to mail it;
she'll sell you one."

"At full price," Barris said, equally mad.

The holos, Arctor thought, will have miles and miles of this on
their expensive tapes. Not miles and miles of dead tape but miles and
miles of tripped out tape.

It was not what went on while Robert Arctor sat before a holo-
scanner that mattered so much, he considered; it was what took
place—at least for him . . . for whom? . . . for Fred—while Bob
Arctor was elsewhere or asleep and others were within scanning
range. So I should split, he thought, as I planned it out, leaving these
guys, and sending other people I know over here. I should make my
house superaccessible from now on.

And then a dreadful, ugly thought rose inside him. Suppose when I
play the tapes back I see Donna when she's in here—opening a win-

dow with a spoon or knife blade—and slipping in and destroying my possessions and stealing. *Another* Donna: the chick as she really is, or anyhow as she is when I can't see her. The philosophical "when a tree falls in the forest" number. What is Donna like when no one is around to watch her?

Does, he wondered, the gentle lovely shrewd and very kind, super-kind girl transform herself instantly into something sly? Will I see a change which will blow my mind? Donna or Luckman, anyone I care about. Like your pet cat or dog when you're out of the house . . . the cat empties a pillowcase and starts stuffing your valuables in it: electric clock and bedside radio, shaver, all it can stuff in before you get back; another cat entirely while you're gone, ripping you off and pawning it all, or lighting up your joints, or walking on the ceiling, or phoning people long distance . . . God knows. A nightmare, a weird other world beyond the mirror, a terror city reverse thing, with unrecognizable entities creeping about; Donna crawling on all fours, eating from the animals' dishes . . . any kind of psychedelic wild trip, unfathomable and horrid.

Hell, he thought; for that matter, maybe Bob Arctor rises up in the night from deep sleep and does trips like that. Has sexual relations with the wall. Or mysterious freaks show up who he's never seen before, a whole bunch of them, with special heads that swivel all the way around, like owls'. And the audio-scanners will pick up the far-out demented conspiracies hatched out by him and them to blow up the men's room at the Standard station by filling the toilet with plastic explosives for God knows what brain-charred purpose. Maybe this sort of stuff goes on every night while he just imagines he's asleep—and is gone by day.

Bob Arctor, he speculated, may learn more new information about himself than he is ready for, more than he will about Donna in her little leather jacket, and Luckman in his fancy duds, and even Barris—maybe when nobody's around Jim Barris merely goes to sleep. And sleeps until they reappear.

But he doubted it. More likely Barris whipped out a hidden transmitter from the mess and chaos of his room—which, like all the other rooms in the house, had now for the first time come under twenty-four-hour scanning—and sent a cryptic signal to the other bunch of cryptic motherfuckers with whom he currently conspired for whatever people like him or them conspired for. Another branch, Bob Arctor reflected, of the authorities.

On the other hand, Hank and those guys downtown would not be too happy if Bob Arctor left his house, now that the monitors had been expensively and elaborately installed, and was never seen again: never showed up on any of the tape. He could not therefore take off in order to fulfill his personal surveillance plans at the expense of theirs. After all, it was their money.

In the script being filmed, he would at all times have to be the star actor. Actor, Arctor, he thought. Bob the Actor who is being hunted; he who is the El Primo huntee.

They say you never recognize your own voice when you first hear it played back on tape. And when you see yourself on video tape, or like this, in a 3-D hologram, you don't recognize yourself visually either. You imagined you were a tall fat man with black hair, and instead you're a tiny thin woman with no hair at all . . . is that it? I'm sure I'll recognize Bob Arctor, he thought, if by nothing else than by the clothes he wears or by a process of elimination. What isn't Barris or Luckman and lives here must be Bob Arctor. Unless it's one of the dogs or cats. I'll try to keep my professional eye trained on something which walks upright.

"Barris," he said, "I'm going out to see if I can score some beans." Then he pretended to remember he had no car; he got that sort of expression. "Luckman," he said, "is your Falcon running?"

"No," Luckman said thoughtfully, after consideration, "I don't think so."

"Can I borrow your car, Jim?" Arctor asked Barris.

"I wonder . . . if you can handle my car," Barris said.

This always arose as a defense when anyone tried to borrow Barris's car, because Barris had had secret unspecified modifications done on it, in its

(a) suspension
(b) engine
(c) transmission
(d) rear end
(e) drive train
(f) electrical system
(g) front end and steering
(h) as well as clock, cigar lighter, ashtray, glove compartment. In particular the glove compartment. Barris kept it locked always. The radio, too, had been cunningly *changed* (never explained how or why). If you tuned one station you got only one-minute-apart blips. All the push-buttons brought in a single transmission that made no sense, and, oddly, there was never any rock played over it. Sometimes when they were accompanying Barris on a buy and Barris parked and got out of the car, leaving them, he turned the particular station on in a special fashion very loud. If they changed it while he was gone he became incoherent and refused to

speak on the trip back or ever to explain. He had not explained yet. Probably when set to that frequency his radio transmitted

(a)   to the authorities.
(b)   to a private paramilitary political organization.
(c)   to the Syndicate.
(d)   to extraterrestrials of higher intelligence.

"By that I mean," Barris said, "it will cruise at—"

"Aw fuck!" Luckman broke in harshly. "It's an ordinary six-cylinder motor, you humper. When we park it in downtown L.A. the parking-lot jockey drives it. So why can't Bob? You asshole."

Now, Bob Arctor had a few devices too, a few covert modifications built into his own car radio. But he didn't talk about them. Actually, it was Fred who had. Or anyhow somebody had, and they did a few things a little like what Barris claimed his several electronic assists did, and then on the other hand they did not.

For example, every law-enforcement vehicle emits a particular full-spectrum interference which sounds on ordinary car radios like a failure in the spark-suppressors of that vehicle. As if the police car's ignition is faulty. However, Bob Arctor, as a peace officer, had been allocated a gadget which, when he had mounted it within his car radio, told him a great deal, whereas the noises told other people—most other people—no information at all. These other people did not even recognize the static as information-bearing. First of all, the different subsounds told Bob Arctor how close the law-enforcement vehicle was to his own and, next, what variety of department it represented: city or county, Highway Patrol, or federal, whatever. He, too, picked up the one-minute-apart blips which acted as a time check for a parked vehicle; those in the parked vehicle could determine how many minutes they had waited without any obvious arm gestures. This was useful, for instance, when they had agreed to hit a house in exactly three minutes. The *zt zt zt* on their car radio told them precisely when three minutes had passed.

He knew, too, about the AM station that played the top-ten-type tunes on and on plus an enormous amount of DJ chatter in between, which sometimes was not chatter, in a sense. If that station had been tuned to, and the racket of it filled your car, anyone casually overhearing it would hear a conventional pop music station and typical boring DJ talk, and either not hang around at all or flash on in any way to the fact that the so-called DJ suddenly, in exactly the same muted chatty style of voice in which he said, "Now here's a number for Phil and Jane, a new Cat Stevens tune called—" occasionally said something more like "Vehicle blue will proceed a mile north to Bastanchury and the other units will—" and so on. He had never—with all the many dudes and chicks who rode with him, even when he had been obliged to keep tuned to police info-instruct, such as when a major bust was going down or any big action was in progress which might involve him—had anyone notice. Or if they noticed, they probably thought they were personally spaced and paranoid and forgot it.

And also he knew about the many unmarked police vehicles like old Chevys jacked up in the back with loud (illegal) pipes and racing stripes, with wild-looking hip types driving them erratically at high speed—he knew from what his radio emitted in the way of the special information-carrying static at all frequencies when one buzzed him or shot past. He knew to ignore.

Also, when he pushed the bar that supposedly switched from AM to FM on his car radio, a station on a particular frequency groaned out indefinite Muzak-type music, but this noise being transmitted to his car was filtered out, unscrambled, by the microphone-transmitter within his radio, so that whatever was said by those in his car at the time was picked up by his equipment and broadcast to the authorities; but this one funky station playing away, no matter how loud, was not received by them and did not interfere at all; the grid eliminated it.

What Barris *claimed* to have did bear a certain resemblance to what he, Bob Arctor, as an undercover law-enforcement officer did have in his own car radio; but beyond that, in regard to other modifications such as suspension, engine, transmission, etc., there had been no alterations whatsoever. That would be uncool and obvious. And secondly, millions of car freaks could make equally hairy modifications in their cars, so he simply had gotten allocation for a fairly potent mill for his wheels and let it go at that. Any highpowered vehicle can overtake and leave behind any other. Barris was full of shit about that; a Ferrari has suspension and handling and steering that no "special secret modifications" can match, so the hell with it. And cops can't drive sports cars, even cheap ones. Let alone Ferraris. Ultimately it is the driver's skill that decides it all.

He did have one other law-enforcement allocation, though. Very unusual tires. They had more than steel bands inside, like Michelin had introduced years ago in their X types. These were all metal and wore out fast, but they had advantages in speed and acceleration. Their disadvantage was their cost, but he got them free, from his allocation service, which was not a Dr. Pepper machine like the money one. This worked fine, but he could get allocations only when absolutely necessary. The tires he put on himself, when no one was watching. As he had put in the radio alterations.

The only fear about the radio was not detection by someone snooping, such as Barris, but simple theft. Its added devices made it expensive to replace if it got ripped off; he would have to talk fast.

Naturally, too, he carried a gun hidden in his car. Barris in all his lurid acid-trip, spaced-out fantasies would never have designed its hiding place, where it actually was. Barris would have directed there to be an exotic spot of concealment for it, like in the steering column, in a hollow chamber. Or inside the gas tank, hanging down on a wire like the shipment of coke in the classic flick *Easy Rider,* that place as a stash place, incidentally, being about the worst spot on a hog. Every law-enforcement officer who had caught the film flashed right away on what clever psychiatrist types had elaborately figured out: that the two bikers wanted to get caught and if possible killed. His gun, in his car, was in the glove compartment.

The pseudo-clever stuff that Barris continually alluded to about his own vehicle probably bore some resemblance to reality, the reality of Arctor's own modified car, because many of the radio gimmicks which Arctor carried were SOP and had been demonstrated on late-night TV, on network talk shows, by electronic experts who had helped design them, or read about them in trade journals, or seen them, or gotten fired from police labs and harbored a grudge. So the average citizen (or, as Barris always said in his quasi-educated lofty way, the *typical* average citizen) knew by now that no black-and-white ran the risk of pulling over a fast-moving souped-up, racing-striped '57 Chevy with what appeared to be a wild teen-ager spaced out behind the wheel on Coors beer—and then finding he'd halted an undercover nark vehicle in hot pursuit of its quarry. So the typical average citizen these days knew how and why all those nark vehicles as they roared along, scaring old ladies and straights into indignation and letter-writing, continually signaled their identity back and forth to one another and their peers . . . what difference did it make? But what *would* make a difference—a dreadful one—would be if the punks, the hot-rodders, the bikers, and especially the dealers and runners and pushers, managed to build and incorporate into their own similar cars such sophisticated devices.

They could then whiz right on by. With impunity.

"I'll walk, then," Arctor said, which was what he had wanted to do anyhow; he had set up both Barris and Luckman. He *had* to walk.

"Where you going?" Luckman said.

"Donna's." Getting to her place on foot was almost impossible; saying this ensured neither man accompanying him. He put on his coat and set off toward the front door. "See you guys later."

"My car—" Barris continued by way of more cop-out.

"If I tried to drive your car," Arctor said, "I'd press the wrong button and it'd float up over the Greater L.A. downtown area like the Goodyear blimp, and they'd have me dumping borate on oil-well fires."

"I'm glad you can appreciate my position," Barris was muttering as Arctor shut the door.

Seated before the hologram cube of Monitor Two, Fred in his scramble suit watched impassively as the hologram changed continually before his eyes. In the safe apartment other watchers watched other holograms from other source points, mostly playbacks. Fred, however, watched a live hologram unfolding; it recorded, but he had by-passed the stored tape to pick up the transmission at the instant it emanated from Bob Arctor's allegedly run-down house.

Within the hologram, in broad-band color, with high resolution, sat Barris and Luckman. In the best chair in the living room, Barris sat bent over a hash pipe he had been putting together for days. His face had become a mask of concentration as he wound white string around and around the bowl of the pipe. At the coffee table Luckman hunched over a Swanson's chicken TV dinner, eating in big clumsy mouthfuls while he watched a western on TV. Four beer cans —empties—lay squashed by his mighty fist on the table; now he reached for a fifth half-full can, knocked it over, spilled it, grabbed it, and cursed. At the curse, Barris peered up, regarded him like Mime in *Siegfried,* then resumed work.

Fred continued to watch.

"Fucking late-night TV," Luckman gargled, his mouth full of food, and then suddenly he dropped his spoon and leaped staggering to his feet, tottered, spun toward Barris, both hands raised, gesturing, saying nothing, his mouth open and half-chewed food spilling from it onto his clothes, onto the floor. The cats ran forward eagerly.

Barris halted in his hash-pipe making, gazed up at hapless Luckman. In a frenzy, now gargling horrid noises, Luckman with one hand swept the coffee table bare of beer cans and food; everything clattered down. The cats sped off, terrified. Still, Barris sat gazing fixedly at him. Luckman lurched a few steps toward the kitchen; the scanner there, on its cube before Fred's horrified eyes, picked up Luckman as he groped blindly in the kitchen semidarkness for a glass, tried to turn on the faucet and fill it with water. At the monitor, Fred jumped up; transfixed, on Monitor Two he saw Barris, still seated, return to painstakingly winding string around and around the bowl of his hash pipe. Barris did not look up again; Monitor Two showed him again intently at work.

The aud tapes clashed out great breaking, tearing sounds of agony: human strangling and the furious din of objects hitting the floor as Luckman hurled pots and pans and dishes and flatware about in an attempt to attract Barris's attention. Barris, amid the noise, continued methodically at his hash pipe and did not look up again.

In the kitchen, on Monitor One, Luckman fell to the floor all at once, not slowly, onto his knees, but completely, with a sodden thump, and lay spread-eagled. Barris continued winding the string of his hash pipe, and now a small snide smile appeared on his face, at the corners of his mouth.

On his feet, Fred stared in shock, galvanized and paralyzed simultaneously. He reached for the police phone beside the monitor, halted, still watched.

For several minutes Luckman lay on the kitchen floor without moving as Barris wound and wound the string, Barris bent over like an intent old lady knitting, smiling to himself, smiling on and on, and rocking a trifle; then abruptly Barris tossed the hash pipe away, stood up, gazed acutely at Luckman's form on the kitchen floor, the broken water glass beside him, all the debris and pans and broken plates, and then Barris's face suddenly reacted with mock dismay. Barris tore off his shades, his eyes widened grotesquely, he flapped his arms in helpless fright, he ran about a little here and there, then scuttled toward Luckman, paused a few feet from him, ran back, panting now.

He's building up his act, Fred realized. He's getting his panic-and-discovery act together. Like he just came onto the scene. Barris, on the cube of Monitor Two, twisted about, gasped in grief, his face dark red, and then he hobbled to the phone, yanked it up, dropped it, picked it up with trembling fingers . . . he has just discovered that Luckman, alone in the kitchen, has choked to death on a piece of food, Fred realized; with no one there to hear him or help him. And now Barris is frantically trying to summon help. Too late.

Into the phone, Barris was saying in a weird, high-pitched slow voice, "Operator, is it called the inhalator squad or the resuscitation squad?"

"Sir," the phone tab squawked from its speaker by Fred, "is there someone unable to breathe? Do you wish—"

"It, I believe, is a cardiac arrest," Barris was saying now in his low, urgent, professional-type, calm voice into the phone, a voice deadly with awareness of peril and gravity and the running out of time. "Either that or involuntary aspiration of a bolus within the—"

"What is the address, sir?" the operator broke in.

"The address," Barris said, "let's see, the address is—"

Fred, aloud, standing, said, "Christ."

Suddenly Luckman, lying stretched out on the floor, heaved convulsively. He shuddered and then barfed up the material obstructing his throat, thrashed about, and opened his eyes, which stared in swollen confusion.

"Uh, he appears to be all right now," Barris said smoothly into the phone. "Thank you; no assistance is needed after all." He rapidly hung the phone up.

"Jeez," Luckman muttered thickly as he sat up. "Fuck." He wheezed noisily, coughing and struggling for air.

"You okay?" Barris asked, in tones of concern.

"I must have gagged. Did I pass out?"

"Not exactly. You did go into an altered state of consciousness, though. For a few seconds. Probably an alpha state."

"God! I soiled myself!" Unsteadily, swaying with weakness, Luckman managed to get himself to his feet and stood rocking back and forth dizzily, holding on to the wall for support. "I'm really getting degenerate," he muttered in disgust. "Like an old wino." He headed toward the sink to wash himself, his steps uncertain.

Watching all this, Fred felt the fear drain from him. The man would be okay. But Barris! What sort of person was he? Luckman had recovered despite him. What a freak, he thought. What a kinky freak. Where's his head at, just to stand idle like that?

"A guy could cash in that way," Luckman said as he splashed water on himself at the sink.

Barris smiled.

"I got a really strong physical constitution," Luckman said, gulping water from a cup. "What were you doing while I was lying there? Jacking off?"

"You saw me on the phone," Barris said. "Summoning the paramedics. I moved into action at—"

"Balls," Luckman said sourly, and went on gulping down fresh clean water. "I know what you'd do if I dropped dead—you'd rip off my stash. You'd even go through my pockets."

"It's amazing," Barris said, "the limitation of the human anatomy, the fact that food and air must share a common passage. So that the risk of—"

Silently, Luckman gave him the finger.

A screech of brakes. A horn. Bob Arctor looked swiftly up at the night traffic. A sports car, engine running, by the curb; inside it, a girl waving at him.

Donna.

"Christ," he said again. He strode toward the curb.

Opening the door of her MG, Donna said, "Did I scare you? I passed you on my way to your place and then I flashed on it that it was you truckin' along, so I made a U-turn and came back. Get in."

Silently he got in and shut the car door.

"Why are you out roaming around?" Donna said. "Because of your car? It's still not fixed?"

"I just did a freaky number," Bob Arctor said. "Not like a fantasy trip. Just . . ." He shuddered.

Donna said, "I have your stuff."

"What?" he said.

"A thousand tabs of death."

"Death?" he echoed.

"Yeah, high-grade death. I better drive." She shifted into low, took off and out onto the street; almost at once she was driving along too fast. Donna always drove too fast, and tailgated, but expertly.

"That fucking Barris!" he said. "You know how he works? He doesn't kill anybody he wants dead; he just hangs around until a situation arises where they die. And he just sits there while they die. In fact, he sets them up to die while he stays out of it. But I'm not sure how. Anyhow, he arranges to allow them to fucking die." He lapsed into silence then, brooding to himself. "Like," he said, "Barris wouldn't wire plastic explosives into the ignition system of your car. What he'd do—"

"Do you have the money?" Donna said. "For the stuff? It's really Primo, and I need the money right now. I have to have it tonight because I have to pick up some other things."

"Sure." He had it in his wallet.

"I don't like Barris," Donna said as she drove, "and I don't trust him. You know, he's crazy. And when you're around him you're crazy too. And then when you're not around him you're okay. You're crazy right now."

"I am?" he said, startled.

"Yes," Donna said calmly.

"Well," he said. "Jesus." He did not know what to say to that. Especially since Donna was never wrong.

"Hey," Donna said with enthusiasm, "could you take me to a rock concert? At the Anaheim Stadium next week? Could you?"

"Right on," he said mechanically. And then it flashed on him what Donna had said—asking him to take her out. *"Alll riiiight!"* he said, pleased; life flowed back into him. Once again, the little dark-haired chick whom he loved so much had restored him to caring. "Which night?"

"It's Sunday afternoon. I'm going to bring some of that oily dark hash and get really loaded. They won't know the difference; there'll be thousands of heads there." She glanced at him, critically. "But you've got to wear something neat, not those funky clothes you sometimes put on. I mean——" Her voice softened. "I want you to look foxy because you are foxy."

"Okay," he said, charmed.

"I'm taking us to my place," Donna said as she shot along through the night in her little car, "and you do have the money and you will give it to me, and then we'll drop a few of the tabs and kick back and get really mellow, and maybe you'd like to go buy us a fifth of Southern Comfort and we can get bombed as well."

"Oh wow," he said, with sincerity.

"What I really genuinely want to do tonight," Donna said as she shifted down and swiveled the car onto her own street and into her driveway, "is go to a drive-in movie. I bought a paper and read what's on, but I couldn't find anything good except at the Torrance Drive-in, but it's already started. It started at five-thirty. Bummer."

He examined his watch. "Then we've missed——"

"No, we could still see most of it." She shot him a warm smile as she stopped her car and shut off the engine. "It's all the *Planet of the Apes* pictures, all eleven of them; they run from 7:30 P.M. all the way through to 8 A.M. tomorrow morning. I'll go to work directly from the drive-in, so I'll have to change now. We'll sit there at the movie loaded and drinking Southern Comfort all night. Wow, can you dig it?" She peered at him hopefully.

"All night," he echoed.

"Yeah yeah yeah." Donna hopped out and came around to help him open his little door. "When did you last see all the *Planet of the Apes* pictures? I saw most of them earlier this year, but then I got sick toward the last ones and had to split. It was a ham sandwich they vended me there at the drive-in. That really made me mad; I missed the last picture, where they reveal that all the famous people in history like Lincoln and Nero were secretly apes and running all human history from the start. That's why I want to go back now so bad." She lowered her voice as they walked toward her front door. "They burned me by vending that ham sandwich, so what I did—— don't rat on me——the next time we went to the drive-in, the one in La Habra, I stuck a bent coin in the slot and a couple more in other vending machines for good measure. Me and Larry Talling——you remember Larry, I was going with him?——bent a whole bunch of quarters and fifty-cent pieces using his vise and a big wrench. I made sure all the vending machines were owned by the same firm, of course. And then we fucked up a bunch of them, practically all of them, if the truth were known." She unlocked her front door with her key, slowly and gravely, in the dim light.

"It is not good policy to burn you, Donna," he said as they entered her small neat place.

"Don't step on the shag carpet," Donna said.

"Where'll I step, then?"

"Stand still, or on the newspapers."

"Donna—"

"Now don't give me a lot of heavy shit about having to walk on the newspapers. Do you know how much it cost me to get my carpet shampooed?" She stood unbuttoning her jacket.

"Thrift," he said, taking off his own coat. "French peasant thrift. Do you ever throw anything away? Do you keep pieces of string too short for any—"

"Someday," Donna said, shaking her long black hair back as she slid out of her leather jacket, "I'm going to get married and I'll need all that, that I've put away. When you get married you need everything there is. Like, we saw this big mirror in the yard next door; it took three of us over an hour to get it over the fence. Someday—"

"How much of what you've got put away did you buy," he asked, "and how much did you steal?"

"*Buy?*" She studied his face uncertainly. "What do you mean by *buy?*"

"Like when you buy dope," he said. "A dope deal. Like now." He got out his wallet. "I give you money, right?"

Donna nodded, watching him obediently (actually, more out of politeness) but with dignity. With a certain reserve.

"And then you hand me a bunch of dope for it," he said, holding out the bills. "What I mean by *buy* is an extension into the greater world of human business transactions of what we have present now, with us, as dope deals."

"I think I see," she said, her large dark eyes placid but alert. She was willing to learn.

"How many—like when you ripped off that Coca-Cola truck you were tailgating that day—how many bottles of Coke did you rip off? How many crates?"

"A month's worth," Donna said. "For me and my friends."

He glared at her reprovingly.

"It's a form of barter," she said.

"What do—" He started to laugh. "What do you give back?"

"I give of myself."

Now he laughed out loud. "To who? To the driver of the truck, who probably had to make good—"

"The Coca-Cola Company is a capitalist monopoly. No one else can make Coke but them, like the phone company does when you want to phone someone. They're all capitalist monopolies. Do you know"—her dark eyes flashed—"that the formula for Coca-Cola is a carefully guarded secret handed down through the ages, known only to a few persons all in the same family, and when the last of them dies that's memorized the formula, there will be no more Coke? So there's a backup written formula in a safe somewhere," she added meditatively. "I wonder where," she ruminated to herself, her eyes flickering.

"You and your rip-off friends will never find the Coca-Cola formula, not in a million years."

"WHO THE FUCK WANTS TO MANUFACTURE COKE ANYHOW WHEN YOU CAN RIP IT OFF THEIR TRUCKS? They've got a lot of trucks. You see them driving constantly, real slow. I tailgate them every chance I get; it makes them mad." She smiled a secret, cunning, lovely little impish smile at him, as if trying to beguile him into her strange reality, where she tailgated and tailgated a slow truck and got madder and madder and more impatient and then, when it pulled off, instead of shooting on by like other drivers would, she pulled off too, and stole everything the truck had on it. Not so much because she was a thief or even for revenge but because by the time it finally pulled off she had looked at the crates of Coke so long that she had figured out what she could do with all of them. *Her impatience had turned to ingenuity.* She had loaded her car—not the MG but the larger Camaro she had been driving then, before she had totaled it—with crates and crates of Coke, and then for a month she and all her jerk friends had drunk all the free Coke they wanted to, and then after that—

She had turned the empties back in at different stores for the deposits.

"What'd you do with the bottle caps?" he once asked her. "Wrap them in muslin and store them away in your cedar chest?"

"I threw them away," Donna said glumly. "There's nothing you can do with Coke bottle caps. There's no contests or anything any more." Now she disappeared into the other room, returned presently with several polyethylene bags. "You wanta count these?" she inquired. "There's a thousand *for sure.* I weighed them on my gram scale before I paid for them."

"It's okay," he said. He accepted the bags and she accepted the money and he thought, Donna, once more I could send you up, but I probably never will no matter what you do even if you do it to me, because there is something wonderful and full of life about you and sweet and I would never destroy it. I don't understand it, but there it is.

"Could I have ten?" she asked.

"Ten? Ten tabs back? Sure." He opened one of the bags—it was hard to untie, but he had the skill—and counted her out precisely ten. And then ten for himself. And retied the bag. And then carried all the bags to his coat in the closet.

"You know what they do in cassett-tape stores now?" Donna said energetically when he returned. The ten tabs were nowhere in sight; she had already stashed them. "Regarding tapes?"

"They arrest you," he said, "if you steal them."

"They always did that. Now what they do—you know when you carry an LP or a tape to the counter and the clerk removes the little price tag that's gummed on? Well, guess what. Guess what I found out almost the hard way." She threw herself down in a chair, grinned in anticipation, and brought forth a foil-wrapped tiny cube, which he identified as a fragment of hash even before she unwrapped it. "That isn't only a gummed-on price sticker. There's also a tiny fragment of some kind of alloy in it, and if that sticker isn't removed by the clerk at the counter, and you try to go out through the door with it, then an alarm goes off."

"How did you find out almost the hard way?"

"Some teenybopper tried to walk out with one under her coat ahead of me and the alarm went off and they grabbed her and the pigs came."

"How many did *you* have under your coat?"

"Three."

"Did you also have dope in your car?" he said. "Because once they got you for the tape rip-off, they'd impound your car, because you'd be downtown looking out, and the car would be routinely towed away and then they'd find the dope and send you up for that, too. I'll bet that wasn't locally, either; I'll bet you did that where—" He had started to say, Where you don't know anybody in law enforcement who would intervene. But he could not say that, because he meant himself; were Donna ever busted, at least where he had any pull, he would work his ass off to help her. But he could do nothing, say, up in L. A. County. And if it ever happened, which eventually it would, there it would happen: too far off for him to hear or help. He had a scenario start rolling in his head then, a horror fantasy: Donna, much like Luckman, dying with no one hearing or caring or doing anything; they might hear, but they, like Barris, would remain impassive and inert until for her it was all over. She would not literally die, as Luckman had—had? He meant *might*. But she, being an addict to Substance D, would not only be in jail but she would have to withdraw, cold turkey. And since she was dealing, not just using—and there was a rap for theft as well—she would be in for a while, and a lot of other things, dreadful things, would happen to her. So when she came back out she would be a different Donna. The soft, careful expression that he dug so much, the warmth—that would be altered into God knew what, anyhow something empty and too much used. Donna translated into a thing; and so it went, for all of them someday, but for Donna, he hoped, far and away beyond his own lifetime. And not where he couldn't help.

"Spunky," he said to her now, unhappily, "without Spooky."

"What's that?" After a moment she understood. "Oh, that TA therapy. But when I do hash . . ." She had gotten out her very own little round ceramic hash pipe, like a sand dollar, which she had made herself, and was lighting it. "Then I'm Sleepy." Gazing up at him, bright-eyed and happy, she laughed and extended to him the precious hash pipe. "I'll supercharge you," she declared. "Sit down."

As he seated himself, she rose to her feet, stood puffing the hash pipe into lively activity, then waddled at him, bent, and as he opened his mouth—like a baby bird, he thought, as he always thought when she did this—she exhaled great gray forceful jets of hash smoke into him, filling him with her own hot and bold and incorrigible energy, which was at the same time a pacifying agent that relaxed and mellowed them both out together: she who supercharged and Bob Arctor who received.

"I love you, Donna," he said. This supercharging, this was the substitute for sexual relations with her that he got, and maybe it was better; it was worth so much; it was so intimate, and very strange viewed that way, because first she could put something inside him, and then, if she wanted, he put something into her. An even exchange, back and forth, until the hash ran out.

"Yeah, I can dig it, your being in love with me," she said, chuckled, sat down beside him, grinning, to take a hit from the hash pipe now, for herself.

CHAPTER NINE

"Hey, Donna, man," he said. "Do you like cats?"

She blinked, red-eyed. "Drippy little things. Moving along about a foot above the ground."

"Above, no, *on* the ground."

"Drippy. Behind furniture."

"Little spring flowers, then," he said.

"Yes," she said. "I can dig it—little spring flowers, with yellow in them. That first come up."

"Before," he said. "Before anyone."

"Yes." She nodded, eyes shut, off in her trip. "Before anyone stomps them, and they're—gone."

"You know me," he said. "You can read me."

She lay back, setting down the hash pipe. It had gone out. "No more," she said, and her smile slowly dwindled away.

"What's wrong?" he said.

"Nothing." She shook her head and that was all.

"Can I put my arms around you?" he said. "I want to hold you. Okay? Hug you, like. Okay?"

Her dark, enlarged, unfocused weary eyes opened. "No," she said. "No, you're too ugly."

"What?" he said.

"No!" she said, sharply now. "I snort a lot of coke; I have to be super careful because I snort a lot of coke."

"*Ugly?*" he echoed, furious at her. "Fuck you, Donna."

"Just leave my body alone," she said, staring at him.

"Sure," he said. "Sure." He got to his feet and backed away. "You better believe it." He felt like going out to his car, getting his pistol from the glove compartment, and shooting her face off, bursting her skull and eyes to bits. And then that passed, that hash hate and fury. "Fuck it," he said dismally.

"I don't like people to grope my body," Donna said. "I have to watch out for that because I do so much coke. Someday I have it planned I'm going over the Canadian border with four pounds of coke in it, in my snatch. I'll say I'm a Catholic and a virgin. Where are you going?" Alarm had her now; she half rose.

"I'm taking off," he said.

"Your car is at your place. I drove you." The girl struggled up, tousled and confused and half asleep, wandered toward the closet to get her leather jacket. "I'll drive you back. But you can see why I have to protect my snatch. Four pounds of coke is worth—"

"No fucking way," he said. "You're too stoned to drive ten feet, and you never fucking let anybody else drive that little roller skate of yours."

Facing him, she yelled wildly, "That's because nobody else can fucking drive my car! Nobody else ever gets it right, no man especially! Driving or anything else! You had your hands down into my—"

And then he was somewhere outside in the darkness, roaming, without his coat, in a strange part of town. Nobody with him. Fucking alone, he thought, and then he heard Donna hurrying along after him, trying to catch up with him, panting for breath, because she did so much pot and hash these days that her lungs were half silted up with resins. He halted, stood without turning, waiting, feeling really down.

Approaching him, Donna slowed, panted, "I am dreadfully sorry I've hurt your feelings. By what I said. I was out of it."

"Yeah," he said. *"Too ugly!"*

"Sometimes when I've worked all day and I'm super super tired, the first hit I take just spaces me. You wanta come back? Or what? You wanta go to the drive-in? What about the Southern Comfort? I can't buy it . . . they won't sell it to me," she said, and paused. "I'm underage, right?"

"Okay," he said. Together they walked back.

"That sure is good hash, isn't it?" Donna said.

Bob Arctor said, "It's black sticky hash, which means it's saturated in opium alkaloids. What you're smoking is opium, not hash— do you know that? That's why it costs so much—do you know that?" He heard his voice rise; he stopped walking. "You aren't doing hash, sweetie. You're doing opium, and that means a lifetime habit at a cost of . . . what's 'hash' selling for now a pound? And you'll be smoking and nodding off and nodding off and not being able to get your car in gear and rear-ending trucks and needing it every day before you go to work—"

"I need to now," Donna said. "Take a hit before I go to work. And at noon and as soon as I get home. That's why I deal, to buy my hash. Hash is mellow. Hash is where it's at."

"Opium," he repeated. "What's *hash* sell for now?"

"About ten thousand dollars a pound," Donna said. "The good kind."

"Christ! As much as smack."

"I would never use a needle. I never have and I never will. You last about six months when you start shooting, whatever you shoot. Even tap water. You get a habit—"

"You *have* a habit."

Donna said, "We all do. You take Substance D. So what? What's the difference now? I'm happy; aren't you happy? I get to come home and smoke high-grade hash every night . . . it's my trip. Don't try to change me. Don't ever try to change me. Me or my morals. I am what I am. And I get off on hash. It's my life."

"You ever seen pictures of an old opium smoker? Like in China in the old days? Or a hash smoker in India now, what they look like later on in life?"

Donna said, "I don't expect to live long. So what? I don't *want* to be around long. Do you? Why? What's in this world? And have you ever seen— Shit, what about Jerry Fabin; look at someone too far into Substance D. What's there really in this world, Bob? It's a stopping place to the next where they punish us here because we were born evil—"

"You *are* a Catholic."

"We're being punished here, so if we can get off on a trip now and then, fuck it, *do it*. The other day I almost cashed in driving my MG to work. I had the eight-track stereo on and I was smoking my hash pipe and I didn't see this old dude in an 'eighty-four Ford Imperator—"

"You are dumb," he said. "Super dumb."

"I am, you know, going to die early. Anyhow. Whatever I do. Probably on the freeway. I got hardly any brakes on my MG, you realize that? And I've picked up four speeding tickets this year already. Now I got to go to traffic school. It's a bummer. For six whole months."

"So someday," he said, "I will all of a sudden never lay eyes on you again. Right? Never again."

"Because of traffic school? No, after the six months—"

"In the marble orchard," he explained. "Wiped out before you're allowed under California law, fucking goddamn California law, to purchase a can of beer or a bottle of booze."

"Yeah!" Donna exclaimed, alerted. "The Southern Comfort! Right on! Are we going to do a fifth of Southern Comfort and take in the *Ape* flicks? Are we? There's still like eight left, including the one—"

"Listen to me," Bob Arctor said, taking hold of her by the shoulder; she instinctively pulled away.

"No," she said.

He said, "You know what they ought to let you do one time? Maybe just one time? Let you go in legally, just once, and buy a can of beer."

"Why?" she said wonderingly.

"A present to you because you are good," he said.

"They served me once!" Donna exclaimed in delight. "At a bar! The cocktail waitress—I was dressed up and like with some people —asked me what I wanted and I said, 'I'll have a vodka collins,' and she served me. It was at the La Paz, too, which is a really neat place. Wow, can you believe it? I memorized that, the vodka collins, from an ad. So if I ever got asked at a bar, like that, I'd sound cool. Right?" She suddenly put her arm through his, and hugged him as they walked, something she almost never did. "It was the most all-time super trip of my life."

"Then I guess," he said, "you have your present. Your one present."

"I can dig it," Donna said. "I can dig it! Of course they told me later—these people I was with—I should have ordered a Mexican drink like a tequila sunrise, because, see, it's a Mexican kind of bar, there with the La Paz Restaurant. Next time I'll know that; I've got that taped in my memory banks, if I go there again. You know what I'm going to do someday, Bob? I'm going to move north to Oregon and live in the snow. I'm going to shovel snow off the front walk every morning. And have a little house and garden with vegetables."

He said, "You have to save up for that. Save all your money. It costs."

Glancing at him, suddenly shy, Donna said, "He'll get me that. What's-his-name."

"Who?"

"You know." Her voice was soft, sharing her secret. Imparting it to him because he, Bob Arctor, was her friend and she could trust him. "Mister Right. I know what he'll be like—he'll drive an Aston-Martin and he'll take me north in it. And that's where the little old-fashioned house will be in the snow, north from here." After a pause she said, "Snow is supposed to be nice, isn't it?"

He said, "Don't you know?"

"I never have been in the snow except once in San Berdoo up in those mountains and then it was half sleet and muddy and I fucking fell. I don't mean snow like that; I mean *real* snow."

Bob Arctor, his heart heavy in a certain way, said, "You feel positive about all this? It'll really happen?"

"It'll happen!" She nodded. "It's in the cards for me."

They walked on then, in silence. Back to her place, to get her MG. Donna, wrapped up in her own dreams and plans; and he—he recalled Barris and he recalled Luckman and Hank and the safe apartment, and he recalled Fred.

"Hey, man," he said, "can I go with you to Oregon? When you do take off finally?"

She smiled at him, gently and with acute tenderness, with the answer no.

And he understood, from knowing her, that she meant it. And it would not change. He shivered.

"Are you cold?" she asked.

"Yeah," he said. "Very cold."

"I got that good MG heater in my car," she said, "for when we're at the drive-in . . . you'll warm up there." She took his hand, squeezed it, held it, and then, all at once, she let it drop.

But the actual touch of her lingered, inside his heart. That remained. In all the years of his life ahead, the long years without her, with never seeing her or hearing from her or knowing anything about her, if she was alive or happy or dead or what, that touch stayed locked within him, sealed in himself, and never went away. That one touch of her hand.

He brought a cute little needle-freak named Connie home with him that night, to ball her in exchange for him giving her a bag of ten mex hits.

Skinny and lank-haired, the girl sat on the edge of his bed, combing her odd hair; this was the first time she had ever come along with him—he had met her at a head party—and he knew very little about her, although he'd carried her phone number for weeks. Being a needle-freak, she was naturally frigid, but this wasn't a downer; it made her indifferent to sex in terms of her own enjoyment, but on the other hand, she didn't mind what sort of sex it was.

This was obvious just watching her. Connie sat half-dressed, her shoes off, a bobby pin in her mouth, gazing off listlessly, evidently doing a private trip in her head. Her face, elongated and bony, had a strength to it; probably, he decided, because the bones, especially the jaw lines, were pronounced. On her right cheek was a zit. Undoubtedly she neither cared about nor noticed that, either; like sex, zits meant little to her.

Maybe she couldn't tell the difference. Maybe, to her, a longtime needle-freak, sex and zits had similar or even identical qualities. What a thought, he thought, this glimpse into a hype's head for a moment.

"Do you have a toothbrush I can use?" Connie said; she had begun to nod a little, and to mumble, as hypes tended to do this time of night. "Aw screw it—teeth are teeth. I'll brush them . . ." Her voice had sunk so low he couldn't hear her, although he knew from the movement of her lips that she was droning on.

"Do you know where the bathroom is?" he asked her.

"What bathroom?"

"In this house."

Rousing herself, she resumed reflexively combing. "Who are those guys out there this late? Rolling joints and rattling on and on? They live here with you, I guess. Sure they do. Guys like that must."

"Two of them do." Arctor said.

Her dead-codfish eyes turned to fix their gaze on him. "You're queer?" Connie asked.

"I try not to be. That's why you're here tonight."

"Are you putting up a pretty good battle against it?"

"You better believe it."

Connie nodded. "Yes, I suppose I'm about to find out. If you're a latent gay you probably want me to take the initiative. Lie down and I'll do you. Want me to undress you? Okay, you just lie there and I'll do it all." She reached for his zipper.

Later, in the semidarkness he drowsed, from—so to speak—his own fix. Connie snored on beside him, lying on her back with her arms at her sides outside the covers. He could see her dimly. They sleep like Count Dracula, he thought, junkies do. Staring straight up until all of a sudden they sit up, like a machine cranked from position A to position B. "It—must—be—day," the junkie says, or anyhow the tape in his head says. Plays him his instructions, the mind of a junkie being like the music you hear on a clock radio . . . it sometimes sounds pretty, but it is only there to make you do something. The music from the clock radio is to wake you up; the music from the junkie is to get you to become a means for him to obtain more junk, in whatever way you can serve. He, a machine, will turn you into *his* machine.

Every junkie, he thought, is a recording.

Again he dozed, meditating about these bad things. And eventually the junkie, if it's a chick, has nothing to sell but her body. Like Connie, he thought; Connie right here.

Opening his eyes, he turned toward the girl beside him and saw Donna Hawthorne.

Instantly he sat up. Donna! he thought. He could make out her face clearly. No doubt. Christ! he thought, and reached for the bedside light. His fingers touched it; the lamp tumbled and fell. The girl, however, slept on. He still stared at her, and then by degrees he saw Connie again, hatchet-faced, bleak-jawed, sunken, the gaunt face of the out-of-it junkie, Connie and not Donna; one girl, not the other.

He lay back and, miserable, slept somewhat again, wondering what it meant and so forth and on and on, into darkness.

"I don't care if he stunk," the girl beside him muttered later on, dreamily, in her sleep. "I still loved him."

He wondered who she meant. A boy friend? Her father? A tomcat? A childhood precious stuffed toy? Maybe all of them, he thought. But the words were "I loved," not "I still love." Evidently he, whatever or whoever he had been, was gone now. Maybe, Arctor reflected, they (whoever they were) had made her throw him out, because he stank so bad.

Probably so. He wondered how old she had been then, the remembering worn-out junkie girl who dozed beside him.

CHAPTER TEN

In his scramble suit, Fred sat before a battery of whirling holo-playbacks, watching Jim Barris in Bob Arctor's living room reading a book on mushrooms. Why mushrooms? Fred wondered, and sped the tapes at high-speed forward to an hour later. There sat Barris yet, reading with great concentration and making notes.

Presently Barris set the book down and left the house, passing out of scanning range. When he returned he carried a little brown-paper bag which he set on the coffee table and opened. From it he removed dried mushrooms, which he then began to compare one by one with the color photos in the book. With excessive deliberation, unusual for him, he compared each. At last he pushed one miserable-looking mushroom aside and restored the others to the bag; from his pocket he brought a handful of empty capsules and then with equally great precision began crumbling bits of the one particular mushroom into the caps and sealing each of them in turn.

After that, Barris started phoning. The phone tap automatically recorded the numbers called.

"Hello, this is Jim."

"So?"

"Say, have I scored."

"No shit."

"Psilocybe mexicana."

"What's that?"

"A rare hallucinogenic mushroom used in South American mystery cults thousands of years ago. You fly, you become invisible, understand the speech of animals—"

"No thanks." Click.

Redialing. "Hello, this is Jim."

"Jim? Jim who?"

"With the beard . . . green shades, leather pants. I met you at a happening over at Wanda—"

"Oh yeah. Jim. Yeah."

"You interested in scoring on some organic psychedelics?"

"Well, I don't know . . ." Unease. "You sure this is Jim? You don't sound like him."

"I've got something unbelievable, a rare organic mushroom from South America, used in Indian mystery cults thousands of years ago. You fly, become invisible, your car disappears, you are able to understand the speech of animals—"

"My car disappears all the time. When I leave it in a tow-away zone. Ha-ha."

"I can lay perhaps six caps of this *Psilocybe* on you."

"How much?"

"Five dollars a cap."

"Outrageous! No kidding? Hey, I'll meet you somewhere." Then suspicion. "You know, I believe I remember you—you burned me once. Where'd you get these mushrooms hits? How do I know they're not weak acid?"

"They were brought to the U.S. inside a clay idol," Barris said. "As part of a carefully guarded art shipment to a museum, with this one idol marked. The customs pigs never suspected." Barris added, "If they don't get you off I'll refund your money."

"Well, that's meaningless if my head's been eaten and I'm swinging through the trees."

"I dropped one two days ago myself," Barris said. "To test it out. The best trip I ever had—lots of colors. Better than mescaline, for sure. I don't want my customers burned. I always test my stuff myself. It's guaranteed."

Behind Fred another scramble suit was watching the holo-monitor now too. "What's he peddling? Mescaline, he says?"

"He's been capping mushrooms," Fred said, "that either he picked or someone else picked, locally."

"Some mushrooms are toxic in the extreme," the scramble suit behind Fred said.

A third scramble suit knocked off its own holo scrutiny for a moment and stood with them now. "Certain *Amanita* mushrooms contain four toxins that are red-blood-cell cracking agents. It takes two weeks to die and there's no antidote. It's incalculably painful. Only an expert can tell what mushroom he's picking for sure when they're wild."

"I know," Fred said, and marked the ident numbers of this tape section for department use.

Barris again was dialing.

"What's the statute violation cited on this?" Fred said.

"Misrepresentation in advertising," one of the other scramble suits said, and both laughed and returned to their own screens. Fred continued watching.

On Holo Monitor Four the front door of the house opened and Bob Arctor entered, looking dejected. "Hi."

"Howdy," Barris said, gathering his caps together and thrusting them deep into his pocket. "How'd you make out with Donna?" He chuckled. "In several ways, maybe, eh?"

"Okay, fuck off," Arctor said, and passed from Holo Monitor Four, to be picked up in his bedroom a moment later by scanner five. There, with the door kicked shut, Arctor brought forth a number of plastic bags filled with white tabs; he stood a moment uncertainly and then he stuffed them down under the covers of his bed, out of sight. And took off his coat. He appeared weary and unhappy; his face was drawn.

For a moment Bob Arctor sat on the edge of his unmade bed, all by himself. He at last shook his head, rose, stood uncertain . . . then he smoothed his hair and left the room, to be picked up by the central living-room scanner as he approached Barris. During this time scanner two had witnessed Barris hiding the brown bag of mushrooms under the couch cushions and placing the mushroom textbook back on the bookshelf where it was not noticeable.

"What you been doing?" Arctor asked him.

Barris declared, "Research."

"Into what?"

"The properties of certain mycological entities of a delicate nature." Barris chuckled. "It didn't go too well with little miss big-tits, did it?"

Arctor regarded him and then went into the kitchen to plug in the coffeepot.

"Bob," Barris said, following him leisurely, "I'm sorry if I said anything that offended you." He hung around as Arctor waited for the coffee to heat, drumming and humming aimlessly.

"Where's Luckman?"

"I suppose out somewhere trying to rip off a pay phone. He took your hydraulic axle jack with him; that usually means he's out to knock over a pay phone, doesn't it?"

"My axle jack," Arctor echoed.

"You know," Barris said, "I could assist you professionally in your attempts to hustle little miss—"

Fred shot the tape ahead at high-speed wind. The meter at last read a two-hour passage.

"—pay up your goddamn back rent or goddamn get to work on the cephscope," Arctor was saying hotly to Barris.

"I've already ordered resistors which—"

Again Fred sent the tape forward. Two more hours passed.

Now Holo Monitor Five showed Arctor in his bedroom, in bed, a clock FM radio on to KNX, playing folk rock dimly. Monitor Two in the living room showed Barris alone, again reading about mushrooms. Neither man did much for a long period. Once, Arctor stirred and reached out to increase the radio's volume as a song, evidently one he liked, came on. In the living room Barris read on and on, hardly moving. Arctor again at last lay back in bed unmoving.

The phone rang. Barris reached out and lifted it to his ear. "Hello?"

On the phone tap the caller, a male, said, "Mr. Arctor?"

"Yes, this is," Barris said.

I'll be fucked for a nanny goat, Fred said to himself. He reached to turn up the phone-tap volume level.

"Mr. Arctor," the unidentified caller said in a slow, low voice, "I'm sorry to bother you so late, but that check of yours that did not clear—"

"Oh yes," Barris said. "I've been intending to call you about that. The situation is this, sir. I have had a severe bout of intestinal flu, with loss of body heat, pyloric spasms, cramps . . . I just can't get it all together right now to make that little twenty-dollar check good, and frankly I don't intend to make it good."

"What?" the man said, not startled but hoarsely. Ominously.

"Yes, sir," Barris said, nodding. "You heard me correctly, sir."

"Mr. Arctor," the caller said, "that check has been returned by the bank twice now, and these flu symptoms that you describe—"

"I think somebody slipped me something bad," Barris said, with a stark grin on his face.

"*I* think," the man said, "that you're one of those—" He groped for the word.

"Think what you want," Barris said, still grinning.

"Mr. Arctor," the man said, breathing audibly into the phone, "I am going to the D.A.'s office with that check, and while I'm on the phone I have a couple of things to tell you about what I feel about—"

"Turn on, tune out, and good-by," Barris said, and hung up.

The phone-tap unit had automatically recorded the digits of the caller's own phone, picking them up electronically from an inaudible signal generated as soon as the circuit was in place. Fred read off the number now visible on a meter, then shut off the tape-transport for all his holo-scanners, lifted his own police phone, and called in for a print-out on the number.

"Englesohn Locksmith, 1343 Harbor in Anaheim," the police info operator informed him. "Lover boy."

"Locksmith," Fred said. "Okay." He had that written down and now hung up. A locksmith . . . twenty dollars, a round sum: that suggested a job outside the shop—probably driving out and making a duplicate key. When the "owner's" key had gotten lost.

Theory. Barris had posed as Arctor, phoned Englesohn Locksmith to have a "duplicate" key made illicitly, for either the house or the car or even both. Telling Englesohn he'd lost his whole key ring . . . but then the locksmith, doing a security check, had sprung on Barris a request for a check as I.D. Barris had gone back in the house and ripped off an unfilled-out checkbook of Arctor's and written a check out on it to the locksmith. The check hadn't cleared. But why not? Arctor kept a high balance in his account; a check that small would clear. But if it cleared Arctor would come across it in his statement and recognize it as not his, as Jim Barris's. So Barris had rooted about in Arctor's closets and located—probably at some previous time—an old checkbook from a now abandoned account and used that. The account being closed, the check hadn't cleared. Now Barris was in hot water.

But why didn't Barris just go in and pay off the check in cash? This way the creditor was already mad and phoning, and eventually would take it to the D.A. Arctor would find out. A skyful of shit would land on Barris. But the way Barris had talked on the phone to the already outraged creditor . . . he had slyly goaded him into even further hostility, out of which the locksmith might do anything. And worse—Barris's description of his "flu" was a description of coming off heroin, and anybody would know who knew anything. And Barris had signed off the phone call with a flat-out insinuation that he was a heavy doper and so what about it? Signed all this off as Bob Arctor.

The locksmith at this point knew he had a junkie debtor who'd written him a rubber check and didn't care shit and had no intention of making good. And the junkie had this attitude because obviously he was so wired and spaced and mind-blown on his dope it didn't matter to him. And this was an insult to America. Deliberate and nasty.

In fact, Barris's sign-off was a direct quote of Tim Leary's original funky ultimatum to the establishment and all the straights. And this was Orange County. Full of Birchers and Minutemen. With guns. Looking for just this kind of uppity sass from bearded dopers.

Barris had set Bob Arctor up for a fire-bombing. A bust on the bad check at the least, a fire-bombing or other massive retaliatory strike at worst, without Arctor having any notion what was coming down.

Why? Fred wondered. He noted on his scratch pad the ident code on this tape sequence, plus the phone-tap code as well. What was Barris getting Arctor back for? What the hell had Arctor been up to? Arctor must have burned him pretty bad, Fred thought, for this. This is sheer malice. Little, vile, and evil.

This Barris guy, he thought, is a motherfucker. He's going to get somebody killed.

One of the scramble suits in the safe apartment with him roused him from his introspection. "Do you actually know these guys?" The suit gestured at the now blank holo-monitors Fred had before him. "You in there among them on cover assignment?"

"Yep," Fred said.

"It wouldn't be a bad idea to warn them in some way about this mushroom toxicity he's exposing them to, that clown with the green shades who's peddling. Can you pass it on to them without faulting your cover?"

The other nearly scramble suit called from his swivel chair, "Any time one of them gets violently nauseous—that's sometimes a tip-off on mushroom poisoning."

"Resembling strychnine?" Fred said. A cold in sight grappled with his head then, a rerun of the Kimberly Hawkins dog-shit day and his illness in his car after what—

His.

"I'll tell Arctor," he said. "I can lay it on him. Without him flashing on me. He's docile."

"Ugly-looking, too," one of the scramble suits said. "He the individual came in the door stoop-shouldered and hung over?"

"Aw," Fred said, and swiveled back to his holos. Oh goddamn, he thought, that day Barris gave us the tabs at the roadside—his mind went into spins and double trips and then split in half, directly down the middle. The next thing he knew, he was in the safe apartment's bathroom with a Dixie cup of water, rinsing out his mouth, by himself, where he could think. When you get down to it, I'm Arctor, he thought. I'm the man on the scanners, the suspect Barris was fucking over with his weird phone call with the locksmith, and I was asking, What's Arctor been up to to get Barris on him like that? I'm slushed; my brain is slushed. This is not real. I'm not believing this, watching what is me, is Fred—that was Fred down there without his scramble suit; that's how Fred appears without the suit!

And Fred the other day possibly almost got it with toxic mushroom fragments, he realized. He almost didn't make it here to this safe apartment to get these holos going. But now he has.

Now Fred has a chance. But only barely.

Crazy goddamn job they gave me, he thought. But if I wasn't doing it someone else would be, and they might get it wrong. They'd set him up—set Arctor up. They'd turn him in for the reward; they'd plant dope on him and collect. If anyone, he thought, has to be watching that house, it better ought to be me by far, despite the disadvantages; just protecting everybody against kinky fucking Barris in itself justifies it right there.

And if any other officer monitoring Barris's actions sees what I probably will see, they'll conclude Arctor is the biggest drug runner in the western U.S. and recommend a—Christ!—covert snuff. By our unidentified forces. The ones in black we borrow from back East that tiptoe a lot and carry the scope-site Winchester 803's. The new infrared sniper-scope sights synched with the EE-tropic shells. Those guys who don't get paid at all, even from a Dr. Pepper machine; they just get to draw straws to see which of them gets to be the next U. S. President. My God, he thought, those fuckers can shoot down a passing plane. And make it look like one engine inhaled a flock of birds. Those EE-trophic shells—why fuck me, man, he thought; they'd leave traces of feathers in the ruins of the engines; they'd prime them for that.

This is awful, he thought, thinking about this. Not Arctor as suspect but Arctor as . . . whatever. Target. I'll keep on watching him; Fred will keep on doing his Fred-thing; it'll be a lot better; I can edit and interpret and do a great deal of "Let's wait until he actually" and so on, and, realizing this, he tossed the Dixie cup away and emerged from the safe apartment's bathroom.

"You look done in," one of the scramble suits said to him.

"Well," Fred said, "funny thing happened to me on the way to the grave." He saw in his mind a picture of the supersonic tight-beam projector which had caused a forty-nine-year-old district attorney to have a fatal cardiac arrest, just as he was about to reopen the case of a dreadful and famous political assassination here in California. "I almost got there," he said aloud.

"Almost is almost," the scramble suit said. "It's not there."

"Oh," Fred said. "Yeah. Right."

"Sit down," a scramble suit said, "and get back to work, or for you no Friday, just public assistance."

"Can you imagine listing this job as a job skill on the—" Fred began, but the two other scramble suits were not amused and in fact weren't even listening. So he reseated himself and lit a cigarette. And started up the battery of holos once more.

What I ought to do, he decided, is walk back up the street to the house, right now, while I'm thinking about it, before I get sidetracked, and walk in on Barris real fast and shoot him.

In the line of duty.

I'll say, "Hey, man, I'm hurtin'—can you lay a joint on me? I'll pay you a buck." And he will, and then I'll arrest him, drag him to my car, throw him inside, drive onto the freeway, and then pistolwhip him out of the car in front of a truck. And I can say he fought loose and tried to jump. Happens all the time.

Because if I don't I can never eat or drink any open food or beverage in the house, and neither can Luckman or Donna or Freck or we'll all croak from toxic mushroom fragments, after which Barris will explain about how we were all out in the woods picking them at random and eating them and he tried to dissuade us but we wouldn't listen because we didn't go to college.

Even if the court psychiatrists find him totally burned out and nuts and toss him in forever, somebody'll be dead. He thought, Maybe Donna, for instance. Maybe she'll wander in, spaced on hash, looking for me and the spring flowers I promised her, and Barris will offer her a bowl of Jell-O he made himself special, and ten days later she'll be thrashing in agony in an intensive-care ward and it won't do any good then.

If that happens, he thought, I'll boil him in Drāno, in the bathtub, in hot Drāno, until only bones remain, and then mail the bones to his mother or kids, whichever he has, and if he hasn't either then just toss the bones out at passing dogs. But the deed will be done to that little girl anyhow.

Excuse me, he rolled in his head in fantasy to the other two scramble suits. Where can I get a hundred-pound can of Drāno this time of night?

I've had it, he thought, and turned on the holos so as not to attract any more static from the other suits in the safe room.

On Monitor Two, Barris was talking to Luckman, who apparently had rolled in the front door dead drunk, no doubt on Ripple. "There are more people addicted to alcohol in the U.S.," Barris was telling Luckman, who was trying to find the door to his bedroom, to go pass out, and having a terrible time, "than there are addicts of all other forms of drugs. And brain damage and liver damage from the alcohol plus impurities—"

Luckman disappeared without ever having noticed Barris was

there. I wish him luck, Fred thought. It's not a workable policy, though, not for long. Because the fucker is there.

But now Fred is here, too. But all Fred's got is hindsight. Unless, he thought, unless maybe if I run the holo-tapes backward. Then I'd be there first, before Barris. What I do would precede what Barris does. If with me first he gets to do anything at all.

And then the other side of his head opened up and spoke to him more calmly, like another self with a simpler message flashed to him as to how to handle it.

"The way to cool the locksmith check," it told him, "is to go down there to Harbor tomorrow first thing very early and redeem the check and get it back. Do that first, before you do anything else. Do that right away. Defuse that, at that end. And after that, do the other more serious things, once that's finished. Right?" Right, he thought. That will remove me from the disadvantage list. That's where to start.

He put the tape on fast forward, on and on until he figured from the meters that it would show a night scene with everyone asleep. For a pretext to sign off his workday, here.

It now showed lights off, the scanners on infra. Luckman in his bed in his room; Barris in his; and in his room, Arctor beside a chick, both of them asleep.

Let's see, Fred thought. Connie something. We have her in the computer files as strung out on hard stuff and also turning tricks and dealing. A true loser.

"At least you didn't have to watch your subject have sexual intercourse," one of the other scramble suits said, watching from behind him and then passing on by.

"That's a relief," Fred said, stoically viewing the two sleeping figures in the bed; his mind was on the locksmith and what he had to do there. "I always hate to—"

"A nice thing to do," the scramble suit agreed, "but not too nice to watch."

Arctor asleep, Fred thought. With his trick. Well, I can wind up soon; they'll undoubtedly ball on arising but that's about it for them.

He continued watching, however. The sight of Bob Arctor sleeping . . . on and on, Fred thought, hour after hour. And then he noticed something he had not noticed. *That doesn't look like anybody else but Donna Hawthorne!* he thought. There in bed, in the sack with Arctor.

It doesn't compute, he thought, and reached to snap off the scanners. He ran the tape back, then forward again. Bob Arctor and a chick, but not Donna! It was the junkie chick Connie! He had been right. The two individuals lay there side by side, both asleep.

And then, as Fred watched, Connie's hard features melted and faded into softness, and into Donna Hawthorne's face.

He snapped off the tape again. Sat puzzled. I don't get it, he thought. It's—what they call that? Like a goddamn dissolve! A film technique. Fuck, what is this? Pre-editing for TV viewing? By a director, using special visual effects?

Again he ran the tape back, then forward; when he first came to the alteration in Connie's features he then stopped the transport, leaving the hologram filled with one freeze-frame.

He rotated the enlarger. All the other cubes cut out; one huge cube formed from the previous eight. A single nocturnal scene: Bob Arctor, unmoving, in his bed, the girl unmoving, beside him.

Standing, Fred walked into the holo-cube, into the three-dimensional projection, and stood close to the bed to scrutinize the girl's face.

Halfway between, he decided. Still half Connie; already half Donna. I better turn this over to the lab, he thought; it's been tampered with by an expert. I've been fed fake tape.

Who by? he wondered. He emerged from the holo-cube, collapsed it, and restored the small eight ones. Still sat there, pondering.

Somebody faked in Donna. Superimposed over Connie. Forged evidence that Arctor was laying the Hawthorne girl. Why? As a good technician can do with either audio or video tape and now—as witness—with holo-tapes. Hard to do, but . . .

If this was a click-on, click-off, interval scan, he thought, we'd have a sequence showing Arctor in bed with a girl he probably never did get into bed and never will, but there it is on the tape.

Or maybe it's a visual interruption or breakdown electronically, he pondered. What they call *printing*. Holo-printing: from one section of the tape storage to another. If the tape sits too long, if the recording gain was too high initially, it prints across. Jeez, he thought. It printed Donna across from a previous or later scene, maybe from the living room.

I wish I knew more about the technical side of this, he reflected. I'd better acquire more background on this before jumping the gun. Like another AM station filtering in, interfering—

Crosstalk, he decided. Like that: accidental.

Like ghosts on a TV screen. Functional, a malfunction. A transducer opened up briefly.

Again he rolled the tape. Connie again, and Connie it stayed. And then . . . again Fred saw Donna's face melt back in, and this time the sleeping man beside her in the bed, Bob Arctor, woke up after a moment and sat up abruptly, then fumbled for the light beside him; the light fell to the floor and Arctor sat staring on and on at the sleeping girl, at sleeping Donna.

When Connie's face seeped back, Arctor relaxed, and at last he sank back and again slept. But restlessly.

Well, that shoots down the "technical interference" theory, Fred thought. Printing or crosstalk. *Arctor saw it too*. Woke up, saw it, stared, then gave up.

Christ, Fred thought, and shut off the equipment before him entirely. "I guess that's enough for me for now," he declared, and rose shakily to his feet. "I've had it."

"Saw some kinky sex, did you?" a scramble suit asked. "You'll get used to this job."

"I never will get used to this job," Fred said. "You can make book on that."

CHAPTER ELEVEN

The next morning, by Yellow Cab, since now not only was his cephscope laid up for repairs but so was his car, he appeared at the door of Englesohn Locksmith with forty bucks in cash and a good deal of worry inside his heart.

The store had an old wooden quality, with a more modern sign but many little brass doodads in the windows of a lock type: funky ornate mailboxes, trippy doorknobs made to resemble human heads, great fake black iron keys. He entered, into semigloom. Like a doper's place, he thought, appreciating the irony.

At a counter where two huge key-grinding machines loomed up, plus thousands of key blanks dangling from racks, a plump elderly lady greeted him. "Yes, sir? Good morning."

Arctor said, "I'm here . . .

> *Ihr Instrumente freilich spottet mein,*
> *Mit Rad and Kämmen, Walz' und Bügel:*
> *Ich stand am Tor, ihr solltet Schlüssel sein;*
> *Zwar euer Bart ist kraus, doch hebt ihr nicht die Riegel.*

. . . to pay for a check of mine which the bank returned. It's for twenty dollars, I believe."

"Oh." The lady amiably lifted out a locked metal file, searched for the key to it, then discovered the file wasn't locked. She opened it and found the check right away, with a note attached. "Mr. Arctor?"

"Yes," he said, his money already out.

"Yes, twenty dollars." Detaching the note from the check, she began laboriously writing on the note, indicating that he had shown up and purchased the check back.

"I'm sorry about this," he told her, "but by mistake I wrote the check on a now closed account rather than my active one."

"Umm," the lady said, smiling as she wrote.

"Also," he said, "I'd appreciate it if you'd tell your husband, who called me the other day—"

"My brother Carl," the lady said, "actually." She glanced over her shoulder. "If Carl spoke to you . . ." She gestured, smiling. "He gets overwrought sometimes about checks . . . I apologize if he spoke . . . you know."

"Tell him," Arctor said, his speech memorized, "that when he called I was distraught myself, and I apologize for that, too."

"I believe he did say something about that, yes." She laid out his check; he gave her twenty dollars.

"Any extra charge?" Arctor said.

"No extra charge."

"I was distraught," he said, glancing briefly at the check and then putting it away in his pocket, "because a friend of mine had just passed on unexpectedly."

"Oh dear," the lady said.

Arctor, lingering, said, "He choked to death alone, in his room, on a piece of meat. No one heard him."

"Do you know, Mr. Arctor, that more deaths from that happen than people realize? I read that when you are dining with a friend, and he or she does not speak for a period of time but just sits there, you should lean forward and ask him if he can talk? Because he may not be able to; he may be strangling and can't tell you."

"Yes," Arctor said. "Thanks. That's true. And thanks about the check."

"I'm sorry about your friend," the lady said.

"Yes," he said. "He was about the best friend I had."

"That is so dreadful," the lady said. "How old was he, Mr. Arctor?"

"In his early thirties," Arctor said, which was true: Luckman was thirty-two."

"Oh, how terrible. I'll tell Carl. And thank you for coming all the way down here."

"Thank you," Arctor said. "And thank Mr. Englesohn too, for me. Thank you both so much." He departed, finding himself back out on the warm morning sidewalk, blinking in the bright light and foul air.

He phoned for a cab, and on the journey back to his house sat advising himself as to how well he had gotten out of this net of Barris's with no real overly bad scene. Could have been a lot worse, he pointed out to himself. The check was still there. And I didn't have to confront the dude himself.

He got out the check to see how closely Barris had been able to approximate his handwriting. Yes, it was a dead account; he recognized the color of the check right away, an entirely closed one, and the bank had stamped it ACCOUNT CLOSED. No wonder the locksmith had gone bananas. And then, studying the check as he rode along, Arctor saw that the handwriting was his.

Not anything like Barris's. A perfect forgery. He would never have known it wasn't his, except that he remembered not having written it.

My God, he thought, how many of these has Barris done by now? Maybe he's embezzled me out of half I've got.

Barris, he thought, is a genius. On the other hand, it's probably a tracing reproduction or anyhow mechanically done. But I never made a check out to Englesohn Locksmith, so how could it be a transfer forgery? This is a unique check. I'll turn it over to the department graphologists, he decided, and let them figure out how it was done. Maybe just practice, practice, practice.

As to the mushroom jazz— He thought, I'll just walk up to him and say people told me he's been trying to sell them mushroom hits. And to knock it off. I got feedback from somebody worried, as they should be.

But, he thought, these items are only random indications of what he's up to, discovered on the first replay. *They only represent samples of what I'm up against.* Christ knows what else he's done: he's got all the time in the world to loaf around and read reference books and dream up plots and intrigues and conspiracies and so forth . . . Maybe, he thought abruptly, I better have a trace run on my phone right away to see if it's tapped. Barris has a box of electronic hardware, and even Sony, for example, makes and sells an induction coil that can be used as a phone-tapping device. The phone probably is. It probably has been for quite a while.

I mean, he thought, in addition to my own recent—necessary— phone tap.

Again he studied the check as the cab jiggled along, and all at once he thought, What if I made it out myself? What if Arctor wrote this? I think I did, he thought; I think the motherfucking dingey Arctor himself wrote this check, very fast—the letters slanted—because for some reason he was in a hurry; he dashed it off, got the wrong blank check, and afterward forgot all about it, forgot the incident entirely.

Forgot, he thought, the time Arctor . . .

Was grinsest du mir, hohler Schädel, her?
Als dass dein Hirn, wie meines, einst verwirret
Den leichten Tag gesucht und in der Dämmrung schwer,
Mit Lust nach Wahrheit, jämmerlich geirret.

. . . oozed out of that huge dope happening in Santa Ana, where he met that little blond chick with odd teeth, long blond hair, and a big ass, but so energetic and friendly . . . he couldn't get his car started; he was wired up to his nose. He kept having trouble—there was so much dope dropped and shot and snorted that night, it went on almost until dawn. So much Substance D, and very Primo. Very very Primo. His stuff.

Leaning forward, he said, "Pull over at that Shell station. I'll get out there."

He got out, paid the cab driver, then entered the pay phone, looked up the locksmith's number, phoned him.

The old lady answered. "Englesohn Locksmith, good—"

"This is Mr. Arctor again, I'm sorry to bother you. What address do you have for the call, the service call for which my check was made out?"

"Well, let me see. Just a moment, Mr. Arctor." Bumping of the phone as she set it down.

Distant muffled man's voice: "Who is it? That Arctor?"

"Yes, Carl, but don't say anything, please. He came in just now—"

"Let me talk to him."

Pause. Then the old lady again. "Well, I have this address, Mr. Arctor." She read off his home address.

"That's where your brother was called out to? To make the key?"

"Wait a moment. Carl? Do you remember where you went in the truck to make the key for Mr. Arctor?"

Distant man's rumble: "On Katella."

"Not his home?"

"On Katella!"

"Somewhere on Katella, Mr. Arctor. In Anaheim. No, wait—Carl says it was in Santa Ana, on Main. Does that—"

"Thanks," he said and hung up. Santa Ana. Main. That's where the fucking dope party was, and I must have turned in thirty names and as many license plates that night; that was not your standard party. A big shipment had arrived from Mexico; the buyers were splitting and, as usual with buyers, sampling as they split. Half of them now probably have been busted by buy agents sent out . . . Wow, he thought: I still remember—or never will correctly remember—that night.

But that still doesn't excuse Barris from impersonating Arctor with malice aforethought on that phone call coming in. Except that, by the evidence, Barris had made it up on the spot—improvised. Shit, maybe Barris was wired the other night and did what a lot of dudes do when they're wired: just sort of groove with what's happening.

Arctor wrote the check for a certainty; Barris just happened to pick up the phone. Thought, in his charred head, that it was a cool gag. Being irresponsible only, nothing more.

And, he reflected as he dialed Yellow Cab again, Arctor has not been very responsible in making good on that check over this prolonged period. Whose fault is that? Getting it out once more, he examined the date on the check. A month and a half. Jesus, talk about irresponsibility! Arctor could wind up inside looking out, for that; it's God's mercy that nutty Carl didn't go to the D.A. already. Probably his sweet old sister restrained him.

Arctor, he decided, better get his ass in gear; he's done a few din-gey things himself I didn't know about until now. Barris isn't the only one or perhaps even the primary one. For one thing, there is still to be explained the cause of Barris's intense, concerted malice toward Arctor; a man doesn't set out over a long period of time to burn somebody for no reason. And Barris isn't trying to burn any-body else, not, say, Luckman or Charles Freck or Donna Haw-thorne; he helped get Jerry Fabin to the federal clinic more than anyone else, and he's kind to all the animals in the house.

One time Arctor had been going to send one of the dogs—what the hell was the little black one's name, Popo or something?—to the pound to be destroyed, she couldn't be trained, and Barris had spent hours, in fact days, with Popo, gently training her and talking with her until she calmed down and could be trained and so didn't have to go be snuffed. If Barris had general malice toward all, he wouldn't do numbers, good numbers, like that.

"Yellow Cab," the phone said.

He gave the address of the Shell station.

And if Carl the locksmith had pegged Arctor as a heavy doper, he pondered as he lounged around moodily waiting for the cab, it isn't Barris's fault; when Carl must've pulled up in his truck at 5 A.M. to make a key for Arctor's Olds, Arctor probably was walking on Jell-O sidewalks and up walls and batting off fisheyes and every other kind of good dope-trip thing. Carl drew his conclusions then. As Carl ground the new key, Arctor probably floated around upside down or bounced about on his head, talking sideways. No wonder Carl had not been amused.

In fact, he speculated, maybe Barris is trying to cover up for Arc-tor's increasing fuckups. Arctor is no longer keeping his vehicle in safe condition, as he once did, he's been hanging paper, not deliber-ately but because his goddamn brain is slushed from dope. But, if anything, that's worse. Barris is doing what he can; that's a possi-bility. Only, *his* brain, too, is slushed. *All* their brains are . . .

Dem Wurme gleich' ich, der den Staub durchwühlt,
Den, wie er sich im Staube nährend lebt,
Des Wandrers Tritt vernichtet und begräbt.

. . . slushed and mutually interacting in a slushed way. It's the slushed leading the slushed. And right into doom.

Maybe, he conjectured, Arctor cut the wires and bent the wires and created all the shorts in his cephscope. In the middle of the night. But for what reason?

That would be a difficult one: *why?* But with slushed brains anything was possible, any variety of twisted—like the wires themselves —motives. He'd seen it, during his undercover law-enforcement work, many, many times. This tragedy was not new to him; this would be, in their computer files, just one more case. This was the phase ahead of the journey to the federal clinic, as with Jerry Fabin.

All these guys walked one game board, stood now in different squares various distances from the goal, and would reach it at several times. But all, eventually, would reach it: the federal clinics.

It was inscribed in their neural tissue. Or what remained of it. Nothing could halt it or turn it back now.

And, he had begun to believe, for Bob Arctor most of all. It was his intuition, just beginning, not dependent on anything Barris was doing. A new, professional insight.

And also, his superiors at the Orange County Sheriff's Office had decided to focus on Bob Arctor; they no doubt had reasons which he knew nothing about. Perhaps these facts confirmed one another: their growing interest in Arctor—after all, it had cost the department a bundle to install the holo-scanners in Arctor's house, and to pay him to analyze the print-outs, as well as others higher up to pass judgment on what he periodically turned over—this fitted in with Barris's unusual attention toward Arctor, both having selected Arctor as a Primo target. But what had he seen himself in Arctor's conduct that struck him as unusual? Firsthand, not dependent on these two interests?

As the taxi drove along, he reflected that he would have to watch awhile to come across anything, more than likely; it would not disclose itself to the monitors in a day. He would have to be patient; he would have to resign himself to long-term scrutiny and to put himself in a space where he was willing to wait.

Once he saw something on the holo-scanners, however, some enigmatic or suspicious behavior on Arctor's part, then a three-point fix would exist on him, a third verification of the others' interests. Certainly this would be a confirm. It would justify the expense and time of everyone's interest.

I wonder what Barris knows that we don't know, he wondered. Maybe we should haul him in and ask him. But—better to obtain material developed independently from Barris; otherwise it would be a duplication of what Barris, whoever he was or represented, had.

And then he thought, What the hell am I talking about? I must be nuts. I know Bob Arctor; he's a good person. He's up to nothing. At least nothing unsavory. In fact, he thought, he works for the Orange County Sheriff's Office, covertly. Which is probably . . .

> *Zwei Seelen wohnen, ach! in meiner Brust,*
> *Die eine will sich von der andern trennen:*
> *Die eine hält, in derber Liebeslust,*
> *Sich an die Welt mit klammernden Organen;*
> *Die andre hebt gewaltsam sich vom Dust*
> *Zu den Gefilden hoher Ahnen.*

. . . why Barris is after him.

But, he thought, that wouldn't explain why the Orange County Sheriff's Office is after him—especially to the extent of installing all those holos and assigning a full-time agent to watch and report on him. That wouldn't account for that.

It does not compute, he thought. More, a lot more, is going down in that house, that run-down rubble-filled house with its weed-patch backyard and catbox that never gets emptied and animals walking on the kitchen table and garbage spilling over that no one ever takes out.

What a waste, he thought, of a truly good house. So much could be done with it. A family, children and a woman, could live there. It was designed for that: three bedrooms. Such a waste; such a fucking waste! They ought to take it away from him, he thought; enter the situation and foreclose. Maybe they will. And put it to better use; that house yearns for that. That house has seen so much better days, long ago. Those days could return. If another kind of person had it and kept it up.

The yard especially, he thought, as the cab pulled into the newspaper-splattered driveway.

He paid the driver, got out his door key, and entered the house.

Immediately he felt something watching: the holo-scanners on him. As soon as he crossed his own threshold. Alone—no one but him in the house. Untrue! Him and the scanners, insidious and invisible, that watched him and recorded. Everything he did. Everything he uttered.

Like the scrawls on the wall when you're peeing in a public urinal, he thought. SMILE! YOU'RE ON CANDID CAMERA! I am, he thought, as soon as I enter this house. It's eerie. He did not like it. He felt self-conscious; the sensation had grown since the first day, when they'd arrived home—the "dog-shit day," as he thought of it, couldn't keep from thinking of it. Each day the experience of the scanners had grown.

"Nobody home, I guess," he stated aloud as usual, and was aware that the scanners had picked that up. But he had to take care always: he wasn't supposed to know they were there. Like an actor before a movie camera, he decided, you act like the camera doesn't exist or else you blow it. It's all over.

And for this shit there are no take-two's.

What you get instead is wipeout. I mean, what *I* get. Not the people behind the scanners but me.

What I ought to do, he thought, to get out of this, is sell the house; it's run down anyway. But . . . I love this house. No way!

It's my house.

Nobody can drive me out.

For whatever reasons they would or do want to.

Assuming there's a "they" at all.

Which may just be my imagination, the "they" watching me. Paranoia. Or rather the "it." The depersonalized *it*.

Whatever it is that's watching, it is not a human.

Not by my standards, anyhow. Not what I'd recognize.

As silly as this is, he thought, it's frightening. Something is being done to me and by a mere thing, here in my own house. Before my very eyes.

Within *something's* very eyes; within the sight of some *thing*. Which, unlike little dark-eyed Donna, does not ever blink. What does a scanner see? he asked himself. I mean, really see? Into the head? Down into the heart? Does a passive infrared scanner like they used to use or a cube-type holo scanner like they use these days, the latest thing, see into me—into us—clearly or darkly? I hope it does, he thought, see clearly, because I can't any longer these days see into myself. I see only murk. Murk outside; murk inside. I hope, for everyone's sake, the scanners do better. Because, he thought, if the scanner sees only darkly, the way I myself do, then we are cursed, cursed again and like we have been continually, and we'll wind up dead this way, knowing very little and getting that little fragment wrong too.

From the living-room bookcase he took down a volume at random; it turned out to be, he discovered, *The Picture Book of Sexual Love*. Opening at random, he perceived a page—which showed a man nibbling happily at a chick's right tit, and the chick sighing—and said aloud, as if reading to himself from the book, as if quoting from some famous old-time double-dome philosopher, which he was not:

"Any given man sees only a tiny portion of the total truth, and very often, in fact almost . . .

> *Weh! steck' ich in dem Kerker noch?*
> *Verfluchtes dumpfes Mauerloch,*
> *Wo selbst das liebe Himmelslicht*
> *Trüb durch gemalte Scheiben bricht!*
> *Beschränkt mit diesem Bücherhauf,*
> *Den Würme nagen, Staub bedeckt,*
> *Den bis ans hohe.*

. . . perpetually, he deliberately deceives himself about that little precious fragment as well. A portion of him turns against him and acts like another person, defeating him from inside. A man inside a man. Which is no man at all."

Nodding, as if moved by the wisdom of the nonexisting written words on that page, he closed the large red-bound, gold-stamped *Picture Book of Sexual Love* and restored it to the shelf. I hope the scanners don't zoom in on the cover of this book, he thought, and blow my shuck.

Charles Freck, becoming progressively more and more depressed by what was happening to everybody he knew, decided finally to off himself. There was no problem, in the circles where he hung out, in putting an end to yourself: you just bought into a large quantity of reds and took them with some cheap wine, late at night, with the phone off the hook so no one would interrupt you.

The planning part had to do with the artifacts you wanted found on you by later archeologists. So they'd know from which stratum you came. And also could piece together where your head had been at at the time you did it.

He spent several days deciding on the artifacts. Much longer than he had spent deciding to kill himself, and approximately the same time required to get that many reds. He would be found lying on his back, on his bed, with a copy of Ayn Rand's *The Fountainhead* (which would prove he had been a misunderstood superman rejected by the masses and so, in a sense, murdered by their scorn) and an unfinished letter to Exxon protesting the cancellation of his gas credit card. That way he would indict the system and achieve something by his death, over and above what the death itself achieved.

Actually, he was not as sure in his mind what the death achieved as what the two artifacts achieved; but anyhow it all added up, and he began to make ready, like an animal sensing its time has come and acting out its instinctive programming, laid down by nature, when its inevitable end was near.

At the last moment (as end-time closed in on him) he changed his mind on a decisive issue and decided to drink the reds down with a connoisseur wine instead of Ripple or Thunderbird, so he set off on one last drive, over to Trader Joe's, which specialized in fine wines, and bought a bottle of 1971 Mondavi Cabernet Sauvignon, which set him back almost thirty dollars—all he had.

Back home again, he uncorked the wine, let it breathe, drank a few glasses of it, spent a few minutes contemplating his favorite page of *The Illustrated Picture Book of Sex,* which showed the girl on top, then placed the plastic bag of reds beside his bed, lay down with the Ayn Rand book and unfinished protest letter to Exxon, tried to think of something meaningful but could not, atlhough he kept remembering the girl being on top, and then, with a glass of the Cabernet Sauvignon, gulped down all the reds at once. After that, the deed being done, he lay back, the Ayn Rand book and letter on his chest, and waited.

However, he had been burned. The capsules were not barbiturates, as represented. They were some kind of kinky psychedelics, of a type he had never dropped before, probably a mixture, and new on the market. Instead of quietly suffocating, Charles Freck began to hallucinate. Well, he thought philosophically, this is the story of my life. Always ripped off. He had to face the fact—considering how many of the capsules he had swallowed—that he was in for some trip.

The next thing he knew, a creature from between dimensions was standing beside his bed looking down at him disapprovingly.

The creature had many eyes, all over it, ultra-modern expensive-looking clothing, and rose up eight feet high. Also, it carried an enormous scroll.

"You're going to read me my sins," Charles Freck said.

The creature nodded and unsealed the scroll.

Freck said, lying helpless on his bed, "and it's going to take a hundred thousand hours."

Fixing its many compound eyes on him, the creature from between dimensions said, "We are no longer in the mundane universe. Lower-plane categories of material existence such as 'space' and 'time' no longer apply to you. You have been elevated to the transcendent realm. Your sins will be read to you ceaselessly, in shifts, throughout eternity. The list will never end."

Know your dealer, Charles Freck thought, and wished he could take back the last half-hour of his life.

A thousand years later he was still lying there on his bed with the Ayn Rand book and the letter to Exxon on his chest, listening to them read his sins to him. They had gotten up to the first grade, when he was six years old.

Ten thousand years later they had reached the sixth grade.

The year he had discovered masturbation.

He shut his eyes, but he could still see the multi-eyed, eight-foot-high being with its endless scroll reading on and on.

"And next—" it was saying.

Charles Freck thought, At least I got a good wine.

CHAPTER TWELVE

Two days later Fred, puzzled, watched Holo-Scanner Three as his subject Robert Arctor pulled a book, evidently at random, from his bookshelf in the living room of his house. Dope stashed behind it? Fred wondered, and zoomed the scanner lens in. Or a phone number or address written in it? He could see that Arctor hadn't pulled the book to read; Arctor had just entered the house and still wore his coat. He had a peculiar air about him: tense and bummed out both at once, a sort of dulled urgency.

The zoomar lens of the scanner showed the page had a color photo of a man gnawing on a woman's right nipple, with both individuals nude. The woman was evidently having an orgasm; her eyes had half shut and her mouth hung open in a soundless moan. Maybe Arctor's using it to get off on, Fred thought as he watched. But Arctor paid no attention to the picture; instead, he creakingly recited something mystifying, partly in German obviously to puzzle anyone overhearing him. Maybe he imagined his roommates were somewhere in the house and wanted to bait them into appearing. Fred speculated.

No one appeared. Luckman, Fred knew from having been at the scanners a long while, had dropped a bunch of reds mixed with Substance D and passed out fully dressed in his bedroom, a couple of steps short of his bed. Barris had left entirely.

What is Arctor doing? Fred wondered, and noted the ident code for these sections. He's becoming more and more strange. I can see now what that informant who phoned in about him meant.

Or, he conjectured, those sentences Arctor spoke aloud could be a voice command to some electronic hardware he's installed in the house. Turn on or turn off. Maybe even create an interference field against scanning . . . such as this. But he doubted it. Doubted if it was in any way rational or purposeful or meaningful, except to Arctor.

The guy is nuts, he thought. He really is. From the day he found his cephscope sabotaged—certainly the day he arrived home with his car all fucked up, fucked up in such a way as to almost kill him—

he's been dingey ever since. And to some extent before that, Fred thought. Anyhow, ever since the "dog-shit day," as he knew Arctor called it.

Actually, he could not blame him. That, Fred reflected as he watched Arctor peel off his coat wearily, would blow anyone's mind. But most people would phase back in. He hasn't. He's getting worse. Reading aloud to no one messages that don't exist and in foreign tongues.

Unless he's shucking me, Fred thought with uneasiness. In some fashion figured out he's being monitored and is . . . covering up what he's actually doing? Or just playing head games with us? Time, he decided, will tell.

I say he's shucking us, Fred decided. Some people can tell when they're being watched. A sixth sense. Not paranoia, but a primitive instinct: what a mouse has, any hunted thing. Knows it's being stalked. *Feels* it. He's doing shit for our benefit, stringing us along. But—you can't be sure. There are shucks on top of shucks. Layers and layers.

The sound of Arctor reading obscurely had awakened Luckman according to the scanner covering his bedroom. Luckman sat up groggily and listened. He then heard the noise of Arctor dropping a coat hanger while hanging up his coat. Luckman slid his long muscular legs under him and in one motion picked up a hand ax which he kept on the table by his bed; he stood erect and moved animal-smoothly toward the door of his bedroom.

In the living room, Arctor picked up the mail from the coffee table and started through it. He tossed a large junk-mail piece toward the wastebasket. It missed.

In his bedroom Luckman heard that. He stiffened and raised his head as if to sniff the air.

Arctor, reading the mail, suddenly scowled and said, "I'll be dipped."

In his bedroom Luckman relaxed, set the ax down with a clank, smoothed his hair, opened the door, and stepped out. "Hi. What's happening?"

Arctor said, "I drove by the Maylar Microdot Corporation Building."

"You're shitting me."

"And," Arctor said, "they were taking an inventory. But one of the employees evidently had tracked the inventory outdoors on the heel of his shoe. So they were all outside there in the Maylar Microdot Corporation parking lot with a pair of tweezers and lots and lots of little magnifying glasses. And a little paper bag."

"Any reward?" Luckman said, yawning and beating with his palms on his flat, hard gut.

"They had a reward they were offering," Arctor said. "But they lost that, too. It was a little tiny penny."

Luckman said, "You see very many events of this nature as you're driving along?"

"Only in Orange County," Arctor said.

"How large is the Maylar Microdot Corporation building?"

"About an inch high," Arctor said.

"How much would you estimate it weighs?"

"Including the employees?"

Fred sent the tape spinning ahead at fast wind. When an hour had passed, according to the meter, he halted it momentarily.

"—about ten pounds," Arctor was saying.

"Well, how can you tell, then, when you pass by it, if it's only an inch high and only weighs ten pounds?"

Arctor, now sitting on the couch with his feet up, said, "They have a big sign."

Jesus! Fred thought, and again sent the tape ahead. He halted it at only ten minutes elapsed real time, on a hunch.

"—what's the sign look like?" Luckman was saying. He sat on the floor, cleaning a boxful of grass. "Neon and like that? Colors? I wonder if I've seen it. Is it conspicuous?"

"Here, I'll show it to you," Arctor said, reaching into his shirt pocket. "I brought it home with me."

Again Fred sent the tape at fast forward.

"—you know how you could smuggle microdots into a country without them knowing?" Luckman was saying.

"Just about any way you wanted," Arctor said, leaning back, smoking a joint. The air was cloudy.

"No, I mean a way they'd never flash on," Luckman said. "It was Barris who suggested this to me one day, confidentially; I wasn't supposed to tell anyone, because he's putting it in his book."

"What book? *Common Household Dope and—*"

"No. *Simple Ways to Smuggle Objects into the U.S. and out, Depending on Which Way You're Going.* You smuggle it in with a shipment of dope. Like with heroin. The microdots are down inside the packets. Nobody'd notice, they're so small. They won't—"

"But then some junkie'd shoot up a hit of half smack and half microdots."

"Well, then, he'd be the fuckingest educated junkie you ever did see."

"Depending on what was on the microdots."

"Barris had this other way to smuggle dope across the border. You know how the customs guys, they ask you to declare what you have? And you can't say dope because—"

"Okay, how?"

"Well, see, you take a huge block of hash and carve it in the shape of a man. Then you hollow out a section and put a wind-up motor like a clockworks in it, and a little cassette tape, and you stand in line with it, and then just before it goes through customs you wind up the key and it walks up to the customs man, who says to it, 'Do you have anything to declare?' and the block of hash says, 'No, I don't,' and keeps on walking. Until it runs down on the other side of the border."

"You could put a solar-type battery in it instead of a spring and it could keep walking for years. Forever."

"What's the use of that? It'd finally reach either the Pacific or the Atlantic. In fact, it'd walk off the edge of the Earth, like—"

"Imagine an Eskimo village, and a six-foot-high block of hash worth about—how much would that be worth?"

"About a billion dollars."

"More. Two billion."

"These Eskimos are chewing hides and carving bone spears, and this block of hash worth two billion dollars comes walking through the snow saying over and over. 'No, I don't.' "

"They'd wonder what it meant by that."

"They'd be puzzled forever. There'd be legends."

"Can you imagine telling your grandkids, 'I saw with my own eyes the six-foot-high block of hash appear out of the blinding fog and walk past, that way, worth two billion dollars, saying, "No, I don't." ' His grandchildren would have him committed."

"No, see, legends build. After a few centuries they'd be saying, 'In my forefathers' time one day a ninety-foot-high block of extremely good quality Afghanistan hash worth eight trillion dollars came at us dripping fire and screaming, "Die, Eskimo dogs!" and we fought and fought with it, using our spears, and finally killed it.' "

"The kids wouldn't believe that either."

"Kids never believe anything any more."

"It's a downer to tell anything to a kid. I once had a kid ask me, 'What was it like to see the first automobile?' Shit, man, I was born in 1962."

"Christ," Arctor said, "I once had a guy I knew burned out on acid ask me that. He was twenty-seven years old. I was only three years older than him. He didn't know anything any more. Later on he dropped some more hits of acid—or what he was sold as acid—

and after that he peed on the floor and crapped on the floor, and when you said something to him, like 'How are you, Don?', he just repeated it after you, like a bird. 'How are you, Don?'"

Silence, then. Between the two joint-smoking men in the cloudy living room. A long, somber silence.

"Bob, you know something . . ." Luckman said at last. "I used to be the same age as everyone else."

"I think so was I," Arctor said.

"I don't know what did it."

"Sure, Luckman," Arctor said, "you know what did it to all of us."

"Well, let's not talk about it." He continued inhaling noisily, his long face sallow in the dim midday light.

One of the phones in the safe apartment rang. A scramble suit answered it, then extended it toward Fred. "Fred."

He shut off the holos and took the phone.

"Remember when you were downtown last week?" a voice said. "Being administered the BG test?"

After an interval of silence Fred said, "Yes."

"You were supposed to come back." A pause at that end, too. "We've processed more recent material on you . . . I have taken it upon myself to schedule you for the full standard battery of percept tests plus other testing. Your time for this is tomorrow, three o'clock in the afternoon, the same room. It will take about four hours in all. Do you remember the room number?"

"No," Fred said.

"How are you feeling?"

"Okay," Fred said stoically.

"Any problems? In your work or outside your work?"

"I had a fight with my girl."

"Any confusion? Are you experiencing any difficulty identifying persons or objects? Does anything you see appear inverted or reversed? And while I'm asking, any space-time or language disorientation?"

"No," he said glumly. "No to all of the above."

"We'll see you tomorrow at Room 203," the psychologist deputy said.

"What material of mine did you find to be—"

"We'll take that up tomorrow. Be there. All right? And, Fred, don't get discouraged." *Click.*

Well, click to you too, he thought, and hung up.

With irritation, sensing that they were leaning on him, making him do something he resented doing, he snapped the holos into print-out once more; the cubes lit up with color and the three-dimensional scenes within animated. From the aud tap more purposeless, frustrating—to Fred—babble emerged:

"This chick," Luckman droned on, "had gotten knocked up, and she applied for an abortion because she'd missed like four periods and she was conspicuously swelling up. She did nothing but gripe about the cost of the abortion; she couldn't get on public assistance for some reason. One day I was over at her place, and this girl friend of hers was there telling her she only had a hysterical pregnancy. 'You just *want* to believe you're pregnant,' the chick was nattering at her. 'It's a guilt trip. And the abortion, and the heavy bread it's going to cost you, that's a penance trip.' So the chick—I really dug her—she looked up calmly and she said, 'Okay, then if it's a hysterical pregnancy I'll get a hysterical abortion and pay for it with hysterical money.'"

Arctor said, "I wonder whose face is on the hysterical five-dollar bill."

"Well, who was our most hysterical President?"

"Bill Falkes. He only *thought* he was President."

"When did he think he served?"

"He imagined he served two terms back around 1882. Later on after a lot of therapy he came to imagine he served only one term—"

With great fury Fred slammed the holos ahead two and a half hours. How long does this garbage go on? he asked himself. All day? Forever?

"—so you take your child to the doctor, to the psychologist, and you tell him how your child screams all the time and has tantrums." Luckman had two lids of grass before him on the coffee table plus a can of beer; he was inspecting the grass. "And lies; the kid lies. Makes up exaggerated stories. And the psychologist examines the kid and his diagnosis is 'Madam, your child is hysterical. You have a hysterical child. But I don't know why.' And then you, the mother, there's your chance and you lay it on him, 'I know why, doctor. It's because I had a hysterical pregnancy.'" Both Luckman and Arctor laughed, and so did Jim Barris; he had returned sometime during the two hours and was with them, working on his funky hash pipe, winding white string.

Again Fred spun the tape forward a full hour.

"—this guy," Luckman was saying, manicuring a box full of grass, hunched over it as Arctor sat across from him, more or less watching, "appeared on TV claiming to be a world-famous impostor. He had posed at one time or another, he told the interviewer, as a great surgeon at Johns Hopkins Medical College, a theoretical

submolecular high-velocity particle-research physicist on a federal
grant at Harvard, as a Finish novelist who'd won the Nobel Prize in
literature, as a deposed president of Argentina married to—"

"And he got away with all that?" Arctor asked. "He never got
caught?"

"The guy never posed as any of those. He never posed as anything
but a world-famous impostor. That came out later in the L. A. *Times*
—they checked up. The guy pushed a broom at Disneyland, or had
until he read this autobiography about this world-famous impostor—
there really was one—and he said, 'Hell, I can pose as all those exotic dudes and get away with it like he did,' and then he decided,
'Hell, why do that; I'll just pose as another impostor.' He made a lot
of bread that way, the *Times* said. Almost as much as the real world-
famous impostor. And he said it was a lot easier."

Barris, off to himself in a corner winding string, said, "we see im-
postors now and then. In our lives. But not posing as subatomic
physicists."

"Narks, you mean," Luckman said. "Yeah, narks. I wonder how
many narks we know. What's a nark look like?"

"It's like asking, What's an impostor look like?" Arctor said. "I
talked one time to a big hash dealer who'd been busted with ten
pounds of hash in his possession. I asked him what the nark who
busted him looked like. You know, the—what do they call them?—
buying agent that came out and posed as a friend of a friend and got
him to sell him some hash."

"Looked," Barris said, winding string, "just like us."

"*More* so," Arctor said. "The hash-dealer dude—he'd already
been sentenced and was going in the following day—he told me,
'They have longer hair than we do.' So I guess the moral of that is,
Stay away from guys looking the same as us."

"There are female narks," Barris said.

"I'd like to meet a nark," Arctor said. "I mean knowingly. Where
I could be positive."

"Well," Barris said, "you could be positive when he claps the cuffs
on you, when that day comes."

Arctor said, "I mean, do narks have friends? What sort of social
life do they have? Do their wives know?"

"Narks don't have wives," Luckman said. "They live in caves and
peep out from under parked cars as you pass. Like trolls."

"What do they eat?" Arctor said.

"People," Barris said.

"How could a guy do that?" Arctor said. "Pose as a nark?"

"*What?*" both Barris and Luckman said together.

"Shit, I'm spaced," Arctor said, grinning. " 'Pose as a nark'—wow." He shook his head, grimacing now.

Staring at him, Luckman said, "POSE AS A NARK? *POSE AS A NARK?*"

"My brains are scrambled today," Arctor said. "I better go crash."

At the holos, Fred cut the tape's forward motion; all the cubes froze, and the sound ceased.

"Taking a break, Fred?" one of the other scramble suits called over to him.

"Yeah," Fred said. "I'm tired. This crap gets to you after a while." He rose and got out his cigarettes. "I can't figure out half what they're saying, I'm so tired. Tired," he added, "of listening to them."

"When you're actually down there with them," a scramble suit said, "it's not so bad; you know? Like I guess you were—on the scene itself up until now, with a cover. Right?"

"I would never hang around with creeps like that," Fred said. "Saying the same things over and over, like old cons. Why do they do what they do, sitting there shooting the bull?"

"Why do we do what we do? This is pretty damn monotonous, when you get down to it."

"But we have to; this is our job. We have no choice."

"Like the cons," a scramble suit pointed out. "We have no choice."

Posing as a nark, Fred thought. What does that mean? Nobody knows . . .

Posing, he reflected, as an impostor. One who lives under parked cars and eats dirt. Not a world-famous surgeon or novelist or politician; nothing that anyone would care to hear about on TV. No life that anyone in their right mind . . .

> I resemble that worm which crawls through dust,
> Lives in the dust, eats dust
> Until a passerby's foot crushes it.

Yes, that expresses it, he thought. That poetry. Luckman must have read it to me, or maybe I read it in school. Funny what the mind pops up. Remembers.

Arctor's freaky words still stuck in his mind, even though he had shut off the tape. I wish I could forget it, he thought. I wish I could, for a while, forget *him*.

"I get the feeling," Fred said, "that sometimes I know what they're going to say before they say it. Their exact words."

"It's called *déjà vu*," one of the scramble suits agreed. "Let me

give you a few pointers. Run the tape ahead over longer break-inter-
vals, not an hour but, say, six hours. Then run it back if there's nothing until you hit something. Back, you see, rather than forward. That
way you don't get into the rhythm of their flow. Six or even eight
ahead, then big jumps back . . . You'll get the hang of it pretty soon,
you'll get so you can sense when you've got miles and miles of nothing or when somewhere you've got something useful."

"And you won't really listen at all," the other scramble suit said,
"until you do actually hit something. Like a mother when she's
asleep—nothing wakes her, even a truck going by, until she hears
her baby cry. That wakes her—that alerts her. No matter how faint
that cry is. The unconscious is selective, when it learns what to listen
for."

"I know," Fred said. "I've got two kids."

"Boys?"

"Girls," he said. "Two little girls."

"That's allll riiight," one of the scramble suits said. "I have one
girl, a year old."

"No names please," the other scramble suit said, and they all
laughed. A little.

Anyhow, there is an item, Fred said to himself, to extract from the
total tape and pass along. That cryptic statement about "posing as a
nark." The other men in the house with Arctor—it surprised them,
too. When I go in tomorrow at three, he thought, I'll take a print of
that—aud alone would do—and discuss it with Hank, along with
what else I obtain between now and then.

But even if that's all I've got to show Hank, he thought, it's a beginning. Shows, he thought, that this around-the-clock scanning of
Arctor is not a waste.

It shows, he thought, that I was right.

That remark was a slip. Arctor blew it.

But what it meant he did not yet know.

But we will, he said to himself, find out. Unpleasant as it is to have to watch and listen to
him and his pals all the time. Those pals of his, he thought, are as
bad as he is. How'd I ever sit around in that house with them all that
time? What a way to live a life; what, as the other officer said just
now, an endless nothing.

Down there, he thought, in the murk, the murk of the mind and
the murk outside as well; murk everywhere. Thanks to what they
are: that kind of individual.

Carrying his cigarette, he walked back to the bathroom, shut and
locked the door, then, from inside the cigarette package, he got out

ten tabs of death. Filling a Dixie cup with water, he dropped all ten tabs. He wished he had brought more tabs with him. Well, he thought, I can drop a few more when I get through work, when I get back home. Looking at his watch, he tried to compute how long that would be. His mind felt fuzzy; how the hell long will it be? he asked himself, wondering what had become of his time sense. Watching the holos has fucked it up, he realized. I can't tell what time it is at all any more.

I feel like I've dropped acid and then gone through a car wash, he thought. Lots of titantic whirling soapy brushes coming at me; dragged along by a chain into tunnels of black foam. What a way to make a living, he thought, and unlocked the bathroom door to go back—reluctantly—to work.

When he turned on the tape-transport once more, Arctor was saying, "—as near as I can figure out, God is dead."

Luckman answered, "I didn't know He was sick."

"Now that my Olds is laid up indefinitely," Arctor said, "I've decided I should sell it and buy a Henway."

"What's a Henway?" Barris said.

To himself Fred said, About three pounds.

"About three pounds," Arctor said.

The following afternoon at three o'clock two medical officers—not the same two—administered several tests to Fred, who was feeling even worse than he had the day before.

"In rapid succession you will see a number of objects with which you should be familiar pass in sequence before—first—your left eye and then your right. At the same time, on the illuminated panel directly before you, outline reproductions will appear simultaneously of several such familiar objects, and you are to match, by means of the punch pencil, what you consider to be the correct outline reproduction of the actual object visible at that instant. Now, these objects will move by you very rapidly, so do not hesitate too long. You will be time-scored as well as scored for accuracy. Okay?"

"Okay," Fred said, punch pencil ready.

A whole flock of familiar objects jogged past him then, and he punched away at the illuminated photos below. This took place for his left eye, and then it all happened again for his right.

"Next, with your left eye covered, a picture of a familiar object will be flashed to your right eye. You are to reach with your left hand, repeat, left hand, into a group of objects and find the one whose picture you saw."

"Okay," Fred said. A picture of a single die was flashed; with his

left hand he groped around among small objects placed before him
until he found a die.

"In the next test, several letters which spell out a word will be
available to your left hand, unseen. You will feel them and then, with
your right hand, write out the word the letters spell."

He did that. They spelled HOT.

"Now name the word spelled."

So he said, "Hot."

"Next, you will reach into this absolutely dark box with both eyes
covered, and with your left hand touch an object in order to identify
it. Then tell us what the object is, without having seen it visually.
After that you will be shown three objects somewhat resembling one
another, and you will tell us which of the three that you see most
resembles the object you manually touched."

"Okay," Fred said, and he did that then, and other tests, for almost an hour. Grope, tell, look at with one eye, select. Grope, tell,
look at with the other eye, select. Write down, draw.

"In this following test you will, with your eyes again covered,
reach out and feel an object with each hand. You are to tell us if the
object presented to your left hand is identical to the object presented
to your right."

He did that.

"Here in rapid succession are pictures of triangles in various posi-
tions. You are to tell us if it is the same triangle or—"

After two hours they had him fit complicated blocks into complicated holes and timed him doing this. He felt as if he was in first
grade again, and screwing up. Doing worse than he had then. Miss
Frinkel, he thought; old Miss Frinkel. She used to stand there and
watch me do this shit back then, flashing me "Die!" messages, like
they say in transactional analysis. Die. Do not be. Witch messages. A
whole bunch of them, until I did finally fuck up. Probably Miss
Frinkel was dead by now. Probably somebody had managed to flash
her a "Die!" message back, and it had caught. He hoped so. Maybe
it had been one of his. As with the psych testers now, he flashed such
messages right back.

It didn't seem to be doing much good now. The test continued.

"What is wrong with this picture? One object among the others
does not belong. You are to mark—"

He did that. And then it was actual objects, one of which did not
belong; he was supposed to reach out and manually remove the
offending object, and then, when the test was over, pick up all the
offending objects from a variety of "sets," as they were called, and

say what characteristic, if any, all the offending objects had in common: if *they* constituted a "set."

He was still trying to do that when they called time and ended the battery of testing and told him to go have a cup of coffee and wait outside until called.

After an interval—which seemed damn long to him—a tester appeared and said, "One more thing, Fred—we want a sample of your blood." He gave him a slip of paper: a lab requisition. "Go down the hall to the room marked 'Pathology Lab' and give them this and then after they have taken a blood sample come back here again and wait."

"Sure," he said glumly, and shuffled off with the requisition.

Traces in the blood, he realized. They're testing for that.

When he had gotten back to Room 203 from the pathology lab he rounded up one of the testers and said, "Would it be all right if I went upstairs to confer with my superior while I'm waiting for your results? He'll be taking off for the day soon."

"Affirmative," the psych tester said. "Since we decided to have a blood sample taken, it will be longer before we can make our evaluation; yes, go ahead. We'll phone upstairs when we're ready for you back here. Hank, is it?"

"Yes," Fred said. "I'll be upstairs with Hank."

The psych tester said, "You certainly seem much more depressed today than you did when we first saw you."

"Pardon?" Fred said.

"The first time you were in. Last week. You were kidding and laughing. Although very tense."

Gazing at him, Fred realized that this was one of the two medical deputies he had originally encountered. But he said nothing; he merely grunted and then left their office, made his way to the elevator. What a downer, he thought. This whole thing. I wonder which of the two medical deputies it is, he wondered. The one with the handle-bar mustache or the other . . . I guess the other. This one has no mustache.

"You will manually feel this object with your left hand," he said to himself, "and at the same time you will look at it with your right. And then in your own words you will tell us—" He could not think out any more nonsense. Not without their help.

When he entered Hank's office he found another man, not in a scramble suit, seated in the far corner, facing Hank.

Hank said, "This is the informant who phoned in about Bob Arctor using the grid—I mentioned him."

"Yes," Fred said, standing there unmoving.

"This man again phoned in, with more information about Bob Arctor; we told him he'd have to step forth and identify himself. We challenged him to appear down here and he did. Do you know him?"

"Sure I do," Fred said, staring at Jim Barris, who sat grinning and fiddling with a pair of scissors. Barris appeared ill at ease and ugly. Super ugly, Fred thought, with revulsion. "You're James Barris, aren't you?" he said. "Have you ever been arrested?"

"His I.D. shows him to be James R. Barris," Hank said, "and that is who he claims to be." He added, "He has no arrest record."

"What does he want?" To Barris, Fred said, "What's your information?"

"I have evidence," Barris said in a low voice, "that Mr. Arctor is part of a large secret covert organization, well funded, with arsenals of weapons at their disposal, using code words, probably dedicated to the overthrow of—"

"That part is speculation," Hank interrupted. "What you suppose it's up to? What's your evidence? Now don't give us anything that is not firsthand."

"Have you ever been sent to a mental hospital?" Fred said to Barris.

"No," Barris said.

"Will you sign a sworn, notarized statement at the D.A.'s office," Fred continued, "regarding your evidence and information? Will you be willing to appear in court *under oath* and—"

"He has already indicated he would," Hank interrupted.

"My evidence," Barris said, "which I mostly don't have with me today, but which I can produce, consists of tape recordings I have made of Robert Arctor's phone conversations. I mean, conversations when he didn't know I was listening."

"What is this organization?" Fred said.

"I believe it to be—" Barris began, but Hank waved him off. "It is political," Barris said, perspiring and trembling a little, but looking pleased, "and against the country. From outside. An enemy against the U.S."

Fred said, "What is Arctor's relationship with the source of Substance D?"

Blinking, then licking his lip and grimacing, Barris said, "It is in my—" He broke off. "When you examine all my information you will—that is, my evidence—you will undoubtedly conclude that Substance D is produced by a foreign nation determined to overthrow the U.S. and that Mr. Arctor has his hands deep within the machinery of this—"

"Can you tell us specific names of anyone else in this organization?" Hank said. "Persons Arctor has met with? You understand that giving false information to the legal authorities is a crime and if you do so you can and probably will be cited."

"I understand that," Barris said.

"Who has Arctor conferred with?" Hank said.

"A Miss Donna Hawthorne," Barris said. "On various pretexts he goes over to her place and colludes with her regularly."

Fred laughed. *"Colludes.* What do you mean?"

"I have followed him," Barris said, speaking slowly and distinctly, "in my own car. Without his knowledge."

"He goes there often?" Hank said.

"Yes, sir," Barris said. "Very often. As often as—"

"She's his girl," Fred said.

Barris said, "Mr. Arctor also—"

Turning to Fred, Hank said, "You think there's any substance in this?"

"We should definitely look at his evidence," Fred said.

"Bring in your evidence," Hank instructed Barris. "All of it. Names we want most of all—names, license-plate numbers, phone numbers. Have you ever seen Arctor deeply involved in large amounts of drugs? More than a user's?"

"Certainly," Barris said.

"What types?"

"Several kinds. I have samples. I carefully took samples . . . for you to analyze. I can bring them in too. Quite a bit, and varied."

Hank and Fred glanced at each other.

Barris, sightlessly gazing straight ahead, smiled.

"Is there anything else you want to say at this time?" Hank said to Barris. To Fred he said, "Maybe we should send an officer with him to get his evidence." Meaning, To make sure he doesn't panic and split, doesn't try to change his mind and pull out.

"There is one thing I would like to say," Barris said. "Mr. Arctor is an addict, addicted to Substance D, and his mind is deranged now. It has slowly become deranged over a period of time, and he is dangerous."

"Dangerous," Fred echoed.

"Yes," Barris declared. "He is already having episodes such as occur with brain damage from Substance D. The optic chiasm must be deteriorated, since a weak ipsilateral component . . . But also—" Barris cleared his throat. "Deterioration, as well, in the corpus callosum."

"This kind of unsupported speculation," Hank said, "as I already informed you, warned you, is worthless. Anyhow, we will send an officer with you to get your evidence. All right?"

Grinning, Barris nodded. "But naturally—"

"We'll arrange for an officer out of uniform."

"I might—" Barris gestured. "Be murdered. Mr. Arctor, as I say—"

Hank nodded. "All right, Mr. Barris, we appreciate this, and your extreme risk, and if it works out, if your information is of significant value in obtaining a conviction in court, then naturally—"

"I'm not here for that reason," Barris said. "The man is sick. Brain-damaged. From Substance D. The reason I am here—"

"We don't care why you're here," Hank said. "We only care whether your evidence and material amount to anything. The rest is your problem."

"Thank you, sir," Barris said, and grinned and grinned.

CHAPTER THIRTEEN

Back at Room 203, the police psychology testing lab, Fred listened without interest as his test results were explained to him by both the psychologists.

"You show what we regard more as a competition phenomenon than impairment. Sit down."

"Okay," Fred said stoically, sitting down.

"Competition," the other psychologist said, "between the left and right hemispheres of your brain. It's not so much a single signal, defective or contaminated; it's more like two signals that interfere with each other by carrying conflicting information."

"Normally," the other psychologist explained, "a person uses the left hemisphere. The self-system or ego, or consciousness, is located there. It is dominant, because it's in the left hemisphere always that the speech center is located; more precisely, bilateralization involves a verbal ability or valency in the left, with spatial abilities in the right. The left can be compared to a digital computer; the right to an analogic. So bilateral function is not mere duplication; both percept systems monitor and process incoming data differently. But for you, neither hemisphere is dominant and they do *not* act in a compensatory fashion, each to the other. One tells you one thing, the other another."

"It's as if you have two fuel gauges on your car," the other man said, "and one says your tank is full and the other registers empty. They can't both be right. They conflict. But it's—in your case—not one functioning and one malfunctioning; it's . . . Here's what I mean. Both gauges study exactly the same amount of fuel: the same fuel, the same tank. Actually they test the same thing. You as the driver have only an indirect relationship to the fuel tank, via the gauge or, in your case, gauges. In fact, the tank could fall off entirely and you wouldn't know until some dashboard indicator told you or finally the engine stopped. There should never be two gauges reporting conflicting information, because as soon as that happens you have no knowledge of the condition being reported on *at all*. This is not the same as a gauge and a backup gauge, where the backup one cuts in when the regular one fouls up."

Fred said, "So what does this mean?"

"I'm sure you know already," the psychologist to the left said. "You've been experiencing it, without knowing why or what it is."

"The two hemispheres of my brain are competing?" Fred said.

"Yes."

"Why?"

"Substance D. It often causes that, functionally. This is what we expected; this is what the tests confirm. Damage having taken place in the normally dominant left hemisphere, the right hemisphere is attempting to compensate for the impairment. But the twin functions do not fuse, because this is an abnormal condition the body isn't prepared for. It should never happen. *Cross-cuing,* we call it. Related to split-brain phenomena. We could perform a right hemispherectomy, but—"

"Will this go away," Fred interrupted, "when I get off Substance D?"

"Probably," the psychologist on the left said, nodding. "It's a functional impairment."

The other man said, "It may be organic damage. It may be permanent. Time'll tell, and only after you are off Substance D for a long while. And off entirely."

"What?" Fred said. He did not understand the answer—was it yes or no? Was he damaged forever or not? Which had they said?

"Even if it's brain-tissue damage," one of the psychologists said, "there are experiments going on now in the removal of small sections from each hemisphere, to abort competing gestalt-processing. They believe eventually this may cause the original hemisphere to regain dominance."

"However, the problem there is that then the individual may only receive *partial* impressions—incoming sense data—for the rest of his life. Instead of two signals, he gets half a signal. Which is equally impairing, in my opinion."

"Yes, but partial noncompeting function is better than no function, since twin competing cross-cuing amounts to zero recept form."

"You see, Fred," the other man said, "you no longer have—"

"I will never drop any Substance D again," Fred said. "For the rest of my life."

"How much are you dropping now?"

"Not much." After an interval he said, "More, recently. Because of job stress."

"They undoubtedly should relieve you of your assignments," one psychologist said. "Take you off everything. You *are* impaired, Fred. And will be a while longer. At the very least. After that, no one can be sure. You may make a full comeback; you may not."

"How come," Fred grated, "that even if both hemispheres of my brain are dominant they don't receive the same stimuli? Why can't their two whatevers be synchronized, like stereo sound is?"

Silence.

"I mean," he said, gesturing, "the left hand and the right hand when they grip an object, the same object, should—"

"Left-handedness versus right-handedness, as for example what is meant by those terms with, say, a mirror image—in which the left hand 'becomes' the right hand . . ." The psychologist leaned down over Fred, who did not look up. "How would you define a left-hand glove compared to a right-hand glove so a person who had no knowledge of those terms could tell you which you meant? And not get the other? The mirror opposite?"

"A left-hand glove . . ." Fred said, and then stopped.

"It is as if one hemisphere of your brain is perceiving the world as reflected in a mirror. Through a mirror. See? So left becomes right, and all that that implies. And we don't know yet what that does imply, to see the world reversed like that. Topologically speaking, a lefthand glove is a right-hand glove *pulled through infinity*."

"Through a mirror," Fred said. A darkened mirror, he thought; a darkened scanner. And St. Paul meant, by a mirror, not a glass mirror—they didn't have those then—but a reflection of himself when he looked at the polished bottom of a metal pan. Luckman, in his theological readings, had told him that. Not through a telescope or lens system, which does not reverse, not through anything but seeing his own face reflected back up at him, reversed—pulled through infinity. Like they're telling me. It is not *through* a glass but as reflected *back* by a glass. And that reflection that returns to you: it is you, it is your face, but it isn't. And they didn't have cameras in those old days, and so that's the only way a person saw himself: backward.

I have seen myself backward.

I have in a sense begun to see the entire universe backward. With the other side of my brain!

"Topology," one psychologist was saying. "A little-understood science or math, whichever. As with the black holes in space, how—"

"Fred is seeing the world from inside out," the other man was declaring at the same moment. "From in front and from behind both, I guess. It's hard for us to say how it appears to him. Topology is the branch of math that investigates the properties of a geometric or other configuration that are unaltered if the thing is subjected to a one-to-one, *any* one-to-one, continuous transformation. But applied to psychology . . ."

"And when that occurs to objects, who knows what they're going to look like then? They'd be unrecognizable. As when a primitive sees a photograph of himself the first time, he doesn't recognize it as himself. Even though he's seen his reflection many times, in streams, from metal objects. Because his reflection is reversed and the photograph of himself isn't. So he doesn't know it's the identical person."

"He's accustomed only to the reversed reflected image and thinks he looks like that."

"Often a person hearing his own voice played back—"

"That's different. That has to do with the resonance in the sinus—"

"Maybe it's you fuckers," Fred said, "who're seeing the universe backward, like in a mirror. Maybe I see it right."

"You see it *both ways.*"

"Which is the—"

A psychologist said, "They used to talk about seeing only 'reflections' of reality. Not reality itself. The main thing wrong with a reflection is not that it isn't real, *but that it's reversed.* I wonder." He had an odd expression. "Parity. The scientific principle of parity. Universe and reflected image, the latter we take for the former, for some reason . . . because we lack bilateral parity."

"Whereas a photograph can compensate for the lack of bilateral hemispheric parity; it's not the object but it's not reversed, so that objection would make photographic images not images at all but the true form. Reverse of a reverse."

"But a photo can get accidentally reversed, too, if the negative is flipped—printed backward; you usually can tell only if there's writing. But not with a man's face. You could have two contact prints of a given man, one reversed, one not. A person who'd never met him couldn't tell which was correct, but he could see they were different and couldn't be superimposed."

"There, Fred, does that show you how complex the problem of formulating the distinction between a left-hand glove and—"

"Then shall it come to pass the saying that is written," a voice said. "Death is swallowed up. In victory." Perhaps only Fred heard it. "Because," the voice said, "as soon as the writing appears backward, then you know which is illusion and which is not. The confusion ends, and death, the last enemy, Substance Death, is swallowed not down into the body but up—in victory. Behold, I tell you the sacred secret now: *we shall not all sleep in death.*"

The mystery, he thought, the explanation, he means. Of a secret. A sacred secret. We shall not die.

    The reflections shall leave

      And it will happen fast.

We shall all be changed, and by that he means reversed back, suddenly. In the

      twinkling of an eye!

Because, he thought glumly as he watched the police psychologists writing out their conclusions and signing them, we are fucking backward right now, I guess, every one of us; everyone and every damn thing, and distance, and even time. But how long, he thought, when a print is being made, a contact print, when the photographer discovers he's got the negative reversed, how long does it take to flip it? To reverse it again so it's like it's supposed to be?

A fraction of a second.

I understand, he thought, what that passage in the Bible means, Through a glass darkly. But my percept system is as fucked up as ever. Like they say. I understand but am helpless to help myself.

Maybe, he thought, since I see both ways at once, correctly and reversed, I'm the first person in human history to have it flipped and not-flipped simultaneously, and so get a glimpse of what it'll be when it's right. Although I've got the other as well, the regular. And which is which?

Which is reversed and which is not?

When do I see a photograph, when a reflection?

And how much allotment for sick pay or retirement or disability do I get while I dry out? he asked himself, feeling horror already, deep dread and coldness everywhere. *Wie kalt ist es in diesem unterirdischen Gewölbe! Das ist natürlich, es ist ja tief.* And I have to withdraw from the shit. I've seen people go through that. Jesus Christ, he thought, and shut his eyes.

"This may sound like metaphysics," one of them was saying, "but the math people say we may be on the verge of a new cosmology so much—"

The other said excitedly, "The infinity of time, which is expressed as eternity, as a loop! Like a loop of cassette tape!"

He had an hour to kill before he was supposed to be back in Hank's office, to listen to and inspect Jim Barris's evidence.

The building's cafeteria attracted him, so he walked that way, among those in uniform and those in scramble suits and those in slacks and ties.

Meanwhile, the psychologists' findings presumably were being taken up to Hank. They would be there when he arrived.

This will give me time to think, he reflected as he wandered into the cafeteria and lined up. Time. Suppose, he thought, time is round, like the Earth. You sail west to reach India. They laugh at you, but finally there's India in front, not behind. In time—maybe the Crucifixion lies ahead of us as we all sail along, thinking it's back east.

Ahead of him a secretary. Tight blue sweater, no bra, almost no skirt. It felt nice, checking her out; he gazed on and on, and finally she noticed him and edged off with her tray.

The First and Second Coming of Christ the same event, he thought; time a cassette loop. No wonder they were sure it'd happen, He'd be back.

He watched the secretary's behind, but then he realized that she could not possibly be noticing him back as he noticed her because in his suit he had no face and no ass. But she senses my scheming on her, he decided. Any chick with legs like that would sense it a lot, from every man.

You know, he thought, in this scramble suit I could hit her over the head and bang her forever and who'd know who did it? How could she identify me?

The crimes one could commit in these suits, he pondered. Also lesser trips, short of actual crimes, which you never did; always wanted to but never did.

"Miss," he said to the girl in the tight blue sweater, "you certainly have nice legs. But I suppose you recognize that or you wouldn't be wearing a microskirt like that."

The girl gasped. "Eh," she said. "Oh, now I know who you are."

"You do?" he said, surprised.

"Pete Wickam," the girl said.

"What?" he said.

"Aren't you Pete Wickam? You always are sitting across from me —aren't you, Pete?"

"Am I the guy," he said, "who's always sitting there and studying your legs and scheming a lot about you know what?"

She nodded.

"Do I have a chance?" he said.

"Well, it depends."

"Can I take you out to dinner some night?"

"I guess so."

"Can I have your phone number? So I can call you?"

The girl murmured, "You give me yours."

"I'll give it to you," he said, "if you'll sit with me right now, here, and have whatever you're having with me while I'm having my sandwich and coffee."

"No, I've got a girl friend over there—she's waiting."

"I could sit with you anyhow, both of you."

"We're going to discuss something private."

"Okay," he said.

"Well, then I'll see you, Pete." She moved off down the line with her tray and flatware and napkin.

He obtained his coffee and sandwich and found an empty table and sat by himself, dropping little bits of sandwich into the coffee and staring down at it.

They're fucking going to pull me off Arctor, he decided. I'll be in Synanon or New-Path or some place like that withdrawing and they'll station someone else to watch him and evaluate him. Some asshole who doesn't know jack shit about Arctor—they'll have to start all over from the beginning.

At least they can let me evaluate Barris's evidence, he thought. Not put me on temsuspens until after we go over that stuff, whatever it is.

If I did bang her and she got pregnant, he ruminated, the babies— no faces. Just blurs. He shivered.

I know I've got to be taken off. But why necessarily right away? If I could do a few more things . . . process Barris's info, participate in the decision. Or even just sit there and see what he's got. Find out for my own satisfaction finally what Arctor is up to. Is he anything? Is he not? They owe it to me to allow me to stay on long enough to find that out.

If I could just listen and watch, not say anything.

He sat there on and on, and later he noticed the girl in the tight blue sweater and her girl friend, who had short black hair, get up from their table and start to leave. The girl friend, who wasn't too foxy, hesitated and then approached Fred where he sat hunched over his coffee and sandwich fragments.

"Pete?" the short-haired girl said.

He glanced up.

"Um, Pete," she said nervously. "I just have a sec. Um, Ellen wanted to tell you this, but she chickened out. Pete, she would have gone out with you a long time ago, like maybe a month ago, like back in March even. If—"

"If what?" he said.

"Well, she wanted me to tell you that for some time she's wanted to clue you into the fact that you'd do a whole lot better if you used like, say, Scope."

"I wish I had known," he said, without enthusiasm.

"Okay, Pete," the girl said, relieved now and departing. "Catch you later." She hurried off, grinning.

Poor fucking Pete, he thought to himself. Was that for real? Or just a mind-blowing put-down of Pete by a pair of malice-head types who cooked it up seeing him—me—sitting here alone. Just a nasty little dig to— Aw, the hell with it, he thought.

Or it could be true, he decided as he wiped his mouth, crumpled up his napkin, and got heavily to his feet. I wonder if St. Paul had bad breath. He wandered from the cafeteria, his hands again shoved down in his pockets. Scramble suit pockets first and then inside that real suit pockets. Maybe that's why Paul was always in jail the latter part of his life. They threw him in for that.

Mindfucking trips like this always get laid on you at a time like this, he thought as he left the cafeteria. She dumped that on me on top of all the other bummers today—the big one out of the composite wisdom of the ages of psychological-testing pontification. That and then this. Shit, he thought. He felt even worse now than he had before; he could hardly walk, hardly think; his mind buzzed with confusion. Confusion and despair. Anyhow, he thought, Scope isn't any good; Lavoris is better. Except when you spit it out it looks like you're spitting blood. Maybe Micrin, he thought. That might be best.

If there was a drugstore in this building, he thought, I could get a bottle and use it before I go upstairs to face Hank. That way— maybe I'd feel more confident. Maybe I'd have a better chance.

I could use, he reflected, anything that'd help, anything at all. Any hint, like from that girl, any suggestion. He felt dismal and afraid. *Shit,* he thought, *what am I going to do?*

If I'm off everything, he thought, then I'll never see any of them again, any of my friends, the people I watched and knew. I'll be out of it; I'll be maybe retired the rest of my life—anyhow, I've seen the last of Arctor and Luckman and Jerry Fabin and Charles Freck and most of all Donna Hawthorne. I'll never see any of my friends again, for the rest of eternity. It's over.

Donna. He remembered a song his great-uncle used to sing years ago, in German. *"Ich seh', wie ein Engel im rosigen Duft / Sich tröstend zur Seite mir stellet,"* which his great-uncle had explained to him meant "I see, dressed like an angel, standing by my side to give me comfort," the woman he loved, the woman who saved him (in the song). In the song, not in real life. His great-uncle was dead, and it was a long time ago he'd heard those words. His great-uncle, German-born, singing in the house, or reading aloud.

>*Gott! Welch Dunkel hier! O grauenvolle Stille!*
>*Od' ist es um mich her. Nichts lebet auszer mir . . .*

>God, how dark it is here, and totally silent.
>Nothing but me lives in this vacuum . . .

Even if my brain's not burned out, he realized, by the time I'm back on duty somebody else will have been assigned to them. Or they'll be dead or in the bucket or in federal clinics or just scattered, scattered, scattered. Burned out and destroyed, like me, unable to figure out what the fuck is happening. It has reached an end in any case, anyhow, for me. I've without knowing it already said good-by.

All I could ever do sometime, he thought, is play the holo-tapes back, to remember.

"I ought to go to the safe apartment . . ." He glanced around and became silent. I ought to go to the safe apartment and rip them off now, he thought. While I can. Later they might be erased, and later I would not have access. Fuck the department, he thought; they can bill me against my back salary. By every ethical consideration those tapes of that house and the people in it belong to me.

And now those tapes, they're all I've got left out of all this; that's all I can hope to carry away.

But also, he thought rapidly, to play the tapes back I need the entire holo transport cube-projection resolution system there in the safe apartment. I'll need to disassemble it and cart it out of there piece by piece. The scanners and recording assemblies I won't need: just transport, playback components, and especially all the cube-projection gear. I can do it bit by bit; I have a key to that apartment. They'll require me to turn in the key, but I can get a dupe made right here before I turn it in; it's a conventional Schlag lock key. Then I can do it! He felt better, realizing this; he felt grim and moral and a little angry. At everyone. Pleasure at how he would make matters okay.

On the other hand, he thought, if I ripped off the scanners and recording heads and like that, I could go on monitoring. On my own. Keep surveillance alive, as I've been doing. For a while at least. But I mean, everything in life is just for a while—as witness this.

The surveillance, he thought, essentially should be maintained. And, if possible, by me. I should always be watching, watching and figuring out, even if I never do anything about what I see; even if I just sit there and observe silently, not seen: that is important, that I as a watcher of all that happens should be at my place.

Not for their sake. For mine.

Yeah, he amended, for theirs too. In case something happens, like when Luckman choked. If someone is watching—if I am watching—I can notice and get help. Phone for help. Bring assistance to them right away, the right kind.

Otherwise, he thought, they could die and no one would be the wiser. Know or even fucking care.

In wretched little lives like that, someone must intervene. Or at least mark their sad comings and goings. Mark and if possible permanently record, so they'll be remembered. For a better day, later on, when people will understand.

In Hank's office he sat with Hank and a uniformed officer and the sweating, grinning informant Jim Barris, while one of Barris's cassette tapes played on the table in front of them. Beside it, a second cassette recorded what it was playing, for a department duplicate.

". . . Oh, hi. Look, I can't talk."

"When, then?"

"Call you back."

"This can't wait."

"Well, what is it?"

"We intend to—"

Hank reached out, signaling to Barris to halt the tape. "Would you identify the voices for us, Mr. Barris?" Hank said.

"Yes," Barris eagerly agreed. "The female's voice is Donna Hawthorne, the male's is Robert Arctor."

"All right," Hank said nodding, then glancing at Fred. He had Fred's medical report before him and was glancing at it. "Go ahead with your tape."

". . . half of Southern California tomorrow night," the male's voice, identified by the informant as Bob Arctor's, continued. "The Air Force Arsenal at Vandenberg AFB will be hit for automatic and semiautomatic weapons—"

Hank stopped reading the medical report and listened, cocking his scramble-suit-blurred head.

To himself and now to all in the room, Barris grinned; his fingers fiddled with paper clips taken from the table, fiddled and fiddled, as if knitting with metal webs of wire, knitting and fiddling and sweating and knitting.

The female, identified as Donna Hawthorne, said, "What about that disorientation drug the bikers ripped off for us? When do we carry that crud up to the watershed·area to—"

"The organization needs the weapons first," the male's voice explained. "That's step B."

"Okay, but now I gotta go; I got a customer."

Click. Click.

Barris aloud, shifting in his chair, said, "I can identify the biker gang mentioned. It is mentioned on another—"

"You have more material of this sort?" Hank said. "To build up background? Or is this tape substantially it?"

"Much more."

"But it's this same sort of thing."

"It refers, yes, to the same conspiratorial organization and its plans, yes. This particular plot."

"Who are these people?" Hank said. "What organization?"

"They are a world-wide—"

"Their names. You're speculating."

"Robert Arctor, Donna Hawthorne, primarily. I have coded notes here, too . . ." Barris fumbled with a grubby notebook, half dropping it as he tried to open it.

Hank said, "I'm impounding all this stuff here, Mr. Barris, tapes and what you've got. Temporarily they're our property. We'll go over them ourselves."

"My handwriting, and the enciphered material which I—"

"You'll be on hand to explain it to us when we get to that point or feel we want anything explained." Hank signaled the uniformed cop, not Barris, to shut off the cassette. Barris reached toward it. At once the cop stopped him and pushed him back. Barris, blinking, gazed around, still fixedly smiling. "Mr. Barris," Hank said, "you will not be released, pending our study of this material. You're being charged, as a formality to keep you available, with giving false information to the authorities knowingly. This is, of course, only a pretext for your own safety, and we all realize that, but the formal charge will be lodged anyhow. It will be passed on to the D.A. but marked for hold. Is that satisfactory?" He did not wait for an answer; instead, he signaled the uniformed cop to take Barris out, leaving the evidence and shit and what-not on the table.

The cop led grinning Barris out. Hank and Fred sat facing each other across the littered table. Hank said nothing; he was reading the psychologists' findings.

After an interval he picked up his phone and dialed an in-building number. "I've got some unevaluated material here—I want you to go over it and determine how much of it is fake. Let me know about that, and then I'll tell you what to do with it next. It's about twelve pounds; you'll need one cardboard box, size three. Okay, thanks." He hung up. "The electronics and crypto lab," he informed Fred, and resumed reading.

Two heavily armed uniformed lab technicians appeared, bringing with them a lock-type steel container.

"We could only find this," one of them apologized as they carefully filled it with the items on the table.

"Who's down there?"

"Hurley."

"Have Hurley go over this sometime today for sure, and report when he's got a spurious index-factor for me. It must be today; tell him that."

The lab technicians locked the metal box and lugged it out of the office.

Tossing the medical-findings report on the table, Hank leaned back and said, "What do you— Okay, what's your response to Barris's evidence so far?"

Fred said, "That is my medical report you have there, isn't it?" He reached to pick it up, then changed his mind. "I think what he played, the little he played, it sounded genuine to me."

"It's a fake," Hank said. "Worthless."

"You may be right," Fred said, "but I don't agree."

"The arsenal they're talking about at Vandenberg is probably the OSI Arsenal." Hank reached for the phone. To himself, aloud, he said, "Let's see—who's the guy at OSI I talked to that time . . . he was in on Wednesday with some pictures . . ." Hank shook his head and turned away from the phone to confront Fred. "I'll wait. It can wait for the prelim spurious report. Fred?"

"What does my medical—"

"They say you're completely cuckoo."

Fred (as best he could) shrugged. "Completely?"

Wie kalt ist es in diesem unterirdischen Gewölbe!

"Possibly two brain cells still light up. But that's about all. Mostly short circuits and sparks."

Das ist natürlich, es ist ja tief.

"Two, you say," Fred said. "Out of how many?"

"I don't know. Brains have a lot of cells, I understand—trillions."

"More possible connections between them," Fred said, "than there are stars in the universe."

"If that's so, then you're not batting too good an average right now. About two cells out of—maybe sixty-five trillion?"

"More like sixty-five trillion trillion," Fred said.

"That's worse than the old Philadelphia Phillies under Connie Mack. They used to end the season with a percentage—"

"What do I get," Fred said, "for saying it happened on duty?"

"You get to sit in a waiting room and read a lot of *Saturday Evening Posts* and *Cosmopolitans* free."

"Where's that?"

"Where would you like?"

Fred said, "Let me think it over."

"I'll tell you what I'd do," Hank said. "I wouldn't go into a Federal clinic; I'd get about six bottles of good bourbon, I. W. Harper, and go up into the hills, up into the San Bernadino Mountains near one of the lakes, by myself, and just stay there all alone until it's over. Where no one can find me."

"But it may never be over," Fred said.

"Then never come back. Do you know anyone who has a cabin up there?"

"No," Fred said.

"Can you drive okay?"

"My—" He hesitated, and a dreamlike strength fell over him, relaxing him and mellowing him out. All the spatial relationships in the room shifted; the alteration affected even his awareness of time. "It's in the . . ." He yawned.

"You don't remember."

"I remember it's not functioning."

"We can have somebody drive you up. That would be safer, anyhow."

Drive me up where? he wondered. Up to what? Up roads, trails, paths, hiking and striding through Jell-O, like a tomcat on a leash who only wants to get back indoors, or get free.

He thought, *Ein Engel, der Gattin, so gleich, der führt mich zur Freiheit ins himmlische Reich.* "Sure," he said, and smiled. Relief. Pulling forward against the leash, trying and striving to get free, and then to lie down. "What do you think about me now," he said, "now that I've proved out like this—burned out, temporarily, anyhow. Maybe permanently."

Hank said, "I think you're a very good person."

"Thank you," Fred said.

"Take your gun with you."

"*What?*" he said.

"When you go off to the San Bernadino Mountains with the fifths of I. W. Harper. Take your gun."

"You mean for if I don't come out of it?"

Hank said, "Either way. Coming down off the amount they say you're on . . . Have it there with you."

"Okay."

"When you get back," Hank said, "call me. Let me know."

"Hell, I won't have my suit."

"Call me anyhow. With or without your suit."

Again he said, "Okay." Evidently it didn't matter. Evidently that was over.

"When you go pick up your next payment, there'll be a different amount. A considerable change this one time."

Fred said, "I get some sort of bonus for this, for what happened to me?"

"No. Read your penal code. An officer who willingly becomes an addict and does not promptly report it is subject on a misdemeanor charge—a fine of three thousand dollars and/or six months. You'll probably just be fined."

"*Willingly?*" he said, marveling.

"Noboby held a gun to your head and shot you up. Nobody dropped something in your soup. You knowingly and willingly took an addictive drug, brain-destructive and disorienting."

"I had to!"

Hank said, "You could have pretended to. Most officers manage to cope with it. And from the quantity they say you were dropping, you had to have been—"

"You're treating me like a crook. I am not a crook."

Picking up a clipboard and pen, Hank began to figure. "How much are you at, paywise? I can calculate it now if—"

"Could I pay the fine later on? Maybe in a series of monthly installments over like two years?"

Hank said, "Come on, Fred."

"Okay," he said.

"How much per hour?"

He couldn't remember.

"Well, then, how many logged hours?"

That, neither.

Hank tossed his clipboard back down. "Want a cigarette?" He offered Fred his pack.

"I'm getting off that, too," Fred said. "Everything. Including peanuts and . . ." He couldn't think. They both sat there, the two of them, in their scramble suits, both silent.

"Like I tell my kids," Hank began.

"I've got two kids," Fred said. "Two girls."

"I don't believe you do; you're not supposed to."

"Maybe not." He had begun to try to figure out when withdrawal would begin, and then he began to try to figure how many tabs of Substance D he had hidden here and there. And how much money he would have, when he got paid, for scoring.

"Maybe you want me to continue figuring what your payoff amount will consist of," Hank said.

"Okay," he said, and nodded vigorously. "Do that." He sat waiting, tensely, drumming on the table, like Barris.

"How much per hour?" Hank repeated, and then presently reached for his phone. "I'll call payroll."

Fred said nothing. Staring down, he waited. He thought, Maybe Donna can help me. Donna, he thought, please help me now.

"I don't think you're going to make it to the mountains," Hank said. "Even if somebody drives you."

"No."

"Where do you want to go?"

"Let me sit and think."

"Federal clinic?"

"No."

They sat.

He wondered what *not supposed to* meant.

"What about over to Donna Hawthorne's?" Hank said. "From all the information you've brought in and everyone else has, I know you're close."

"Yes." He nodded. "We are." And then he looked up and said, "How do you know that?"

Hank said, "By a process of elimination. I know who you *aren't*, and there aren't an infinite number of suspects in this group—in fact, they're a very small group. We thought they'd lead us up higher, and maybe Barris will. You and I have spent a lot of time rapping together. I pieced it together a long time ago. That you're Arctor."

"I'm *who*?" he said, staring at Hank the scramble suit facing him. "I'm Bob Arctor?" He could not believe it. It made no sense to him. It did not fit anything he had done or thought; it was grotesque.

"Never mind," Hank said. "What's Donna's phone number?"

"She's probably at work." His voice trembled. "The perfume store. The number is—" He couldn't keep his voice steady, and he couldn't remember the number. The hell I am, he said to himself. I'm not Bob Arctor. But who am I? Maybe I'm—

"Get me Donna Hawthorne's number at work," Hank was saying rapidly into the phone. "Here," he said, holding the phone toward Fred. "I'll put you on the line. No, maybe I better not. I'll tell her to pick you up—where? We'll drive you there and drop you off; can't meet her here. What's a good place? Where do you usually meet her?"

"Take me to her place," he said. "I know how to get in."

"I'll tell her you're there and that you're withdrawing. I'll just say I know you and you asked me to call."

"Far out," Fred said. "I can dig it. Thanks, man."

Hank nodded and began to redial, an outside number. It seemed to Fred that he dialed each digit more and more slowly and it went on forever, and he shut his eyes, breathing to himself and thinking, Wow. I'm really out of it.

You really are, he agreed. Spaced, wired, burned out and strung-out and fucked. Completely fucked. He felt like laughing.

"We'll get you over there to her—" Hank began, and then shifted his attention to the phone, saying, "Hey, Donna, this is a buddy of Bob's, you know? Hey, man, he's in a bad way, I'm not jiving you. Hey, he—"

I can dig it, two voices thought inside his mind in unison as he heard his buddy laying it on Donna. And don't forget to tell her to bring me something; I'm really hurting. Can she score for me or something? Maybe supercharge me, like she does? He reached out to touch Hank but could not; his hand fell short.

"I'll do the same for you sometime," he promised Hank as Hank hung up.

"Just sit there until the car's outside. I'll put through the call now." Again Hank phoned, this time saying, "Motor pool? I want an unmarked car and officer out of uniform. What do you have available?"

They, inside the scramble suit, the nebulous blur, shut their eyes to wait.

"It might be I should get you taken to the hospital," Hank said. "You're very bad off; maybe Jim Barris poisoned you. We really are interested in Barris, not you; the scanning of the house was primarily to keep on Barris. We hoped to draw him in here . . . and we did." Hank was silent. "So that's why I knew pretty well that his tapes and the other items were faked. The lab will confirm. But Barris is into something heavy. Heavy and sick, and it has to do with guns."

"I'm a what, then?" he said suddenly, very loud.

"We had to get to Jim Barris and set him up."

"You fuckers," he said.

"The way we arranged it, Barris—if that's who he is—got progressively more and more suspicious that you were an undercover police agent, about to nail him or use him to get higher. So he—"

The phone rang.

"All right," Hank said later. "Just sit, Bob. Bob, Fred, whatever.

Take comfort—we did get the bugger and he's a—well, what you just now called us. You know it's worth it. Isn't it? To entrap him? A thing like that, whatever it is he's doing?"

"Sure, worth it." He could hardly speak; he grated mechanically.

Together they sat.

On the drive to New-Path, Donna pulled off the road where they could see the lights below, on all sides. But the pain had started for him now; she could see 'that, and there wasn't much time left. She had wanted to be with him one more time. Well, she had waited too long. Tears ran down his cheeks, and he had started to heave and vomit.

"We'll sit for a few minutes," she told him, guiding him through the bushes and weeds, across the sandy soil, among the discarded beer cans and debris. "I—"

"Do you have your hash pipe?" he managed to say.

"Yes," she said. They had to be far enough from the road not to be noticed by the police. Or at least far enough so they could ditch the hash pipe if an officer came along. She would see the police car park, its lights off, covertly, a way off, and the officer approach on foot. There would be time.

She thought, Time enough for that. Time enough to be safe from the law. But no time any more for Bob Arctor. His time—at least if measured in human standards—had run out. It was another kind of time which he had entered now. Like, she thought, the time a rat has: to run back and forth, to be futile. To move without planning, back and forth, back and forth. But at least he can still see the lights below us. Although maybe for him it doesn't matter.

They found a sheltered place, and she got out the foil-wrapped fragment of hash and lit the hash pipe. Bob Arctor, beside her, did not seem to notice. He had dirtied himself, but she knew he could not help it. In fact, he probably didn't even know it. They all got this way during withdrawal.

"Here." She bent toward him, to supercharge him. But he did not notice her either. He just sat doubled up, enduring the stomach cramps, vomiting and soiling himself, shivering, and crazily moaning to himself, a kind of song.

She thought then of a guy she had known once, who had seen God. He had acted much like this, moaning and crying, although he had not soiled himself. He had seen God in a flashback after an acid trip; he had been experimenting with water-soluble vitamins, huge doses of them. The orthomolecular formula that was supposed to improve neural firing in the brain, speed it up and synchronize it. With that guy, though, instead of merely becoming smarter, he had seen God. It had been a complete surprise to him.

"I guess," she said, "we never know what's in store for us."

Beside her, Bob Arctor moaned and did not answer.

"Did you know a dude named Tony Amsterdam?"

There was no response.

Donna inhaled from the hash pipe and contemplated the lights spread out below them; she smelled the air and listened. "After he saw God he felt really good, for around a year. And then he felt really bad. Worse than he ever had before in his life. Because one day it came over him, he began to realize, that he was never going to see God again; he was going to live out his whole remaining life, decades, maybe fifty years, and see nothing but what he had always seen. What we see. He was worse off than if he hadn't seen God. He told me one day he got really mad; he just freaked out and started cursing and smashing things in his apartment. He even smashed his stereo. He realized he was going to have to live on and on like he was, seeing nothing. Without any purpose. Just a lump of flesh grinding along, eating, drinking, sleeping, working, crapping."

"Like the rest of us." It was the first thing Bob Arctor had managed to say; each word came with retching difficulty.

Donna said, "That's what I told him. I pointed that out. We were all in the same boat and it didn't freak the rest of us. And he said, 'You don't know what I saw. You don't know.'"

A spasm passed through Bob Arctor, convulsing him, and then he choked out, "Did . . . he say what it was like?"

"Sparks. Showers of colored sparks, like when something goes wrong with your TV set. Sparks going up the wall, sparks in the air. And the whole world was a living creature, wherever he looked. And there were no accidents: everything fitted together and happened on purpose, to achieve something—some goal in the future. And then he saw a doorway. For about a week he saw it wherever he looked—inside his apartment, outdoors when he was walking to the store or driving. And it was always the same proportions, very narrow. He said it was very—pleasing. That's the word he used. He never tried to go through it; he just looked at it, because it was so pleasing. Outlined in vivid red and gold light, he said. As if the sparks had collected into lines, like in geometry. And then after that he never saw it again his whole life, and that's what finally made him so fucked up."

After a time Bob Arctor said, "What was on the other side?"

Donna said, "He said there was another world on the other side. He could see it."

"He . . . never went through it?"

"That's why he kicked the shit out of everything in his apartment; he never thought of going through it, he just admired the doorway and then later he couldn't see it at all and it was too late. It opened for him a few days and then it was closed and gone forever. Again and again he took a whole lot of LSD and those water-soluble vitamins, but he never saw it again; he never found the combination."

Bob Arctor said, "What was on the other side?"

"He said it was always nighttime."

"Nighttime!"

"There was moonlight and water, always the same. Nothing moved or changed. Black water, like ink, and a shore, a beach of an island. He was sure it was Greece, ancient Greece. He figured out the doorway was a weak place in time, and he was seeing back into the past. And then later on, when he couldn't see it any more, he'd be on the freeway driving along, with all the trucks, and he'd get madder than hell. He said he couldn't stand all the motion and noise, everything going this way and that, all the clanking and banging. Anyhow, he never could figure out why they showed him what they showed him. He really believed it was God, and it was the doorway to the next world, but in the final analysis all it did was mess up his head. He couldn't hold on to it so he couldn't cope with it. Every time he met anybody, after a while he'd tell them he'd lost everything."

Bob Arctor said, "That's how I am."

"There was a woman on the island. Not exactly—more a statue. He said it was of the Cyrenaican Aphrodite. Standing there in the moonlight, pale and cold and made out of marble."

"He should have gone through the doorway when he had the chance."

Donna said, "He didn't have the chance. It was a promise. Something to come. Something better a long time in the future. Maybe after he—" She paused. "When he died."

"He missed out," Bob Arctor said. "You get one chance and that's it." He shut his eyes against the pain and the sweat streaking his face. "Anyhow what's a burned-out acid head know? What do any of us know? I can't talk. Forget it." He turned away from her, into the darkness, convulsing and shuddering.

"They show us trailers now," Donna said. She put her arms around him and held on to him as tightly as she could, rocking him back and forth. "So we'll hold out."

"That's what you're trying to do. With me now."

"You're a good man. You've been dealt a bad deal. But life isn't over for you. I care for you a lot. I wish . . ." She continued to hold him, silently, in the darkness that was swallowing him up from inside. Taking over even as she held on to him. "You are a good and kind person," she said. "And this is unfair but it has to be this way. Try to wait for the end. Sometime, a long time from now, you'll see the way you saw before. It'll come back to you." Restored, she thought. On the day when everything taken away unjustly from people will be restored to them. It may take a thousand years, or longer than that, but that day will come, and all the balances will be set right. Maybe, like Tony Amsterdam, you have seen a vision of God that is gone only temporarily; withdrawn, she thought, rather than ended. Maybe inside the terribly burned and burning circuits of your head that char more and more, even as I hold you, a spark of color and light in some disguised form manifested itself, unrecognized, to lead you, by its memory, through the years to come, the dreadful years ahead. A word not fully understood, some small thing seen but not understood; some fragment of a star mixed with the trash of this world, to guide you by reflex until the day . . . but it was so remote. She could not herself truly imagine it. Mingled with the commonplace, something from another world perhaps had appeared to Bob Arctor before it was over. All she could do now was hold him and hope.

But when he found it once again, if they were lucky, pattern-recognition would take place. Correct comparison in the right hemisphere. Even at the subcortical level available to him. And the journey, so awful for him, so costly, so evidently without point, would be finished.

A light shone in her eyes. Standing in front of her, a cop with nightstick and flashlight. "Would you two please stand up?" the officer said. "And show me your identification? You first, miss."

She let go of Bob Arctor, who slid sideways until he lay against the ground; he was unaware of the cop, who had approached them up the hill, stealthily, from a service road below. Getting her wallet out of her purse, Donna motioned the officer away, where Bob Arctor could not hear. For several minutes the officer studied her identification by the muted light of his flashlight, and then he said,

"You're undercover for the federal people."

"Keep your voice down," Donna said.

"I'm sorry." The officer handed the wallet back to her.

"Just fucking take off," Donna said.

The officer shone his light in her face briefly, and then turned away; he departed as he had approached, noiselessly.

When she returned to Bob Arctor, it was obvious that he had

never been aware of the cop. He was aware of almost nothing, now. Scarcely of her, let alone anyone or anything else.

Far off, echoing, Donna could hear the police car moving down the rutted, invisible service road. A few bugs, perhaps a lizard, made their way through the dry weeds around them. In the distance the 91 Freeway glowed in a pattern of lights, but no sound reached them; it was too remote.

"Bob," she said softly. "Can you hear me?"

No answer.

All the circuits are welded shut, she thought. Melted and fused. And no one is going to get them open, no matter how hard they try. And they are going to try.

"Come on," she said, tugging at him, attempting to get him to his feet. "We've got to get started."

Bob Arctor said, "I can't make love. My thing's disappeared."

"They're expecting us," Donna said firmly. "I have to sign you in."

"But what'll I do if my thing's disappeared? Will they still take me in?"

Donna said, "They'll take you."

It requires the greatest kind of wisdom, she thought, to know when to apply injustice. How can justice fall victim, ever, to what is right? How can this happen? She thought, Because there is a curse on this world, and all this proves it; this is the proof right here. Somewhere, at the deepest level possible, the mechanism, the construction of things, fell apart, and up from what remained swam the need to do all the various sort of unclear wrongs the wisest choice has made us act out. It must have started thousands of years ago. By now it's infiltrated into the nature of everything. And, she thought, into every one of us. We can't turn around or open our mouth and speak, decide at all, without doing it. I don't even care how it got started, when or why. She thought, I just hope it'll end some time. Like with Tony Amsterdam; I just hope one day the shower of brightly colored sparks will return, and this time we'll all see it. The narrow doorway where there's peace on the far side. A statue, the sea, and what looks like moonlight. And nothing stirring, nothing to break the calm.

A long, long time ago, she thought. Before the curse, and everything and everyone became this way. The Golden Age, she thought, when wisdom and justice were the same. Before it all shattered into cutting fragments. Into broken bits that don't fit, that can't be put back together, hard as we try.

Below her, in the darkness and distribution of urban lights, a police siren sounded. A police car in hot pursuit. It sounded like a deranged animal, greedy to kill. And knowing that it soon would. She shivered; the night air had become cold. It was time to go.

It isn't the Golden Age now, she thought, with noises like that in the darkness. Do I emit that kind of greedy noise? she asked herself. Am I that thing? Closing in, or having closed in?

Having caught?

. Beside her, the man stirred and moaned as she helped him up. Helped him to his feet and back to her car, step by step, helped him, helped him, helped him continue on. Below them, the noise of the police car had abruptly ceased; it had stopped its quarry. Its job was done. Holding Bob Arctor against her, she thought, Mine is done, too.

The two New-Path staff members stood surveying the thing on their floor that lay puking and shivering and fouling itself, its arms hugging itself, embracing its own body as if to stop itself, against the cold that made it tremble so violently.

"What is it?" one staff member said.

Donna said, "A person."

"Substance D?"

She nodded.

"It ate his head. Another loser."

She said to the two of them, "It's easy to win. Anybody can win." Bending down over Robert Arctor she said, silently,

Good-by.

They were putting an old army blanket over him as she left. She did not look back.

Getting into her car, she drove at once onto the closest freeway, into the thickest traffic possible. From the box of tapes on the floor of the car she took the Carole King *Tapestry* tape, her favorite of all she had, and pushed it into the tape deck; at the same time, she tugged loose the Ruger pistol magnetically mounted out of sight beneath the dashboard. In top gear she tailgated a truck carrying wooden cases of quart bottles of Coca-Cola, and as Carole King sang in stereo she emptied the clip of the Ruger at the Coke bottles a few feet ahead of her.

While Carole King sang soothingly about people sitting down and turning into toads, Donna managed to get four bottles before the gun's clip was empty. Bits of glass and smears of Coke splattered the windshield of her car. She felt better.

Justice and honesty and loyalty are not properties of this world, she thought; and then, by God, she rammed her old enemy, her ancient foe, the Coca-Cola truck, which went right on going without noticing. The impact spun her small car around; her headlights dimmed out, horrible noises of fender against tire shrieked, and then she was off the freeway onto the emergency strip, facing the other direction, water pouring from her radiator, with motorists slowing down to gape.

Come back, you motherfucker, she said to herself, but the Coca-Cola truck was long gone, probably undented. Maybe a scratch. Well, it was bound to happen sooner or later, her war, her taking on a symbol and a reality that outweighed her. Now my insurance rates will go up, she realized as she climbed from her car. In this world you pay for tilting with evil in cold, hard cash.

A late-model Mustang slowed and the driver, a man, called to her, "You want a ride, miss?"

She did not answer. She just kept on going. A small figure on foot facing an infinity of oncoming lights.

CHAPTER FOURTEEN

Magazine clipping thumbtacked to the wall of the lounge at Samarkand House, New-Path's residence building in Santa Ana, California:

> When the senile patient awakens in the morning and asks for his mother, remind him that she is long since dead, that he is over eighty years old and living in a convalescent home, and that this is 1992 and not 1913 and that he must face reality and the fact that

A resident had torn down the rest of the item; it ended there. Evidently it had been clipped from a professional nursing magazine; it was on slick paper.

"What you'll be doing here first," George, the staff member, told him, leading him down the hall, "is the bathrooms. The floors, the basins, especially the toilets. There're three bathrooms in this structure, one on each floor."

"Okay," he said.

"Here's a mop. And a pail. You feel you know how to do this? Clean a bathroom? Start, and I'll watch you and give you pointers."

He carried the pail to the tub on the back porch and he poured soap into it and then ran the hot water. All he could see was the foam of water directly before him; foam and the roar.

But he could hear George's voice, out of sight. "Not too full, because you won't be able to lift it."

"Okay."

"You have a little trouble telling where you are," George said, after a time.

"I'm at New-Path." He set the pail down on the floor and it slopped; he stood staring down at it.

"New-Path where?"

"In Santa Ana."

George lifted the pail up for him, showing him how to grip the wire handle and swing it along as he walked. "Later on I think we'll transfer you to the island or one of the farms. First you have to go through the dishpan."

"I can do that," he said. "Dishpans."

"Do you like animals?"

"Sure."

"Or farming?"

"Animals."

"We'll see. We'll wait until we're acquainted with you better. Anyhow, that'll be a while; everyone is in the dishpan for a month. Everyone who comes in the door."

"I'd sort of like to live in the country," he said.

"We maintain several types of facilities. We'll determine what's best suited. You know, you can smoke here, but it isn't encouraged. This isn't Synanon; they don't let you smoke."

He said, "I don't have any more cigarettes."

"We give each resident one pack a day."

"Money?" He didn't have any.

"It's without cost. There's never any cost. You paid your cost." George took the mop, pushed it down into the pail, showed him how to mop.

"How come I don't have any money?"

"The same reason you don't have any wallet or any last name. It'll be given back to you, all given back. That's what we want to do: give you back what's been taken away from you."

He said, "These shoes don't fit."

"We depend on donations, but new ones only, from stores. Later on maybe we can measure you. Did you try all the shoes in the carton?"

"Yes," he said.

"All right, this is the bathroom here on the basement floor; do it first. Then when that's done, really done well, really perfect, then go upstairs—bring the mop and bucket—and I'll show you the bathroom up there, and then after that the bathroom on the third floor. But you got to get permission to go up there to the third floor, because that's where the chicks live, so ask one of the staff first; never go up there without permission." He slapped him on the back. "All right, Bruce? Understand?"

"Okay," Bruce said, mopping.

George said, "You'll be doing this kind of work, cleaning these bathrooms, until you get so you can do a good job. It doesn't matter what a person does; it's that he gets so he can do it right and be proud of it."

"Will I ever be like I was again?" Bruce asked.

"What you were brought you here. If you become what you were again then sooner or later it'd bring you here again. Next time you might not make it here, even. Isn't that right? You're lucky you got here; you almost didn't get here."

"Somebody else drove me here."

"You're fortunate. The next time they might not. They might dump you on the side of the freeway somewhere and say the hell with it."

He continued mopping.

"The best way is to do the bowls first, then the tub, then the toilets, and the floor last."

"Okay," he said, and put the mop away.

"There's a certain knack to it. You'll master it."

Concentrating, he saw before him cracks in the enamel of the basin; he dribbled cleanser down into the cracks and ran hot water. The steam rose, and he stood within it, unmoving, as the steam grew. He liked the smell.

After lunch he sat in the lounge drinking coffee. No one spoke to him, because they understood he was withdrawing. Sitting drinking from his cup, he could hear their conversation. They all knew one another.

"If you could see out from inside a dead person you could still see, but you couldn't operate the eye muscles, so you couldn't focus. You couldn't turn your head or your eyeballs. All you could do would be wait until some object passed by. You'd be frozen. Just wait and wait. It'd be a terrible scene."

He gazed down at the steam of his coffee, only that. The steam rose; he liked the smell.

"Hey."

A hand touched him. From a woman.

"Hey."

He looked sideways a little.

"How you doing?"

"Okay," he said.

"Feel any better?"

"I feel okay," he said.

He watched his coffee and the steam and did not look at her or any of them; he looked down and down at the coffee. He liked the warmth of the smell.

"You could see somebody when they passed by directly in front of you, and only then. Or whichever way you were looking, no other. If a leaf or something floated over your eye, that would be it, forever. Only the leaf. Nothing more; you couldn't turn."

"Okay," he said, holding the coffee, the cup with both his hands.

"Imagine being sentient but not alive. Seeing and even knowing, but not alive. Just looking out. Recognizing but not being alive. A person can die and still go on. Sometimes what looks out at you from a person's eyes maybe died back in childhood. What's dead in there still looks out. It's not just the body looking at you with nothing in it; there's still something in there but it died and just keeps on looking and looking; it can't stop looking."

Another person said, "That's what it means to die, to not be able to stop looking at whatever's in front of you. Some darn thing placed directly there, with nothing you can do about it such as selecting anything or changing anything. You can only accept what's put there as it is."

"How'd you like to gaze at a beer can throughout eternity? It might not be so bad. There'd be nothing to fear."

Before dinner, which was served to them in the dining room, they had Concept time. Several Concepts were put on the blackboard by different staff members and discussed.

He sat with his hands folded in his lap, watching the floor and listening to the big coffee urn heating up; it went *whoop-whoop,* and the sound frightened him.

"Living and unliving things are exchanging properties."

Seated here and there on folding chairs, everyone discussed that. They seemed familiar with the Concept. Evidently these were parts of New-Path's way of thought, perhaps even memorized and then thought about again and again. *Whoop-whoop.*

"The drive of unliving things is stronger than the drive of living things."

They talked about that. *Whoop-whoop.* The noise of the coffee urn got louder and louder and scared him more, but he did not move or look; he sat where he was, listening. It was hard to hear what they were saying, because of the urn.

"We are incorporating too much unliving drive within us. And exchanging— Will somebody go look at that damn coffeepot to see why it's doing that?"

There was a break while someone examined the coffee urn. He sat staring down, waiting.

"I'll write this again. *'We are exchanging too much passive life for the reality outside us.'* "

They discussed that. The coffee urn became silent, and they trooped over to get coffee.

"Don't you want some coffee?" A voice behind him, touching him. "Ned? Bruce? What's his name—Bruce?"

"Okay." He got up and followed them to the coffee urn. He waited his turn. They watched as he put cream and sugar into his cup. They watched him return to his chair, the same one; he made certain he found it again, to reseat himself and go on listening. The warm coffee, its steam, made him feel good.

"Activity does not necessarily mean life. Quasars are active. And a monk meditating is not inanimate."

He sat looking at the empty cup; it was a china mug. Turning it over, he discovered printing on the bottom, and cracked glaze. The mug looked old, but it had been made in Detroit.

"Motion that is circular is the deadest form of the universe."

Another voice said, "Time."

He knew the answer to that. Time is round.

"Yes, we've got to break now, but does anyone have a fast final comment?"

"Well, following the line of least resistance, that's the rule of survival. Following, not leading."

Another voice, older, said, "Yes, the followers survive the leader. Like with Christ. Not vice versa."

"We better eat, because Rick stops serving exactly at five-fifty now."

"Talk about that in the Game, not now."

Chairs screaked, creaked. He rose too, carried the old mug to the tray of others, and joined them in line out. He could smell cold clothes around him, good smells but cold.

It sounds like they're saying passive life is good, he thought. But there is no such thing as passive life. That's a contradiction.

He wondered what life was, what it meant; maybe he did not understand.

A huge bunch of donated flashy clothes had arrived. Several people stood with armfuls, and some had put shirts on, trying them out and getting approval.

"Hey, Mike. You're a sharp dude."

In the middle of the lounge stood a short stocky man, with curly hair and pug face; he shifted his belt, frowning. "How do you work this here? I don't see how you get it to stay. Why doesn't it loosen?" He had a three-inch buckleless belt with metal rings and he did not know how to cinch the rings. Glancing around, eyes twinkling, he said, "I think they gave me one nobody else could work."

Bruce went over behind him, reached around him, and cinched the belt looped back through the rings.

"Thanks," Mike said. He sorted through several dress shirts, lips pursed. To Bruce he said, "When I get married I'm going to wear one of these."

"Nice," he said.

Mike strolled toward two women at the far end of the lounge; they smiled. Holding a burgundy floral shirt up against himself, Mike said, "I'm going out on the town."

"All right, go in and get dinner!" the house director yelled briskly, in his powerful voice. He winked at Bruce. "How you doing, fella?"

"Fine," Bruce said.

"Sound like you got a cold."

"Yes," he agreed, "it's from coming off. Could I have any Dristan or—"

"No chemicals," the house director said. "Nothing. Hurry on in and eat. How's your appetite?"

"Better," he said, following. They smiled at him, from tables.

After dinner he sat halfway up the wide stairs to the second floor. No one spoke to him; a conference was taking place. He sat there until it finished. Everyone emerged, filling the hall.

He felt them seeing him, and maybe some spoke to him. He sat on the stairs, hunched over, his arms wrapped around him, seeing and seeing. The dark carpet before his eyes.

Presently no more voices.

"Bruce?"

He did not stir.

"Bruce?" A hand touched him.

He said nothing.

"Bruce, come on into the lounge. You're supposed to be in your room in bed, but, see, I want to talk to you." Mike led him by waving him to follow. He accompanied Mike down the stairs and into the lounge, which was empty. When they were in the lounge Mike shut the door.

Seating himself in a deep chair, Mike indicated for him to sit down facing him. Mike appeared tired; his small eyes were ringed, and he rubbed his forehead.

"I been up since five-thirty this morning," Mike said.

A knock; the door started to open.

Very loudly, Mike yelled, "I want nobody to come in here; we're talking. Hear?"

Mumbles. The door shut.

"Y'know, you better change your shirt a couple times a day," Mike said. "You're sweating something fierce."

He nodded.

"What part of the state are you from?"

He said nothing.

"You come to me from now on when you feel this bad. I went

through the same thing, about a year and a half ago. They used to drive me around in cars. Different staff members. You met Eddie? The tall thin drink-a-water that puts down everybody? He drove me for eight days around and around. Never left me alone." Mike yelled suddenly, "Will you get out of here? We're in here talking. Go watch the TV." His voice sank, and he eyed Bruce. "Sometimes you got to do that. Never leave someone alone."

"I see," Bruce said.

"Bruce, be careful you don't take your own life."

"Yes, sir," Bruce said, staring down.

"Don't call me sir!"

He nodded.

"Were you in the Service, Bruce? Is that what it was? You got on the stuff in the Service?"

"No."

"You shoot it or drop it?"

He made no sound.

" 'Sir,' " Mike said. "I've served, myself, ten years in prison. One time I saw eight guys in our row of cells cut their throats in one day. We slept with our feet in the toilet, our cells were that small. That's what prison is, you sleep with your feet in the toilet. You never been in prison, have you?"

"No," he said.

"But on the other hand, I saw prisoners eighty years old still happy to be alive and wanting to stay alive. I remember when I was on dope, and I shot it; I started shooting when I was in my teens. I never did anything else. I shot up and then I went in for ten years. I shot up so much—heroin and D together—that I never did anything else; I never saw anything else. Now I'm off it and I'm out of prison and I'm here. You know what I notice the most? You know what the big difference is I notice? Now I can walk down the street outside and see something. I can hear water when we visit the forest—you'll see our other facilities later on, farms and so forth. I can walk down the street, the ordinary street, and see the little dogs and cats. I never saw them before. All I saw was dope." He examined his wristwatch. "So," he added, "I understand how you feel."

"It's hard," Bruce said, "getting off."

"Everybody here got off. Of course, some go back on. If you left here you'd go back on. You know that."

He nodded.

"No person in this place has had an easy life. I'm not saying your life's been easy. Eddie would. He'd tell you that your troubles are mickey mouse. Nobody's troubles are mickey mouse. I see how bad you feel, but I felt that way once. Now I feel a lot better. Who's your roommate?"

"John."

"Oh yeah. John. Then you must be down in the basement."

"I like it," he said.

"Yeah, it's warm there. You probably get cold a lot. Most of us do, and I remember I did; I shook all the time, and crapped in my pants. Well, I tell you, you won't have to go through this again, if you stay here at New-Path."

"How long?" he said.

"The rest of your life."

Bruce raised his head.

"*I* can't leave," Mike said. "I'd get back on dope if I went out there. I've got too many buddies outside. I'd be back on the corner again, dealing and shooting, and then back in the prison for twenty years. You know—hey—I'm thirty-five years old and I'm getting married for the first time. Have you met Laura? My fiancée?"

He wasn't sure.

"Pretty girl, plump. Nice figure?"

He nodded.

"She's afraid to go out the door. Someone has to go with her. We're going to the zoo . . . we're taking the Executive Director's little boy to the San Diego Zoo next week, and Laura's scared to death. More scared than I am."

Silence.

"You heard me say that?" Mike said. "That I'm scared to go to the zoo?"

"Yes."

"I never have been to a zoo that I can recall," Mike said. "What do you do at a zoo? Maybe you know."

"Look into different cages and open confined areas."

"What kind of animals do they have?"

"All kinds."

"Wild ones, I guess. Normally wild. And exotical ones."

"At the San Diego Zoo they have almost every wild animal," Bruce said.

"They have one of those . . . what are they? Koala bears."

"Yes."

"I saw a commercial on TV," Mike said. "With a koala bear in it. They hop. They resemble a stuffed toy."

Bruce said, "The old Teddy bear, that kids have, that was created based on the koala bear, back in the twenties."

"Is that right. I guess you'd have to go to Australia to see a koala bear. Or are they extinct now?"

"There're plenty in Australia," Bruce said, "but export is banned. Live or the hides. They almost got extinct."

"I never been anywhere," Mike said, "except when I ran stuff from Mexico up to Vancouver, British Columbia. I always took the same route, so I never saw anything. I just drove very fast to get it over with. I drive one of the Foundation cars. If you feel like it, if you feel very bad, I'll drive you around. I'll drive and we can talk. I don't mind. Eddie and some others not here now did it for me. I don't mind."

"Thank you."

"Now we both ought to hit the sack. Have they got you on kitchen stuff in the morning yet? Setting tables and serving?"

"No."

"Then you get to sleep to the same time I do. I'll see you at breakfast. You sit at the table with me and I'll introduce you to Laura."

"When are you getting married?"

"A month and a half. We'd be pleased if you were there. Of course, it'll be here at the building, so everyone will attend."

"Thank you," he said.

He sat in the Game and they screamed at him. Faces, all over, screaming; he gazed down.

"Y'know what he is? A kissy-facy!" One shriller voice made him peer up. Among the awful screaming distortions one Chinese girl, howling. "You're a kissy-facy, that's what you are!"

"Can you fuck yourself? Can you fuck yourself?" the others chanted at him, curled up in a circle on the floor.

The Executive Director, in red bell-bottoms and pink slippers, smiled. Glittery little broken eyes, like a spook's. Rocking back and forth, his spindly legs tucked under him, without a pillow.

"Let's see you fuck yourself!"

The Executive Director seemed to enjoy it when his eyes saw something break; his eyes glinted and filled with mirth. Like a dramatic stage queer, from some old court, draped in flair, colorful, he peeped around and enjoyed. And then from time to time his voice warbled out, grating and monotonous, like a metal noise. A scraping mechanical hinge.

"The kissy-facy!" the Chinese girl howled at him; beside her another girl flapped her arms and bulged her cheeks, plop-plop. "Here!" the Chinese girl howled, swiveled around to jut her rump at him, pointing to it and howling at him, "Kiss my ass, then, kissy-facy! He wants to kiss people, kiss this, kissy-facy!"

"Let's see you fuck yourself!" the family chanted. "Jack yourself off, kissy-facy!"

He shut his eyes, but his ears still heard.

"You pimp," the Executive Director said slowly to him. Monotonously. "You fuck. You dong. You shit. You turd prick. You—" On and on.

His ears still brought in sounds, but they blended. He glanced up once when he made out Mike's voice, audible during a lull. Mike sat gazing at him impassively, a little reddened, his neck swollen in the too-tight collar of his dress shirt.

"Bruce," Mike said, "what's the matter? What brought you here? What do you want to tell us? Can you tell us anything about yourself at all?"

"Pimp!" George screamed, bouncing up and down like a rubber ball. "What were you, pimp?"

The Chinese girl leaped up, shrieking, "Tell us, you cocksucking fairy whore pimp, you ass-kisser, you fuck!"

He said, "I am an eye."

"You turd prick," the Executive Director said. "You weakling. You puke. You suck-off. You snatch."

He heard nothing now. And forgot the meaning of the words, and, finally, the words themselves.

Only, he sensed Mike watching him, watching and listening, hearing nothing; he did not know, he did not recall, he felt little, he felt bad, he wanted to leave.

The Vacuum in him grew. And he was actually a little glad.

It was late in the day.

"Look in here," a woman said, "where we keep the freaks."

He felt frightened as she opened the door. The door fell aside and noise spilled out of the room, the size surprising him; but he saw many little children playing.

That evening he watched two older men feed the children milk and little foods, sitting in a separate small alcove near the kitchen. Rick, the cook, gave the two older men the children's food first while everyone waited in the dining room.

Smiling at him, a Chinese girl, carrying plates to the dining room, said, "You like kids?"

"Yes," he said.

"You can sit with the kids and eat there with them."

"Oh," he said.

"You can feed them later on like in a month or two." She hesitated. "When we're positive you won't hit them. We have a rule: the children can't never be hit for anything they do."

"Okay," he said. He felt warmed into life, watching the children eat; he seated himself, and one of the smaller children crept up on his lap. He began spooning food to the child. Both he and the child felt, he thought, equally warm. The Chinese girl smiled at him and then passed on with the plates to the dining room.

For a long time he sat among the children, holding first one and then another. The two older men quarreled with the children and criticized each other's way of feeding. Bits and hunks and smudges of food covered the table and floor; startled, he realized that the children had been fed and were going off into their big playroom to watch cartoons on TV. Awkwardly, he bent down to clean up spilled food.

"No, that's not your job!" one of the elderly men said sharply. "I'm supposed to do that."

"Okay," he agreed, rising, bumping his head on the edge of the table. He held spilled food in his hand and he gazed at it, wonderingly.

"Go help clear the dining room!" the other older man said to him. He had a slight speech impediment.

One of the kitchen help, someone from the dishpan, said to him in passing, "You need permission to sit with the kids."

He nodded, standing there, puzzled.

"That's for the old folk," the dishpan person said. "Baby-sitting." He laughed. "That can't do nothing else." He continued by.

One child remained. She studied him, large-eyed, and said to him, "What's your name?"

He answered nothing.

"I said, what's your name?"

Reaching cautiously, he touched a bit of beef on the table. It had cooled now. But, aware of the child beside him, he still felt warm; he touched her on the head, briefly.

"My name is Thelma," the child said. "Did you forget your name?" She patted him. "If you forget your name, you can write it on your hand. Want me to show you how?" She patted him again.

"Won't it wash off?" he asked her. "If you write it on your hand, the first time you do anything or take a bath it'll wash off."

"Oh, I see." She nodded. "Well, you could write it on the wall, over your head. In your room where you sleep. Up high where it won't wash off. And then when you want to know your name better you can—"

"Thelma," he murmured.

"No, that's *my* name. You have to have a different name. And that's a girl's name."

"Let's see," he said, meditating.

"If I see you again I'll give you a name," Thelma said. "I'll make one up for you. 'Kay?"

"Don't you live here?" he said.

"Yes, but my mommy might leave. She's thinking about taking us, me and my brother, and leaving."

He nodded. Some of the warmth left him.

All of a sudden, for no reason he could see, the child ran off.

I should work out my own name, anyhow, he decided; it's my responsibility. He examined his hand and wondered why he was doing that; there was nothing to see. Bruce, he thought; that's my name. But there ought to be better names than that, he thought. The warmth that remained gradually departed, as had the child.

He felt alone and strange and lost again. And not very happy.

One day Mike Westaway managed to get sent out to pick up a load of semirotten produce donated by a local supermarket to New-Path. However, after making sure no staff member had tailed him, he made a phone call and then met Donna Hawthorne at a McDonald's fast-food stand.

They sat together outside, with Cokes and hamburgers between them on the wooden table.

"Have we really been able to duke him?" Donna asked.

"Yes," Westaway said. But he thought, The guy's so burned out. I wonder if it matters. I wonder if we accomplished anything. And yet it had to be like this.

"They're not paranoid about him."

"No," Mike Westaway said.

Donna said, "Are you personally convinced they're growing the stuff?"

"Not me. It's not what I believe. It's them." Those who pay us, he thought.

"What's the name mean?"

"*Mors ontologica*. Death of the spirit. The identity. The essential nature."

"Will he be able to act?"

Westaway watched the cars and people passing; he watched moodily as he fooled with his food.

"You really don't know."

"Never can know until it happens. A memory. A few charred brain cells flicker on. Like a reflex. React, not act. We can just hope. Remember what Paul says in the Bible: faith, hope, and giving away your money." He studied the pretty, dark-haired young girl across from him and could perceive, in her intelligent face, why Bob Arctor — No, he thought; I always have to think of him as Bruce. Otherwise I cop out to knowing too much: things I shouldn't, couldn't, know. Why Bruce thought so much of her. Thought when he was capable of thought.

"He was very well drilled," Donna said, in what seemed to him an extraordinarily forlorn voice. And at the same time an expression of sorrow crossed her face, straining and warping its lines. "Such a cost to pay," she said then, half to herself, and drank from her Coke.

He thought, But there is no other way. To get in there. *I* can't get in. That's established by now; think how long I've been trying. They'd only let a burned-out husk like Bruce in. Harmless. He would have to be . . . the way he is. Or they wouldn't take the risk. It's their policy.

"The government asks an awful lot," Donna said.

"Life asks an awful lot."

Raising her eyes, she confronted him, darkly angry. "In this case the federal government. Specifically. From you, me. From——" She broke off. "From what was my friend."

"He's still your friend."

Fiercely Donna said, "What's left of him."

What's left of him Mike Westaway thought, is still searching for you. After its fashion. He too felt sad. But the day was nice, the people and cars cheered him, the air smelled good. And there was the prospect of success; that cheered him the most. They had come this far. They could go the rest of the way.

Donna said, "I think, really, there is nothing more terrible than the sacrifice of someone or something, a living thing, without its ever knowing. If it *knew*. If it understood and volunteered. But——" She gestured. "He doesn't know; he never did know. He didn't volunteer——"

"Sure he did. It was his job."

"He had no idea, and he hasn't any idea now, because now he hasn't any ideas. You know that as well as I do. And he will never again in his life, as long as he lives, have any ideas. Only reflexes. And this didn't happen accidentally; it was supposed to happen. So we have this . . . bad karma on us. I feel it on my back. Like a corpse. I'm carrying a corpse—Bob Arctor's corpse. Even while he's technically alive." Her voice had risen; Mike Westaway gestured, and, with visible effort, she calmed herself. People at other wooden tables, enjoying their burgers and shakes, had glanced inquiringly.

After a pause Westaway said, "Well, look at it this way. They can't interrogate something, someone, who doesn't have a mind."

"I've got to get back to work," Donna said. She examined her wristwatch. "I'll tell them everything seems okay, according to what you told me. In your opinion."

"Wait for winter," Westaway said.

"Winter?"

"It'll take until then. Never mind why, but that's how it is; it will work in winter or it won't work at all. We'll get it then or not at all." Directly at the solstice, he thought.

"An appropriate time. When everything's dead and under the snow."

He laughed. "In California?"

"The winter of the spirit. *Mors ontologica*. When the spirit is dead."

"Only asleep," Westaway said. He rose. "I have to split, too. I have to pick up a load of vegetables."

Donna gazed at him with sad, mute, afflicted dismay.

"For the kitchen," Westaway said gently. "Carrots and lettuce. That kind. Donated by McCoy's Market, for us poor at New-Path. I'm sorry I said that. It wasn't meant to be a joke. It wasn't meant to be anything." He patted her on the shoulder of her leather jacket. And as he did so it came to him that probably Bob Arctor, in better, happier days, had gotten this jacket for her as a gift.

"We have worked together on this a long time," Donna said in a moderate, steady voice. "I don't want to be on this much longer. I want it to end. Sometimes at night, when I can't sleep, I think, shit, we are colder than they are. The adversary."

"I don't see a cold person when I look at you," Westaway said. "Although I guess I really don't know you all that well. What I do see, and see clearly, is one of the warmest persons I ever knew."

"I am warm on the outside, what people see. Warm eyes, warm face, warm fucking fake smile, but inside I am cold all the time, and full of lies. I am not what I seem to be; I am awful." The girl's voice remained steady, and as she spoke she smiled. Her pupils were large and mellow and without guile. "But, then, there's no other way. Is there? I figured that out a long time ago and made myself like this. But it really isn't so bad. You get what you want this way. And everybody is this way to a degree. What I am that's actually so bad—I am a liar. I lied to my friend, I lied to Bob Arctor all the time. I even told him one time not to believe anything I said, and of course he just believed I was kidding; he didn't listen. But if I told him, then it's his responsibility not to listen, not to believe me any more, after I said that. I warned him. But he forgot as soon as I said it and went right on. Kept right on truckin'."

"You did what you had to. You did more than you had to."

The girl started away from the table. "Okay, then there really isn't anything for me to report, so far. Except your confidence. Just that he's duked in and they accept him. They didn't get anything out of him in those—" She shuddered. "Those gross games."

"Right."

"I'll see you later." She paused. "The federal people aren't going to want to wait until winter."

"But winter it is," Westaway said. "The winter solstice."

"The what?"

"Just wait," he said. "And pray."

"That's bullshit," Donna said. "Prayer, I mean. I prayed a long time ago, a lot, but not any more. We wouldn't have to do this, what we're doing, if prayer worked. It's another shuck."

"Most things are." He followed after the girl a few steps as she departed, drawn to her, liking her. "I don't feel you destroyed your friend. It seems to me you've been as much destroyed, as much the victim. Only on you it doesn't show. Anyhow, there was no choice."

"I'm going to hell," Donna said. She smiled suddenly, a broad, boyish grin. "My Catholic upbringing."

"In hell they sell you nickel bags and when you get home there's M-and-M's in them."

"M-and-M's made out of turkey turds," Donna said, and then all at once she was gone. Vanished away into the hither-and-thither-going people; he blinked. Is this how Bob Arctor felt? he asked himself. Must have. There she was, stable and as if forever; then—nothing. Vanished like fire or air, an element of the earth back into the earth. To mix with the everyone-else people that never cease to be. Poured out among them. The evaporated girl, he thought. Of transformation. That comes and goes as she will. And no one, nothing, can hold on to her.

I seek to net the wind, he thought. And so had Arctor. Vain, he thought, to try to place your hands firmly on one of the federal drug-abuse agents. They are furtive. Shadows which melt away when their job dictates. As if they were never really there in the first place. Arctor, he thought, was in love with a phantom of authority, a kind of hologram, through which a normal man could walk, and emerge on the far side, alone. Without ever having gotten a good grip on it—on the girl itself.

God's M.O., he reflected, is to transmute evil into good. If He is active here, He is doing that now, although our eyes can't perceive it; the process lies hidden beneath the surface of reality, and emerges only later. To, perhaps, our waiting heirs. Paltry people who will not know the dreadful war we've gone through, and the losses we took, unless in some footnote in a minor history book they catch a notion. Some brief mention. With no list of the fallen.

There should be a monument somewhere, he thought, listing those who died in this. And, worse, those who didn't die. Who had to live on, past death. Like Bob Arctor. The saddest of all.

I get the idea Donna is a mercenary, he thought. Not on salary. And they are the most wraithlike. They disappear forever. New names, new locations. You ask yourself, where is she now? And the answer is—

Nowhere. Because she was not there in the first place.

Reseating himself at the wooden table, Mike Westaway finished eating his burger and drinking his Coke. Since it was better than what they were served at New-Path. Even if the burger had been made from ground-up cows' anuses.

To call Donna back, to seek to find her or possess her . . . I seek what Bob Arctor sought, so maybe he is better off now, this way. The tragedy in his life already existed. To love an atmospheric spirit. That was the real sorrow. Hopelessness itself. Nowhere on the printed page, nowhere in the annals of man, would her name appear: no local habitation, no name. There are girls like that, he thought, and those you love the most, the ones where there is no hope because it has eluded you at the very moment you close your hands around it.

So maybe we saved him from something worse, Westaway concluded. And, while accomplishing that, put what remained of him to use. To good and valuable use.

If we turn out lucky.

"Do you know any stories?" Thelma asked one day.

"I know the story about the wolf," Bruce said.

"The wolf and the grandmother?"

"No," he said. "The black-and-white wolf. It was up in a tree, and again and again it dropped down on the farmer's animals. Finally one time the farmer got all his sons and all his sons' friends and they stood around waiting for the black-and-white wolf in the tree to drop down. At last the wolf dropped down on a mangy-looking brown animal, and there in his black-and-white coat he was shot by all of them."

"Oh," Thelma said. "That's too bad."

"But they saved the hide," he continued. "They skinned the great black-and-white wolf that dropped from the tree and preserved his beautiful hide, so that those to follow, those who came later on, could see what he had been like and could marvel at him, at his strength and size. And future generations talked about him and related many stories of his prowess and majesty, and wept for his passing."

"Why did they shoot him?"

"They had to," he said. "You must do that with wolves like that."

"Do you know any other stories? Better ones?"

"No," he said, "that's the only story I know." He sat remembering
how the wolf had enjoyed his great springing ability, his leaping
down again and again in his fine body, but now that body was gone,
shot down. And for meager animals to be slaughtered and eaten anyhow. Animals with no strength that never sprang, that took no pride
in their bodies. But anyhow, on the good side, those animals trudged
on. And the black-and-white wolf had never complained; he had said
nothing even when they shot him. His claws had still been deep in his
prey. For nothing. Except that that was his fashion and he liked to
do it. It was his only way. His only style by which to live. All he
knew. And they got him.

"Here's the wolf!" Thelma exclaimed, leaping about clumsily.
"Voob, voob!" She grabbed at things and missed, and he saw with
dismay that something was wrong with her. He saw for the first time,
distressed and wondering how it could happen, that she was impaired.

He said, "You are not the wolf."

But even so, as she groped and hobbled, she stumbled; even so, he
realized, the impairment continued. He wondered how it could be
that . . .

> Ich unglücksel'ger Atlas! Eine Welt,
> Die ganze Welt der Schmerzen muss ich tragen,
> Ich trage Unerträgliches, und brechen
> Will mir das Herz im Leibe.

. . . such sadness could exist. He walked away.

Behind him she still played. She tripped and fell. How must that
feel? he wondered.

He roamed along the corridor, searching for the vacuum cleaner.
They had informed him that he must carefully vacuum the big playroom where the children spent most of the day.

"Down the hall to the right." A person pointed. Earl.

"Thanks, Earl," he said.

When he arrived at a closed door he started to knock, and then instead he opened it.

Inside the room an old woman stood holding three rubber balls,
which she juggled. She turned toward him, her gray stringy hair falling on her shoulders, grinning at him with virtually no teeth. She
wore white bobby socks and tennis shoes. Sunken eyes, he saw;
sunken eyes, grinning, empty mouth.

"Can you do this?" she wheezed, and threw all three balls up into the air. They fell back, hitting her, bouncing down to the floor. She stooped over, spitting and laughing.

"I can't do that," he said, standing there dismayed.

"I can." The thin old creature, her arms cracking as she moved, raised the balls, squinted, tried to get it right.

Another person appeared at the door beside Bruce and stood with him, also watching.

"How long has she been practicing?" Bruce said.

"Quite a while." The person called, "Try again. You're getting close!"

The old woman cackled as she bent to fumble to pick the balls up once again.

"One's over there," the person beside Bruce said. "Under your night table."

"Ohhhh!" she wheezed.

They watched the old woman try again and again, dropping the balls, picking them back up, aiming carefully, balancing herself, throwing them high into the air, and then hunching as they rained down on her, sometimes hitting her head.

The person beside Bruce sniffed and said, "Donna, you better go clean yourself. You're not clean."

Bruce, stricken, said, "That isn't Donna. Is that Donna?" He raised his head to peer at the old woman and he felt great terror; tears of a sort stood in the old woman's eyes as she gazed back at him, but she was laughing, laughing as she threw the three balls at him, hoping to hit him. He ducked.

"No, Donna, don't do that," the person beside Bruce said to her. "Don't hit people. Just keep trying to do what you saw on TV, you know, catch them again yourself and throw them right back up. But go clean yourself now; you stink."

"Okay," the old woman agreed, and hurried off, hunched and little. She left the three rubber balls still rolling on the floor.

The person beside Bruce shut the door, and they walked along the hall. "How long has Donna been here?" Bruce said.

"A long time. Since before I came, which was six months ago. She started trying to juggle about a week ago."

"Then it isn't Donna," he said. "If she's been here that long. Because I just got here a week ago." And, he thought, Donna drove me here in her MG. I remember that, because we had to stop while she got the radiator filled back up. And she looked fine then. Sad-eyed, dark, quiet and composed in her little leather jacket, her boots, with her purse that has the rabbit's foot dangling. Like she always is.

He continued on then, searching for the vacuum cleaner. He felt a great deal better. But he didn't understand why.

CHAPTER FIFTEEN

Bruce said, "Could I work with animals?"

"No," Mike said, "I think I'm going to put you on one of our farms. I want to try you with plants for a while, a few months. Out in the open, where you can touch the ground. With all these rocket-ship space probes there's been too much trying to reach the sky. I want you to make the attempt to reach—"

"I want to be with something living."

Mike explained, "The ground is living. The Earth is still alive. You can get the most help there. Do you have any agricultural background? Seeds and cultivation and harvesting?"

"I worked in an office."

"You'll be outside from now on. If your mind comes back it'll have to come back naturally. You can't make yourself think again. You can only keep working, such as sowing crops or tilling on our vegetable plantations—as we call them—or killing insects. We do a lot of that, driving insects out of existence with the right kind of sprays. We're very careful, though, with sprays. They can do more harm than good. They can poison not only the crops and the ground but the person using them. Eat his head." He added, "Like yours has been eaten."

"Okay," Bruce said.

You have been sprayed, Mike thought as he glanced at the man, so that now you've become a bug. Spray a bug with a toxin and it dies; spray a man, spray his brain, and he becomes an insect that clacks and vibrates about in a closed circle forever. A reflex machine, like an ant. Repeating his last instruction.

Nothing new will ever enter his brain, Mike thought, because that brain is gone.

And with it, that person who once gazed out. That I never knew.

But maybe, if he is placed in the right spot, in the right stance, he can still see down, and see the ground. And recognize that it is there. And place something which is alive, something different from himself, in it. To grow.

Since that is what he or it can't do any longer: this creature beside me has died, and so can never again grow. It can only decay gradually until what remains, too, is dead. And then we cart that off.

There is little future, Mike thought, for someone who is dead. There is, usually, only the past. And for Arctor-Fred-Bruce there is not even the past; there is only this.

Beside him, as he drove the staff car, the slumped figure jiggled. Animated by the car.

I wonder, he thought, if it was New-Path that did this to him. Sent a substance out to get him like this, to make him this way *so they would ultimately receive him back?*

To build, he thought, their civilization within the chaos. If "civilization" it really is.

He did not know. He had not been at New-Path long enough; their goals, the Executive Director had informed him once, would be revealed to him only after he had been a staff member another two years.

Those goals, the Executive Director had said, had nothing to do with drug rehabilitation.

No one but Donald, the Executive Director, knew where the funding for New-Path originated. Money was always there. Well, Mike thought, there is a lot of money in manufacturing Substance D. Out in various remote rural farms, in small shops, in several facilities labeled "schools." Money in manufacturing it, distributing it, and finally selling it. At least enough to keep New-Path solvent and growing—and more. Sufficient for a variety of ultimate goals.

Depending on what New-Path intended to do.

He knew something—U. S. Drug Restriction knew something—that most of the public, even the police, did not know.

Substance D, like heroin, was organic. Not the product of a lab.

So he meant quite a bit when he thought, as he frequently did, that all those profits could well keep New-Path solvent—*and growing*.

The living, he thought, should never be used to serve the purposes of the dead. But the dead—he glanced at Bruce, the empty shape beside him—should, if possible, serve the purposes of the living.

That, he reasoned, is the law of life.

And the dead, if they could feel, might feel better doing so.

The dead, Mike thought, who can still see, even if they can't understand: they are our camera.

CHAPTER SIXTEEN

Under the sink in the kitchen he found a small bone fragment, down with the boxes of soap and brushes and buckets. It looked human, and he wondered if it was Jerry Fabin.

This made him remember an event from a long way back in his life. Once he had lived with two other guys and sometimes they had kidded about owning a rat named Fred that lived under their sink. And when they got really broke one time, they told people, they had to eat poor old Fred.

Maybe this was one of his bone fragments, the rat who had lived under their sink, who they had made up to keep them company.

Hearing them talking in the lounge.

"This guy was more burned out than he showed. I felt so. He drove up to Ventura one day, cruising all over to find an old friend back inland toward Ojai. Recognized the house on sight without the number, stopped, and asked the people if he could see Leo. 'Leo died. Sorry you didn't know.' So this guy said then, 'Okay, I'll come back again on Thursday.' And he drove off, he drove back down the coast, and I guess he went back up on Thursday again looking for Leo. How about that?"

He listened to their talk, drinking his coffee.

"—works out, the phone book has only one number in it; you call that number for whoever you want. Listed on page after page . . . I'm talking about a totally burned-out society. And in your wallet you have that number, *the* number, scribbled down on different slips and cards, for different people. And if you forget the number, you couldn't call *anybody*."

"You could dial Information."

"It's the same number."

He still listened; it was interesting, this place they were describing. When you called it, the phone number was out of order, or if it wasn't they said, "Sorry, you have the wrong number." So you called it again, the same number, and got the person you wanted.

When a person went to the doctor—there was only one, and he specialized in everything—there was only one medicine. After he had diagnosed you he prescribed the medicine. You took the slip to the pharmacy to have it filled, but the pharmacist never could read what the doctor had written, so he gave you the only pill he had, which was aspirin. And it cured whatever you had.

If you broke the law, there was only the one law, which everybody broke again and again. The cop laboriously wrote it all up, which law, which infraction each time, the same one. And there was always the same penalty for any breaking of the law, from jaywalking to treason: the penalty was the death penalty, and there was agitation to have the death penalty removed, but it could not be because then, for like jaywalking, there would be no penalty at all. So it stayed on the books and finally the community burned out entirely and died. No, not burned out—they had been that already. They faded out, one by one, as they broke the law, and sort of died.

He thought, I guess when people heard that the last one of them had died they said, I wonder what those people were like. Let's see— well, we'll come back on Thursday. Although he was not sure, he laughed, and when he said that aloud, so did everyone else in the lounge.

"Very good, Bruce," they said.

That got to be a sort of tag line then; when somebody there at Samarkand House didn't understand anything or couldn't find what he was sent to get, like a roll of toilet paper, they said, "Well, I guess I'll come back on Thursday." Generally, it was credited to him. His saying. Like with comics on TV who said the same tag-line thing again and again each week. It caught on at Samarkand House and meant something to them all.

Later, at the Game one night, when they gave credit in turn to each person for what he had brought to New-Path, such as Concepts, they credited him with bringing humor there. He had brought with him an ability to see things as funny no matter how bad he felt. Everybody in the circle clapped, and, glancing up, startled, he saw the ring of smiles, everybody's eyes warm with approval, and the noise of their applause remained with him for quite a period, inside his heart.

CHAPTER SEVENTEEN

In late August of that year, two months after he entered New-Path, he was transferred to a farm facility in the Napa Valley, which is located inland in Northern California. It is the wine country, where many fine California vineyards exist.

Donald Abrahams, the Executive Director of New-Path Foundation, signed the transfer order. On the suggestion of Michael Westaway, a member of his staff who had become especially interested in seeing what could be done with Bruce. Particularly since the Game had failed to help him. It had, in fact, made him more deteriorated.

"Your name is Bruce," the manager of the farm said, as Bruce stepped clumsily from the car, lugging his suitcase.

"My name is Bruce," he said.

"We're going to try you on farming for a period, Bruce."

"Okay."

"I think you'll like it better here, Bruce."

"I think I'll like it," he said. "Better here."

The farm manager scrutinized him. "They gave you a haircut recently."

"Yes, they gave me a haircut." Bruce reached up to touch his shaved head.

"What for?"

"They gave me a haircut because they found me in the women's quarters."

"That the first you've had?"

"That is the *second* one I've had." After a pause Bruce said, "One time I got violent." He stood, still holding the suitcase; the manager gestured for him to set it down on the ground. "I broke the violence rule."

"What'd you do?"

"I threw a pillow."

"Okay, Bruce," the manager said. "Come with me and I'll show you where you'll be sleeping. We don't have a central building residence here; each six persons have a little cabin. They sleep and fix their meals there and live there when they're not working. There's no Game sessions, here, just the work. No more Games for you, Bruce."

Bruce seemed pleased; a smile appeared on his face.

"You like mountains?" The farm manager indicated to their right. "Look up. Mountains. No snow, but mountains. Santa Rosa is to the left; they grow really great grapes on those mountain slopes. We don't grow any grapes. Various other farm products, but no grapes."

"I like mountains," Bruce said.

"Look at them." The manager again pointed. Bruce did not look. "We'll round up a hat for you," the manager said. "You can't work out in the fields with your head shaved without a hat. Don't go out to work until we get you a hat. Right?"

"I won't go to work until I have a hat," Bruce said.

"The air is good here," the manager said.

"I like air," Bruce said.

"Yeah," the manager said, indicating for Bruce to pick up his suitcase and follow him. He felt awkward, glancing at Bruce: he didn't know what to say. A common experience for him, when people like this arrived. "We all like air, Bruce. We really all do. We do have that in common." He thought, We do still have that.

"Will I be seeing my friends?" Bruce asked.

"You mean from back where you were? At the Santa Ana facility?"

"Mike and Laura and George and Eddie and Donna and—"

"People from the residence facilities don't come out to the farms," the manager explained. "These are closed operations. But you'll probably be going back once or twice a year. We have gatherings at Christmas and also at—"

Bruce had halted.

"The next one," the manager said, again motioning for him to continue walking, "is at Thanksgiving. We'll be sending workers back to their residences-of-origin for that, for two days. Then back here again until Christmas. So you'll see them again. If they haven't been transferred to other facilities. That's three months. But you're not supposed to make any one-to-one relationships here at New-Path —didn't they tell you that? You're supposed to relate only to the family as a whole."

"I understand that," Bruce said. "They had us memorize that as part of the New-Path Creed." He peered around and said, "Can I have a drink of water?"

"We'll show you the water source here. You've got one in your cabin, but there's a public one for the whole family here." He led Bruce toward one of the prefab cabins. "These farm facilities are closed, because we've got experimental and hybrid crops and we want to keep insect infestation out. People come in here, even staff, track in pests on their clothes, shoes, and hair." He selected a cabin at random. "Yours is 4-G," he decided. "Can you remember it?"

"They look alike," Bruce said.

"You can nail up some object by which to recognize it, this cabin. That you can easily remember. Something with color in it." He pushed open the cabin door; hot stinking air blew out at them. "I think we'll put you in with the artichokes first," he ruminated. "You'll have to wear gloves—they've got stickers."

"Artichokes," Bruce said.

"Hell, we've got mushrooms here too. Experimental mushroom farms, sealed in, of course—all domestic mushroom growers need to seal in their yield—to keep pathogenic spores from drifting in and contaminating the beds. Fungus spores, of course, are airborne. That's a hazard to all mushroom growers."

"Mushrooms," Bruce said, entering the dark, hot cabin. The manager watched him enter.

"Yes, Bruce," he said.

"Yes, Bruce," Bruce said.

"Bruce," the manager said. "Wake up."

He nodded, standing in the stale gloom of the cabin, still holding his suitcase. "Okay," he said.

They nod off as soon as it's dark, the manager said to himself. Like chickens.

A vegetable among vegetables, he thought. Fungus among fungus. Take your pick.

He yanked on the overhead electric light of the cabin, and then began to show Bruce how to operate it. Bruce did not appear to care; he had caught a glimpse of the mountains now, and stood gazing at them fixedly, aware of them for the first time.

"Mountains, Bruce, mountains," the manager said.

"Mountains, Bruce, mountains," Bruce said, and gazed.

"Echolalia, Bruce, echolalia," the manager said.

"Echolalia, Bruce—"

"Okay, Bruce," the manager said, and shut the cabin door behind him, thinking, I believe I'll put him among the carrots. Or beets. Something simple. Something that won't puzzle him.

And another vegetable in the other cot, there. To keep him company. They can nod their lives away together, in unison. Rows of them. Whole acres.

They faced him toward the field, and he saw the corn, like ragged projections. He thought, Garbage growing. They run a garbage farm.

He bent down and saw growing near the ground a small flower, blue. Many of them in short tinkly tinky stalks. Like stubble. Chaff.

A lot of them, he saw now that he could get his face close enough to make them out. Fiends, within the taller rows of corn. Here concealed within, as many farmers planted: one crop inside another, like concentric rings. As, he remembered, the farmers in Mexico plant their marijuana plantations: circled—ringed—by tall plants, so the *federales* won't spot them by jeep. But then they're spotted from the air.

And the *federales*, when they locate such a pot plantation down there—they machine-gun the farmer, his wife, their children, even the animals. And then drive off. And their copter search continues, backed by the jeeps.

Such lovely little blue flowers.

"You're seeing the flower of the future," Donald, the Executive Director of New-Path, said. "But not for you."

"Why not for me?" Bruce asked.

"You've had too much of a good thing already," the Executive Director said. He chuckled. "So get up and stop worshiping—this isn't your god any more, your idol, although it was once. A transcendent vision, is that what you see growing here? You look as if it is." He tapped Bruce firmly on the shoulder, and then, reaching down his hand, he cut the sight off from the frozen eyes.

"Gone," Bruce said. "Flowers of spring gone."

"No, you simply can't see them. That's a philosophical problem you wouldn't comprehend. Epistemology—the theory of knowledge."

Bruce saw only the flat of Donald's hand barring the light, and he stared at it a thousand years. It locked; it had locked; it will lock for him, lock forever for dead eyes outside time, eyes that could not look away and a hand that would not move away. Time ceased as the eyes gazed and the universe jelled along with him, at least for him, froze over with him and his understanding, as its inertness became complete. There was nothing he did not know; there was nothing left to happen.

"Back to work, Bruce," Donald, the Executive Director, said.

"I saw," Bruce said. He thought, I knew. That was it: I saw Substance D growing. I saw death rising from the earth, from the ground itself, in one blue field, in stubbled color.

The farm-facility manager and Donald Abrahams glanced at each other and then down at the kneeling figure, the kneeling man and the *Mors ontologica* planted everywhere, within the concealing corn.